STAR WARS®

THE CLONE WARS®

DARTH MAUL
SHADOW CONSIPIRACY

By Jason Fry

SCHOLASTIC INC.

www.starwars.com
www.scholastic.com

ISBN 978-0-545-47063-6

12 11 10 9 8 7 6 5 4 3 2 1   12 13 14 15 16 17/0
Printed in the U.S.A.   40
First printing, September 2012

Contents

PART ONE:
REVIVAL

CHAPTER ONE

Unlike the vast majority of the galaxy's flesh-and-blood beings, security droids didn't get bored or scared. They were content to patrol the Cybloc Transfer Station, their electronic eyes surveying the same corridors, warehouses, and offices they saw every night.

On this particular night the power went out, plunging the station into darkness. But the security droids weren't worried. Their computer brains calmly switched to high alert, elevating the threat level expected by one step and increasing the sensitivity of their monitoring sensors.

Four droids entered one of the warehouse's many offices. The station's emergency lighting glimmered on the black-and-white plating encasing their circuits.

The warehouse was empty.

"Fan out—I want a scan of the entire perimeter," ordered the lead deputy, whose designation was LD-112. His plating was gold and black, so the station's organic workers could look at a group of droids and tell who was in charge.

The droids began scanning the area, blasters ready.

"SD-357, have you found anyone in the south passage?" LD-112 asked, photoreceptors glowing. While waiting for a response, he took a moment to run through a list of potential reasons for the power outage. It was a long list. MALFUNCTION and SOLAR FLARE were at the top. INTRUSION and ACT OF WAR were at the bottom.

LD-112 reached out to open the door on the other side of the empty office. He peered down the corridor and saw it was empty as well.

"Three-fifty-seven, where are you?" LD-112 asked.

Suddenly, an object flew into view at the end of the corridor. LD-112's visual sensors took a few milliseconds to examine it, then forwarded their analysis to his central processing unit, which concluded with 99.35 percent confidence that the object was the body of a security droid. Further analysis determined that there was a 91.21 percent chance that the body was that of SD-357.

Behind the fallen security droid stood a dark figure. The legs were mechanical, ending in four claws, while the rest of the body was apparently organic. The face was black with red tattoos, fiery yellow eyes, and a crown of curved, wicked-looking horns. In its hand was a lightsaber with a crimson blade.

The newcomer speared the fallen security droid, which expired in a shower of sparks.

A flesh-and-blood guard might have panicked at that point, but LD-112's electronic brain allowed him to perform several tasks in less than a quarter of a second.

First, he marked SD-357 as in need of serious maintenance and likely no longer functional. This alerted headquarters of the need to reorder replacement parts, and possibly a new droid.

Second, his sensors scanned the dark figure, searching several databases for a match. Searches against station workers, current ship crews, and known galactic criminals all came back with INSUFFICIENT DATA.

Third, he erased most of the list of potential reasons for the power outage and moved INTRUSION to the top.

Fourth, he yelled, "INTRUDERS!" and charged into the hallway, firing his blaster.

"You are trespassing on intergalactic—" he warned.

LD-112 never reached the intruder. Suddenly, he was in the air, though his sensors failed to determine why. Then his metal head was collapsing in on itself, crushed by some unseen pressure. He was logging a request for emergency maintenance when the main and auxiliary power cables to his brain snapped and his logic modules went offline.

Darth Maul strode into the office on his mechanical legs, still holding the droid deputy in the air with the Force. Behind him came another horned warrior, thickly muscled and covered with yellow tattoos. He was holding a double-bladed saber.

The new arrival, Savage Opress, slashed through one of the security droids, then raised his head, lifting the two remaining droids into the air. Their legs kicked briefly before he called upon the Force and slammed them against the wall.

Maul let LD-112's motionless body drop and the two Zabraks began to search the office. A safe stood in the corner. Savage plunged his saber into the locking mechanism. When the safe's metal housing bubbled around the plasma blade, Savage deactivated his saber and opened the safe.

Inside were credit chips—hundreds of them.

Savage grinned.

"Look, brother—a fortune," he said, his voice a low growl.

Maul was unimpressed.

"True fortune will be the demise of Kenobi," he said. His voice was smooth and mannered. He sounded like a well-educated son from a rich family in the Core Worlds, not a fiery-eyed warrior who broke into warehouses in the Outer Rim and ran droids through with a lightsaber.

Maul nodded at the credit chips.

"Credit chips are meaningless without a plan to survive," Maul told Savage. "The Jedi will hunt us. We will be forced to make a stand."

"And we will deal with them," Savage said.

"There are too many," Maul replied. "To continue, we need one singular vision. *My* vision."

Savage drew his shoulders back, his massive chest forward.

"Brother, let us share our strength," he said. "There is no need for dominance between us."

Savage's words sounded calm, reasonable. But Maul noticed his brother's body language. It was different than what Savage was saying. It told him Savage was prepared to fight.

In response, Maul also drew himself up to his full height, the motors in his mechanical legs whirring.

"Always two there are, my brother," Maul said. "A Master and an apprentice. And you are the apprentice."

Maul turned away, but heard the snap-hiss of Savage igniting his lightsaber.

"So it is time for a lesson," Maul said calmly.

Savage's saber howled as he flung himself at his brother in a brutal attack. The assault would have ended with most opponents cut in two and lying on the deck in lifeless halves. But Darth Maul was not most opponents. He parried Savage's slash effortlessly, their red saber blades sparking and chattering where they came in contact with each other. Then Maul twitched his wrists and spun Savage's saber out of his hands. A moment later Savage was lying on the deck, pinned by Maul's metal foot.

"You have grown so powerful," Savage said in amazement, staring up at his brother.

Maul paused for a moment, wondering if that were true. He let the memories come flooding back.

His training under the Sith Lord Darth Sidious, a childhood that was a blur of fear and pain, until he learned to control the fear and no longer noticed the pain.

His elation when Sidious unleashed him upon the galaxy, knowing he was eager to avenge the Sith's ancient defeat by crossing sabers with their Jedi enemies.

His satisfaction at seeing the Jedi Qui-Gon Jinn fall, mortally wounded by Maul's own Sith saber.

His dismay and disbelief to find himself plummeting helplessly into the depths of the planet Naboo, cut in half at the waist by Qui-Gon's apprentice, Obi-Wan Kenobi.

Maul should have died that day, but his rage and hatred had allowed him to fight back against fate, to summon the Force and survive. He had fallen, but he had lived. Somehow he had survived, making his way across the Outer Rim to the junk piles of Lotho Minor. There he had dwelled amid trash and madness, remembering only that he'd been ruined and cheated.

And there, he'd been found by Savage—a brother he hadn't known existed. Savage had brought him out of the darkness and back to Dathomir—his homeworld when he was an infant, before Sidious took him. The Nightsister witch Mother Talzin had used her arts to heal him. She had restored his memories, or at least the ones that could be recovered. She had replaced his rusty spiderlike legs with better ones, more suitable for the Sith warrior he once again knew himself to be.

And now Kenobi would pay—Kenobi, and then so many others. Savage was right. Maul's power was growing, because he had a purpose again, and a vision.

Maul kept his clawed foot on Savage's chest for another moment, to make sure both of them understood who was the Master and who was the apprentice. Then he shut off his saber and stepped away from his fallen brother.

"I shall complete your training," Maul said, extending his hand to help Savage to his feet. "Not as your brother, but as your Master."

CHAPTER TWO

The distress signal is coming from here—the Meridian sector," Obi-Wan Kenobi told Adi Gallia. "Cybloc system."

Their tri-winged *Eta*-class shuttle had just emerged from hyperspace, winking into existence not far from Cybloc Prime, the system's third planet. Adi sat in the pilot's chair—Obi-Wan was infamous in the Jedi Order for his dislike of flying, which he regarded as a task best left for droids. Adi, for her part, was one of the Order's best pilots, having led a squadron of Jedi starfighters into battle above Geonosis under the call sign Shooting Star.

Adi's brown eyes narrowed as she threaded the shuttle through Cybloc's necklace of moons, verifying that they were on the correct heading for Cybloc XII. She slid the shuttle into the moon's upper atmosphere, keeping one eye on the scopes as she considered their pursuit of Darth Maul and Savage Opress.

"It is close enough to the earlier attack," Adi said.

"I have a feeling it's them," Obi-Wan agreed.

Master Yoda had been the first to feel the disturbance in the Force. Through meditation, he had discovered its source—Obi-Wan's ancient enemy had somehow returned from the dead. Obi-Wan had been shocked, and certain Yoda was wrong. Hadn't he literally cut Darth Maul in two, watching as the two halves of the Sith warrior's body tumbled into the depths of Naboo?

But events had soon proved Yoda correct. The holographic message had come from the remote world of Raydonia. It had been terrible to watch. As the Jedi looked on in horror, Maul slaughtered an entire village of helpless people, and promised to do far worse if Obi-Wan didn't come to face him—and do so alone. Obi-Wan had agreed to do so, determined that this time he would finish what he'd started.

Obi-Wan still remembered his first sight of Maul on Raydonia—in fact, he doubted he would ever be able to forget it. The ruined Sith warrior had stood on a roof, surrounded by burning buildings, and stared down at him.

"You may have forgotten me, but I will never forget you," Maul had said in that strangely beautiful voice that should have belonged to a diplomat or a HoloNet media star. "You cannot imagine the depths I would go to to stay alive, fueled by my singular hatred for you."

Then they had fought—and Obi-Wan had been ambushed by another old enemy, the Zabrak warrior Savage Opress. The two Zabraks had overpowered Obi-Wan and dragged him onto their ship. Only the intervention of the assassin Asajj Ventress—Count Dooku's former apprentice and Obi-Wan's sworn enemy—had saved him from whatever dark plan Maul had for him.

After that the Jedi had sought everywhere for word of Maul and Savage. There were rumors that Maul was on the shadow world of Umbara, pursuing some secret agenda. Then reports began coming in from across the Outer Rim—two horned and tattooed warriors, murdering and pillaging, leaving chaos and terror in their wake. And now, if the reports were correct, their crime spree had taken them here, to Cybloc.

The teal hull of Cybloc Transfer Station appeared ahead, atop a tower that rose from Cybloc's surface far below. Adi docked the shuttle and they made their way through the station's corridors to the warehouse, where Superintendent Morlimur Snugg was waiting for them. Snugg was a Snivvian, a snaggletoothed alien with black eyes and wide nostrils from the distant planet Cadomai, wearing a blue jumpsuit. He led them into the wrecked office, indicating the disabled security droids and the empty safe.

"They oughta be flush—chips were all unlocked, no way to trace 'em," Snugg said. His speech had the frontier twang of the Outer Rim. "All done by two of the crabbiest Zabraks this side of the Hydian."

"They were alone?" Obi-Wan asked.

"Yup," Snugg said. "What were they? Couple of Jedi gone rogue?"

Obi-Wan and Adi shared a look.

"They're not Jedi," Obi-Wan said.

The superintendent frowned, his eyes settling on Obi-Wan's lightsaber, where it hung from his belt.

"Spark up that lightsaber for me," he said.

That wasn't the way most civilians addressed a Jedi, Obi-Wan thought with mild amusement. But he liked Snugg's no-nonsense manner, and figured he must have some reason for wanting an up-close look at an ignited lightsaber.

Obi-Wan hefted the hilt of his saber and activated the blade. It flared to life, a meter of brilliant blue energy.

"Mm-hmm," said Snugg. "The droids that got attacked said that theirs were red."

If he'd thought the two Jedi would be surprised by this, he was wrong.

"They are Sith, and we need to find them before they strike again," Obi-Wan said gravely.

"Well, they took my cargo ship," Snugg replied. "The droid survivors said they heard something about the Sertar sector."

Adi considered that. The Sertar sector was farther out in the Outer Rim, toward the galactic edge. Its worlds were mostly poor, backwater planets on little-used trade routes. It seemed an odd destination for a pair of Sith warriors flush with credits. But Obi-Wan didn't look surprised.

"What is in the Sertar sector?" Adi asked Obi-Wan, puzzled.

"That's where Florrum is," Obi-Wan replied.

"You've been there?" Adi asked. "What can we expect?"

Obi-Wan's blue eyes twinkled with amusement at some private thought.

"Pirates," he said.

CHAPTER THREE

Above the dull orange globe of the planet Florrum, a *Corona*-class Armed Frigate whirled through space. In the cockpit of the saucer-shaped attack ship, the Weequay pirate Jiro stared out the viewport, eyeing the cargo ship drifting ahead. It was a slab-sided freighter with offset engine pods. Markings on its side read ALC-9.

An Aurore-*class freighter,* thought Jiro. *Curious.*

But then, Jiro reminded himself, a lot of curious things could happen to a starship crossing the unimaginable distances between the stars. Hyperdrives malfunctioned. Life-support·

systems broke down. Crew members mutinied. Lost ships were found decades or centuries later, or never heard from again.

Whatever the reason the freighter was adrift, it was her crew's bad luck to be adrift *here*. Florrum was the territory of Jiro's boss, the Weequay pirate Hondo Ohnaka, and Hondo's gang made a good living intercepting merchant ships and shuttles traveling in this part of the galaxy. The cargoes were resold or divided among Hondo's pirates as booty. The passengers were held for ransom—if they looked valuable enough that somebody would pay for their safe return.

And if they didn't? Well, that was more bad luck.

"Get me a readout on that ship," Jiro ordered the rest of his Weequay crew. The pirates were clad in mismatched pieces of armor, their hair bound up in topknots above their leathery faces, which were pierced with jewelry and marked with tattoos.

"There are life-forms aboard," one of the Weequays said.

"The main reactor and hyperdrive generator are down," another pirate said, looking up from his console. "I think they're stranded."

Jiro laughed. With the cargo ship's critical systems malfunctioning, anyone aboard would be desperate. Well, that was too bad for them. They'd soon find out there were worse things than being stranded.

"And their communications?" Jiro asked.

"Operational, but silenced," a pirate said.

Interesting, Jiro thought. Perhaps the crew was already unconscious, or had given up hope and stopped calling for rescue. Either way, it didn't matter.

"We'll kill anyone on board and take the ship," Jiro said with a grin. "Let's hope they have a wealth of cargo."

The other Weequays grinned back. Hondo insisted taking prisoners was better business than shooting them, but his pirates disliked it. Prisoners were annoying. They panicked and begged and had to be guarded, all of which cut into time better spent on pirate activities such as drinking grog and telling lies.

The pirate ship slowed, docking with the crippled freighter. Jiro and his men marched through the airlock into the hold, which was filled with neatly ordered crates. Jiro pried one open. It was filled with heavy blaster pistols. Another pirate looked up eagerly from a crate he'd opened.

"Pure sansanna spice," he said with a grin.

"Hondo will be pleased," Jiro said. He'd feared the ship might be a slaver: Zygerrians and Thalassians, among others, favored *Aurores* for running slaves. But blasters and spice were easy to transport, and worth more than even he had dared to imagine.

"We drink tonight!" Jiro shouted happily. "Now find me those life-forms—"

Two snap-hisses sounded at the other end of the cargo hold. Startled, Jiro turned and saw two horned warriors standing there, the red glare of their lightsabers making them look like creatures out of a nightmare.

"Jedi!" Jiro yelled.

Blasterfire crackled through the hold. The two warriors deflected the bolts effortlessly. Within seconds the one with red tattoos had seized Jiro by the throat, while the one with yellow tattoos loomed over the other pirates, double-bladed saber held menacingly.

"Do you want to live?" Darth Maul asked Jiro.

Suddenly, Jiro couldn't breathe. His windpipe was being crushed. He stared into the Sith warrior's burning eyes.

"Yes," Jiro gasped. "Very badly."

Maul gestured and the terrible pressure on Jiro's throat was gone.

Savage Opress had opened a safe, turning it so the pirates could see inside. It was filled with credit chips.

"We will make you rich," Savage growled.

"Your skills and talents could serve us well," Maul added. "The choice is yours."

The pirates looked at one another in disbelief. Moments

ago they had been prepared to die. Now they weren't quite sure what was happening.

"Are you . . . are you hiring us?" Jiro asked, thinking this had to be a trick. "What kind of Jedi are you?"

Maul's eyes seemed to burn even more intensely.

"We're not Jedi," he said. "We are lords — crime lords."

Jiro glanced at the safe, thinking to himself that anyone casually showing that many credits probably had a lot more of them lying around. And anyway, if the two warriors were going to kill them, it already would have happened. That meant he could bargain a little.

"We work for Hondo," Jiro said. "You'll have to pay us really well to get us to betray him."

"Money is of no object for men like us," Maul said. "You will have all that you desire and more — if you pledge yourselves to me."

Jiro thought about it. There was such a thing as pushing your luck, he decided. And some choices weren't really choices at all.

"All right," Jiro said. "I'm tired of working for Hondo anyway. I'll call up a couple of the boys and see if they'll join us."

Maul smiled.

CHAPTER FOUR

Hours later, two more *Corona*-class pirate ships had docked with Jiro's ship and the cargo hauler. The captains Jiro had summoned muttered and exchanged nervous looks when they saw the fearsome, half-mechanical Maul and the hulking Savage. But they also saw the crates of blasters and spice, and the piles of credit chips.

"I am certain Captain Hondo will never throw in with you," said the Weequay pirate named Sabo, glancing over at where Savage stood with his lightsaber unlit, but at the ready.

Jiro frowned. Sabo had always been stubborn.

"Hondo's base will soon be ours," Maul warned. "And he will not survive this—unless he embraces the same choice I give you now."

"Ha, I'm in," said Jiro, hoping to get some of the new pirates to commit.

"So am I," rumbled Goru, a hulking Weequay wearing a high-collared vest.

"I'm not sure," said Sabo. "Let's see what Hondo says about that."

Hondo Ohnaka was working at his cluttered office desk when the transmission came in from orbit. He eyed the two tattooed warriors, giving momentary thanks that they were up in space and not down here on the plains of Florrum with him. If Hondo had to talk with people waving laser swords around, he preferred to do it from a distance of at least a few thousand kilometers.

"Two of your lieutenants have already sworn allegiance to me," the hologram of Maul said.

Hondo considered that. He could see that Jiro, Goru, Parsel, and the other pirates were giving the two warriors a healthy respect, which was only wise. But the Weequays didn't look like they were eager to get away from the two

Zabraks, which is what Hondo would have been trying to do.

But wait, Hondo mused. *Didn't Jiro's ship intercept the freighter before summoning the others?*

Aha, Hondo thought. That wasn't fear he was seeing on his men's faces. It was *greed.* The two warriors had promised them something—and pirates didn't put much stock in empty talk. They preferred cold hard credits or goods that were within reach, or would be very soon.

Put all the evidence together, and it told Hondo that the freighter's hold had to be full of good things—and if he were patient, he could get his hands on those good things.

Pilf Mukmuk, Hondo's red-skinned Kowakian monkey-lizard, hopped on his master's shoulder. Hondo glanced at the other pirates in his office. They were staring at the tattooed warriors in fascination and waiting to see what their boss would say.

"Traitors!" Hondo said to Maul. "Scum! I'm so proud . . . but so betrayed!"

The warrior with the mechanical legs was growing impatient. Those legs made him look like some terrifying flightless avian, Hondo thought.

Jiro and Goru walked Sabo over to the cyborg warrior.

"There is a penalty for resistance," Maul said in his unhurried, cultured voice.

He then ignited his saber and slammed it through Sabo's chest.

Hondo went cold. Up there in space, his pirates no longer looked like they were mentally counting credits. Now they looked scared. Things had changed, Hondo thought. The horned warrior wasn't negotiating—he was making demands.

Which was too bad for him—because *no one* told Hondo Ohnaka what to do.

Hondo leaned closer to the holorecorder transmitting his image into space.

"Let me warn you, you're not the first laser-sword-wielding maniacs I've had to deal with," he said. "And Hondo Ohnaka survives every time!"

Hondo could almost feel those terrible eyes burning into him.

"We shall see," Maul said darkly.

CHAPTER FIVE

The Jedi shuttle dropped out of hyperspace at a cautious distance from Florrum. Seated at the controls, Adi Gallia peered at her scope and saw a freighter accompanied by three saucer-shaped attack ships.

The scope identified the freighter: an *Aurore*, designation ALC-9.

"We have a match on the cargo ship," Adi said.

Obi-Wan nodded, pleased by the news. He and Adi had headed for Florrum along the galaxy's better-traveled routes, following the great Perlemian Trade Route to the Shaltin

Tunnels at Lianna, then leaving the tunnels for the gundark trade routes near Brachi. They'd been hoping the Sith brothers would choose slower, less-used routes to Florrum in order to maximize their chances of going undetected, and so allow the two Jedi to catch up. Which they now had.

But the news wasn't all good. A glance at the scopes told Obi-Wan as much.

"It seems Maul and Savage have picked up a pirate escort," he said.

"Maybe to unload the stolen cargo," Adi said.

"I'm not sure Hondo would have an alliance with Maul and his brother," Obi-Wan said cautiously.

Adi glanced at the other Jedi, curious. Obi-Wan's skills as a negotiator had taken him from one side of the galaxy to the other, and he'd met a lot of strange people—including the kinds of beings Jedi Knights didn't normally spend time with. Such company didn't seem to embarrass Obi-Wan, though. He actually appeared to enjoy knowing his way around the seamier side of galactic society.

"So you know this Hondo personally?" Adi asked doubtfully.

The question seemed to amuse Obi-Wan. But Adi thought he also looked a little weary.

"Unfortunately, yes," he said.

Hondo was wondering what he was going to do when one of his lieutenants poked his head back into his office.

"Oi, Hondo — there's a Jedi contacting you," he said. "Says his name is Kenobi."

"Kenobi?" Hondo asked. "Ha! My, aren't we popular today. Put him through."

A moment later, Obi-Wan's image shimmered into being on Hondo's desk.

"Greetings, Hondo," Obi-Wan said politely.

The Jedi was always polite, Hondo thought. Too bad for Obi-Wan that Hondo wasn't in the mood for a nice chat.

"What kind of menace have you brought to my planet now?" demanded Hondo. "First you lose this system and Grievous comes in and destroys my entire stronghold, leaving me here to just rummage through the leftovers of my once-great empire. And now these two horned men show up. Who are these horny-headed maniacs? They don't seem like normal Jedi —"

Obi-Wan had waited patiently during this rant, but now he interrupted Hondo.

"Not Jedi, Hondo — Sith," Obi-Wan said. "We tracked them here."

"They just threatened to attack me with a group of my men," Hondo said. He looked wounded. "My own men!"

"Yes, we are looking at them right now," Obi-Wan said. "A cargo vessel and three of your starships. They are heading toward you, Hondo."

"Da-da-da," Hondo said impatiently. "More to the point, are you going to help me when you get here? Is it going to cost me anything?"

That was very like Hondo, Obi-Wan thought—two of the most dangerous beings in the galaxy were on their way to confront him and quite possibly kill him, and he was worried about credits.

"There's nothing we can do about your men, but we can certainly do something about the Sith," Obi-Wan said.

"Good!" said Hondo. "I'll deal with my men. You deal with those tattooed crazies."

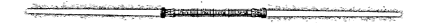

The pirate ships streaked down through Florrum's atmosphere in formation, the cargo ship sitting in the center, protected by the other crafts' weapons, and fighters flying escort. The fighters fired volleys of missiles at Hondo's outpost below, dodging rockets sent up in retaliation. Explosions blossomed on the ground, sending broken equipment and the bodies of pirates into the air.

"Well, that settles it," muttered Hondo. "Those traitors are no longer my men."

The pirate fleet landed outside Hondo's base and pirates loyal to Hondo charged to meet them, defiantly yelling pirate oaths that were impressively creative and thoroughly vile.

"I want their tongues!" Hondo roared, his blood up.

The pirate craft lowered their gangplanks. Pirates raced down the ramps, firing their blasters at their former comrades. Pirates on both sides screamed in agony from glancing hits or fell, dropped in their tracks by laser fire. At the top of the cargo ship's ramp stood Maul and Savage, watching the battle unfold around them.

The two Sith realized there was another ship coming in for a landing—a Jedi shuttlecraft. It crested the canyon wall and touched down neatly on the ridge.

"The Jedi, brother!" Savage yelled. "They've found us!"

"No," Maul said, teeth bared in anger. "It's too soon—my plan isn't finished yet. Too soon."

The Zabraks raced for the ridge, the two bands of battling pirates momentarily forgotten. They arrived as the shuttle's landing ramp descended—but there was no chance to take the two Jedi by surprise. Obi-Wan and Adi had already felt the disturbance in the Force, a wave of anger and malice rolling ahead of Maul and Savage as if a stone had been hurled into a still pool.

Adi and Obi-Wan whirled to face the Sith, lightsabers blazing blue.

"Throwing in with pirates now?" asked Obi-Wan as he assumed a defensive stance. "Oh, how the mighty Sith have fallen."

Maul brought his saber crashing down on Obi-Wan's, trying to turn his fury into a battering ram to demolish the Jedi's defenses. Obi-Wan parried, turning the crimson blade aside, and the two traded rapid blows, their sabers howling, whining bars of light. Savage crossed sabers with Adi, whose Tholothian tendrils whipped first this way and that as she parried and counterattacked.

Obi-Wan and Adi fell back into a defensive stance, moving with the practiced ease of warriors used to operating as a team and becoming a unit whose strengths were greater together than they could be separately. Against them, the Sith's attacks were raw and vicious—animal rage amplified and focused by the dark side of the Force.

The combatants descended down the ridge and continued their battle in the canyon below. Hondo's right flank had crumbled and the pirate chief and his loyalists were retreating toward the main doors of their lair. Obi-Wan pushed Maul back, his mechanical legs whining, and the two leapt to the top of a pirate shuttle, continuing their duel.

"I have plans, Kenobi—and you will not stand in my way this time," Maul said.

He swung his saber viciously. Obi-Wan caught it on his blade and the two continued to trade blows, grunting with effort.

Nearby, Savage and Adi faced each other across the X of their crossed sabers. Teeth gritted, Savage rained blows down on the slim Jedi, roaring as he tried to crash through her defenses. Little by little Adi fell back, all her skill no match for his enormous strength.

Drawing on the Force, Savage hurled Adi into the side of a wrecked shuttle, leaving her momentarily stunned. Before she could recover, he lowered his head and charged, ramming his horns deeply into her body and snapping her head back. Adi gasped and her hands shook.

Obi-Wan heard her cry of surprise and felt her anguish rip through the Force. He shoved Maul away, moving to confront Savage, knocking him off balance as Adi fell to the ground, motionless. Maul sprang after Obi-Wan, aiming a killing blow at him from behind in hopes of catching his Jedi enemy in a moment of distraction. Obi-Wan sensed it coming and whirled with blinding speed, parrying Maul's attack. Then he jumped aside, knowing it would be a fatal mistake to be caught between two Sith.

"Kenobi, this way!" someone yelled.

Obi-Wan realized it was Hondo.

He drew on the Force, shoving Maul and Savage aside. Adi's lightsaber leapt into his hand as he ran for the outpost, then retreated with Hondo and his men into the safety of their lair.

CHAPTER SIX

Inside the Florrum outpost, a weary Obi-Wan found Hondo and his loyal pirates waiting at a T-shaped intersection amid heaps of booty—crates and piles, a large statue, and other ill-gotten gains.

"Take this cannon down the hall," barked Hondo. "We will ambush those traitors there."

A gaggle of pirates hoisted a heavy antipersonnel cannon onto their shoulders and carried it down the corridor.

"Where are the rest of your men?" Obi-Wan asked, alarmed to see how few stood with the pirate chieftain.

"They're setting up an ambush," Hondo said, nodding in the direction his men had gone. "We can use your help. Where is the other Jedi?"

Obi-Wan looked away, momentarily overcome with grief. Adi Gallia had been friends with Qui-Gon Jinn, and it was her investigations that had led to their mission to Naboo to break the Trade Federation blockade. Adi had instructed Obi-Wan when he was an apprentice alongside her own Padawan, Siri Tachi, then been a friend to Anakin Skywalker when so many in the Jedi Order doubted him. And she had helped save Obi-Wan's life at Geonosis, Saleucami, and Lola Sayu. It seemed impossible that she could have passed into the Force, never to fight or teach again.

He managed to get his emotions under control and look back at Hondo.

"She's dead," Obi-Wan said.

Hondo looked shocked.

"They are too powerful for even you?" he asked. "Whoa. Hey. I am speechless."

They heard voices approaching, an excited welter of pirate babble. The voices echoed in the confines of the corridor, making the speakers sound closer than Obi-Wan hoped they actually were.

"I think they went this way—over here," one of the pirates serving Maul called out.

Obi-Wan ignited his saber. Hondo's pirates readied their blasters.

"If I can separate Maul and Savage from your men, can you handle them?" Obi-Wan asked Hondo.

"If you can take care of the horned devils, I assure you I can handle my men," Hondo replied.

Obi-Wan nodded, looking both ways down the corridor that formed the top of the T.

"I shall draw the brothers away," he said. "Once that's done, blast the passageway closed."

Hondo grinned.

"Leave you alone with the two crazies?" he asked. "OK. Good plan!"

They were just in time—Maul raced around the corner, with Savage right behind him, followed by the gang of renegade pirates. Obi-Wan fled down the passage, making sure he'd been spotted. Hondo gave the order to retreat in the opposite direction as the renegade pirates tried to catch up with the two Zabraks.

Maul spotted Hondo and his pirates, and bared his teeth.

"Do not let them escape!" Maul warned his men.

The pirates struggled to keep up with the speedy Sith. Hondo retreated down the corridor, trying to will the Zabraks to hurry, urging their Force or whatever they called it to give them extra speed. He didn't want the Sith to sense the surprise he had planned.

The two Sith reached the intersection and raced after Obi-Wan, while the rebel pirates ran in the other direction, eager to catch Hondo and his loyalists.

Perfect, Hondo thought.

He yelled for his men to fire. Laser blasts ripped through the rock, collapsing the corridor's ceiling and leaving the passage filled with stones and debris. The renegades were now separated from their Sith Masters. Hondo nodded to his own men, who turned the heavy laser cannons so that they faced their former comrades. The renegade pirates stared down the wide barrels of the heavy guns in dismay. They were badly outgunned, and knew it. They stood there for a moment, their faces glum, and then dropped their weapons.

"Are you still willing to fight me?" Hondo demanded. "The horned men aren't interested in helping you — they're only interested in Kenobi."

Jiro pushed his way through the crowd, arms open pleadingly.

"They promised us wealth and power, boss," he said. "Please forgive us! Please don't kill us! We beg of you!"

Hondo raised an eyebrow.

"Kill you?" he asked. "I wouldn't kill you."

Hondo turned to speak to both sets of pirates—those who had betrayed him as well as those who had remained loyal.

"Everyone, the horned men's ship is filled with valuable goods," he said.

A couple of the captured pirates nodded enthusiastically, having seen this wealth for themselves. Hondo's pirates exchanged interested looks.

"As your restored leader," Hondo said, "I say we celebrate our reunification!"

The pirates who had followed Jiro began to grin, thinking that a celebration sounded much better than their own executions. Meanwhile, the pirates who had been shooting at them a moment before were thinking about how rich two tattooed Sith warriors probably were. The two sets of pirates began to grin at each other, hostilities pushed out of their heads by the idea of easy credits and a good, raucous pirate party.

"To the landing pad!" Hondo yelled. The men let out a thunderous cheer and followed him, hollering and whooping, and Hondo was so happy to be surrounded once again by cheerful pirate noise that he found himself laughing as they ran to intercept the Sith.

CHAPTER SEVEN

Maul and Savage walked down the long corridor that led to the landing pad, sabers glowing red. Obi-Wan stood halfway down the passageway, waiting for them.

Obi-Wan had been only a Padawan when he fought Maul on Naboo, more than a decade ago. He'd still been learning to sense the will of the Force, and to keep from letting his emotions distract and overwhelm him. Now Obi-Wan was an experienced duelist, and had long ago found the calm center Qui-Gon had tried to teach him to search for.

Maul had been a well-trained, disciplined warrior on

Naboo—but his real advantage had been the raw power and feral intensity with which he fought. Obi-Wan didn't know where the Sith had spent the long years since he'd tumbled down the shaft of the Theed generator core, and he couldn't imagine what Maul had been doing. But whatever it was, Maul was stronger with the Force than he'd been—stronger, but also colder and more determined. It was the other Zabrak—Mother Talzin's creature Savage—who fought with animal rage.

Obi-Wan knew the Sith would expect him to take up a defensive stance in an effort to keep them at bay. But he also knew that tactic would give him no hope to prevail—he would be worn down until his guard slipped and then he would die, like Adi had.

Surprise was his best bet for survival—and perhaps his only chance.

"Surrender," Maul said quietly. "We are two, and you are no match for us both."

Obi-Wan ignited both Adi's lightsaber and his own.

"You are mistaken," he said—and then he hurled himself at the two Sith, both sabers flashing in his hands.

The two Sith fell back, startled to find Obi-Wan taking the offensive and surprised by the ferocity of his attack. Sabers hissed, their blades striking sparks from the walls, leaving half-melted scrapes and bubbling burns in their wake.

The two Sith maneuvered to pin Obi-Wan against the wall—but there was so little room in the corridor that they got in each other's way. Savage charged in to strike, leaving his left arm exposed for a split second. It was all the time Obi-Wan needed. He lunged and sliced the Zabrak's yellow-and-black arm off at the shoulder.

Savage howled in agony, retreating toward Maul as his brother shoved Obi-Wan backward with a blast of Force power. Maul stared at Obi-Wan, eyes blazing, the hatred boiling inside him. But then he regained control of his emotions, and shut off the surge of animal rage. He had bigger plans now than merely revenge, and settling the score with Obi-Wan Kenobi could wait.

"Come, my apprentice," Maul said to Savage. "This plan has failed, but we will have another opportunity."

He and his wounded brother raced for the landing pad. Behind them, in the gloom, an exhausted Obi-Wan gathered his energy to chase after them.

The pirates were waiting when Maul and Savage emerged into the light of day. The two Sith came to a stop, gazing at the motley band of brigands between them and their cargo ship.

"Jiro, ready the men," Maul ordered. "We're leaving."

But it was Hondo Ohnaka who stepped forward.

"My men aren't going anywhere with you," he sneered. "Look at them, men! How powerful can they be? They are running away from Kenobi!"

The pirates grinned, cackled, and pointed.

"Filth," Maul spat. "You will pay for your insolence."

"Insolence?" Hondo laughed, as Obi-Wan arrived to stand beside him. "We're pirates—we don't even know what that means!"

He turned to his men.

"Open fire!" Hondo yelled. "If we kill these two, their riches will be ours!"

Maul and Savage found themselves surrounded by laser blasts flying in from all angles. The pirates were firing for all they were worth, eager to brag about the day they'd taken down two Sith. Maul and Savage spun their lightsabers in continuous arcs, deflecting bolts in all directions. But there were too many pirates, too many blasters. They couldn't possibly block them all. A bolt got through Maul's defenses, crumpling one of his mechanical legs.

Maul growled, then reached desperately out in the Force, turning his fury into a command. The Jedi shuttle tumbled off the ridge with a groan, crashing down on the landing pad and scattering the pirates. The two brothers raced up the ramp of their ship, which lifted off moments later. As it shrank into the sky, a pirate took aim with a rocket launcher, sending a line of fire streaking after the fleeing ship. The rocket slammed into one of the cargo ship's engines, sending the craft tumbling through the air.

Obi-Wan and Hondo watched as the cargo ship plummeted to the ground, far in the distance. Hondo gestured to several Starhawk speeder bikes parked nearby.

"Well, Kenobi," Hondo said. "Let's get out there and see what riches have fallen from the sky for you and I. Shall we?"

"Very well," said Obi-Wan, peering in the direction of the crash site.

The impact had left a deep crater and scattered twisted metal and ship components across the surface of Florrum. Hondo's pirates were poking through the wreckage, calling dibs on whatever intact goods they could find. There wasn't much.

"There's no sign of those two, boss," said Jiro.

Hondo looked over the wreckage, simultaneously annoyed by the absence of riches and pleased to not have to deal with two dangerous Sith again.

"Well, if the condition of these goods is any indication, your friends have been vaporized," Hondo said.

That was good news, the pirate chief thought—the fewer laser swords being waved around near him, the better. But Obi-Wan looked far from convinced.

"I wouldn't be so sure," he said. "I cut one of them in half once, and he survived."

"Well, isn't that interesting," Hondo said, as Obi-Wan raised his chin and stared up into the sky.

CHAPTER EIGHT

Supreme Chancellor Palpatine sat in his office with Obi-Wan Kenobi, Mace Windu, and Yoda, gazing out at the endless cityscape of Coruscant, capital world of the Republic. He was wondering when Obi-Wan would stop badgering him about two bandits with laser swords who might or might not have survived a crash on a horrible dustball of a planet about as far from the towers and lights of Coruscant as you could get.

Palpatine decided that Obi-Wan wouldn't be finished anytime soon, and that he'd heard enough.

"I think we have closure on this matter, Master Kenobi,"

he said in the polite but firm tone he used when he wished to end one of the Senate's endless yammering debates.

To his annoyance, Kenobi refused to take the hint.

"I disagree, Chancellor," the Jedi said. "Everything we've learned about this is that the Sith are persistent. They will not die."

"I understand your reservations, Master Kenobi," Palpatine said, more firmly now. "But I am afraid we can no longer allow this personal matter of yours to be a Republic concern. It does not appear this Darth Maul is a direct threat to the Republic. We need to redirect your efforts to the cause at hand—stopping Count Dooku and thus ending the Clone Wars."

"Maul was trying to build an army of pirates," Kenobi insisted.

"So let him," Palpatine said dismissively. "Let him play with the rabble. It is of no relevance to the Senate compared to the Separatist threat. Good day, gentlemen."

The three Jedi turned to go, but Palpatine could still hear Kenobi talking. Now he was trying to convince Yoda.

"Something is stirring in the underworld," Kenobi said urgently to the green-skinned Grandmaster of the Jedi Order. "The crime families have had too much free rein since the Jedi have been distracted by the Clone Wars. I fear it is a fertile place for Maul to flourish, if he has indeed survived."

"Right you may be, Obi-Wan—but heed the words of

the Chancellor we must," Yoda replied, inching along with his walking stick. "A personal matter this is for you. Clouded your judgment may be. In time, if he lives, reveal himself again Maul will. And then swiftly we shall act."

Behind them, Palpatine sat alone at his desk. He steepled his fingers together and allowed himself a private, satisfied smile.

PART TWO: EMINENCE

CHAPTER NINE

A white-hulled starship glided through the void, its sharply angled wings gleaming in the unfiltered glare of sunlight in deep space. Below the sleek craft hung the planet Florrum, lair of the pirate Hondo Ohnaka and his gang.

But no pirate craft emerged from the planet's atmosphere to engage this ship. This wasn't a slow, fat-bellied merchant galleon or a luxurious but poorly armed civilian craft. This starship was the *Gauntlet*, a *Kom'rk* transport—nearly seventy meters long, bristling with blaster cannons, and crewed by battle-tested Mandalorian warriors. If Hondo's pirates saw the

Gauntlet on their scopes, they decided it was wiser to let her go about her business.

That was a good decision.

The *Gauntlet*'s sensors locked onto another craft—an escape pod drifting in a low orbit around Florrum. The shadow of the Mandalorian transport fell over the little pod as its crew brought the smaller craft in for docking, aligning their airlocks. The hatches connecting transport and pod opened with a hiss of equalizing atmosphere.

It was freezing inside the cramped pod. A group of armored Mandalorian warriors tramped inside. Each was a walking arsenal, armed with blasters, rockets, flamethrowers, grenades, and knives—not to mention a reputation for being ready to use them. Their gargoyle helmets had T-shaped visors and bore the insignia of the Death Watch.

Behind them came two other figures, also in Mandalorian armor. The first was a large man with a confident, impatient stride. His helmet had two cannons over each ear, tipped up so they looked like horns. Beside him was an armored woman. She was smaller and slimmer than the other warriors. Her helmet's faceplate was white, and its lines were softer and less angular. But her efficient walk and watchful gaze left little doubt that she was as deadly as any of them—and perhaps more so.

Two Zabraks were lying in the dark pod, their tattooed

bodies covered with frost. The Mandalorian leader grabbed one of the Zabraks by the face, inspecting his red and black tattoos and the crown of spikes emerging from his skull. The warrior stirred fitfully, barely conscious. The leader's gaze jumped to the other Zabrak. He was also barely alive, his yellow tattoos dulled by a coating of rime. Then his gaze turned to the lightsabers on their belts.

"You're not a Jedi, are you?" muttered Pre Vizsla. "What are you?"

"Should we rub 'em out?" asked the woman, whose name was Bo-Katan. Vizsla could tell from her voice that she thought that was an excellent idea. But then she usually did.

"No," Vizsla said. "I want to hear their story. If they're an enemy of the Jedi, then they're a friend of mine."

He turned to his warriors and pointed at the frozen Zabraks.

"Load 'em up!" Vizsla ordered.

In his quarters aboard the *Gauntlet*, Pre Vizsla sank into a chair and removed his helmet, revealing a bald head stitched by an ugly-looking scar. He held the lightsabers they'd taken from the two Zabraks, staring at the deadly weapons as he turned them over and over in his hands. Even through his gloves, he could feel the chill of the frozen escape pod still clinging to the metal hilts.

Then he put the weapons down and reached back over his shoulder, extracting a black cylinder from a pocket in his jumpsuit. Vizsla pressed a button and a flat, meter-long blade materialized out of the end of the device. The energy blade was black—rather than producing light, it seemed to suck it in. The black blade was simultaneously fascinating to look at and hurt the eyes. Vizsla held the weapon in front of him and swung it lazily. The blade made a sound like a whistle, or perhaps a scream. Its weight felt comforting in his hand.

The weapon was called the darksaber, and Vizsla's ancestors had stolen it from the Jedi Temple on Coruscant long ago. Vizsla knew nothing about the darksaber's origins, or its history before it fell into Mandalorian hands. Nor did he care—stuff like that was for historians to chatter about. Vizsla only cared that the blade symbolized his right to lead the Death Watch—and that many Jedi had died upon its blade over the centuries. He hoped many more Jedi would meet the same fate in the future.

The Jedi, Vizsla thought, baring his teeth and slashing viciously at the enemies he saw in his imagination. The Mandalorian clans had invaded the Republic thousands of years ago, only to have the Jedi defeat their clans' chieftain, known in every generation as the Mandalore. In their lust for revenge, the Mandalorians had fallen under the sway of the Sith, who were just Jedi with different-colored lightsaber blades. That had led to the Mandalorians' defeat and ruin. The clans had been scattered, the old warrior codes neglected, the title of Mandalore held by brigands and fools.

And then, seven centuries ago, the Jedi had led Republic warships to Mandalore, bombarding the planet until huge areas of its surface were reduced to lifeless expanses of fine white sand. Then the Republic had put traitors in power— weaklings who had destroyed Mandalore's weapons and rejected its warrior codes.

The Death Watch had worked secretly for centuries to overthrow the peace-loving New Mandalorians and restore the clans' honor, a campaign that had culminated with the Great Clan Wars more than a decade ago. That vicious conflict had turned warlord against warlord, splitting clans and even families. The battles of the Great Clan Wars had left terrible new scars on Mandalore's surface, and ended not with the Death Watch's victory, but with the New Mandalorians stronger than ever. A few unrepentant warlords had accepted exile to Concordia, Mandalore's moon. But most had supported the pacifists, and chosen a new Mandalore from among their ranks—Duchess Satine Kryze.

Vizsla snarled at the thought, then raised the darksaber and carved a figure 8 in the air in front of him.

Let me be the one to undo the injustice that has been done, he thought.

Clan Vizsla had been given charge of Concordia and its exiles, and Pre Vizsla himself had become the moon's governor—while secretly plotting against the Duchess, and working to restore the Death Watch. But the hated Jedi had interfered and ruined those plans. First Obi-Wan Kenobi had discovered the Death Watch's weapons factories and rescued Satine. Then Count Dooku, the Jedi turncoat who led the Separatists, had betrayed the Death Watch. Even that hadn't been enough of an insult—Dooku had branded Vizsla with his saber, leaving the scar that snaked across the right side of his face. On Carlac, Ahsoka Tano—brought there by the turncoat Lux Bonteri—had taken the lives of several of Vizsla's warriors.

And now two more lightsaber wielders were in Mandalorian hands. Perhaps Bo-Katan had been right, Vizsla thought. Perhaps he should have left the two Zabraks to die in space.

But if the two Zabraks had lightsabers, that meant they could command the strange power that the Jedi and Sith both called the Force. And powerful enemies of the Jedi might help the Death Watch achieve its goals.

Vizsla held the darksaber before his eyes, staring into the nothingness of its blade. *Soon,* he promised himself. *Soon the Death Watch will declare itself. Soon we will have revenge.*

He deactivated the weapon. Perhaps the two Zabrak refugees would prove useful tools. If not, he would discard them—like any tool found unsuitable for the job.

Darth Maul awakened to find medical droids tending to his damaged legs. Nearby, his brother, Savage Opress, lay unconscious, being worked on by other droids.

Maul didn't recognize his surroundings, but he reached out with the Force and felt the hot pulse of lives around him. They radiated hatred and envy and malice. He could feel that they were not Force-users—in their company, the lowliest Sith apprentice would have been like a bonfire among candles—but he could also sense that they were brutal and capable despite the lack.

Interesting, Maul thought. *Where am I?*

When he'd returned to consciousness, Maul had feared for a moment that he had forgotten everything again, that once again he had escaped death but lost himself in the effort. But this time, the memories had come flooding back at once. He and his brother had dueled Obi-Wan Kenobi on Florrum, but the accursed Jedi had struck off Savage's arm. Maul had led his brother to their freighter, only to find Hondo Ohnaka's turncoat pirates waiting in ambush. One of the pirates had made a lucky shot and damaged Maul's mechanical leg.

The two Sith had escaped in their cargo ship, but just after takeoff a rocket fired from the ground had destroyed one of the ship's engines, sending it spinning out of control. Maul had aimed the ship toward space, locked the throttle on full power, and set the autopilot to keep the ship on course. Then he'd led Savage to an escape pod, ejecting the lifeboat at the top of the doomed cargo ship's trajectory.

They'd been just high enough in the atmosphere for the escape pod's engines to push them the rest of the way to orbit, but then the pod's batteries had run down, starving the two Zabraks of oxygen and warmth. Savage had succumbed first, and eventually even Maul had felt his vision turn gray, then fade to black.

The door to the medical bay opened, admitting a scarred, hard-looking man in Mandalorian armor, followed by a woman and several warriors. The soldiers kept their attention locked on Maul and Savage, blasters ready. The woman removed her helmet. She had green eyes and red hair held in place by a gray headband. Her eyes were cold and calculating as they studied him.

Mandalorians, Maul thought. They were a tough people, still smoldering over ancient defeats and resentments. It gave them focus, made them strong. But rather than use that strength, they wasted it—most Mandalorians were mercenaries, bounty hunters, or thugs.

But still, they were warriors worthy of respect. Long ago at the Orsis Academy, a Mandalorian named Meltch Krakko had helped train Maul in the warrior arts, teaching him tracking and tactics and numerous combat techniques. Krakko was dead—Maul had broken his neck on the same day he'd killed everyone else at the academy.

The hard-looking man held up two lightsabers.

"You're not Jedi," Pre Vizsla said. "So who are you?"

Maul just growled at him.

Bo-Katan, unimpressed, aimed her blaster—but not at Maul. Instead, she leveled it at the helpless Savage.

"We are Sith," Maul said, approving of the Mandalorian woman's ruthlessness.

Now Bo-Katan's blaster was pointed at Maul.

"Do you serve Count Dooku?" Vizsla asked.

"I serve no one," Maul said.

Vizsla looked at Savage and then back at Maul. Maul could see the man's brain working behind his eyes.

"I thought there could only be two Sith," Vizsla said. "A

Master and an apprentice."

"We are brothers," Maul said. "The true Lords of the Sith."

Bo-Katan lowered her blaster. Vizsla looked skeptically at Maul's damaged legs and Savage's stump of an arm. Maul could guess what he was thinking: *For Lords of the Sith, they're sure missing a lot of parts.*

"What happened to your ship?" Vizsla asked.

"Destroyed by Jedi," Maul said.

Vizsla leaned closer.

"Do you know *which* Jedi?" he asked, and Maul could feel his curiosity flaring in the Force.

"Kenobi," Maul growled, the word like a curse.

Vizsla and Bo-Katan looked at each other.

"And what do you seek now, Sith?" Vizsla asked.

"Fortune and power," Maul said.

Vizsla grinned, teeth bared like a predator catching a scent. He turned to the medical droid.

"Repair this one's legs," he ordered. "Do what you can for the other."

The medical droid acknowledged the order.

Vizsla strode out of the medical bay, followed by Bo-Katan.

CHAPTER TEN

They sent a Death Watch warrior to bring Maul to Pre Vizsla's tent.

Walking smoothly on his new humanoid prosthetic legs, Maul stepped out of the tent that housed the medical bay and into the center of a Mandalorian camp, his yellow eyes skipping between the tents and shelters the warriors had set up. A circular fence surrounded the camp. Behind it, a pair of *Kom'rk* transports were parked, their wings raised in landing configuration. The planet was swampy and shrouded in fog, its skies a leaden gray.

"Welcome to Zanbar," the Mandalorian said, his voice harsh through his helmet's speakers.

Maul crossed the space between the medical tent and the main tent, the warrior a step behind him. He stopped before the main tent and the warrior prodded him in the back with a blaster.

"Go on," the Mandalorian said harshly. "Get moving."

It would have been the easiest thing in the galaxy to kill the man. Maul could have done it without turning around. First he'd use the Force to crush the windpipe. Then the blaster would fly out of the weakening hands and into Maul's.

But there was Savage to think of, unconscious and helpless in the medical bay. And Maul had time. He would file away the insult, and avenge it later, when he had time to do the job properly and make it an effective demonstration of the fate awaiting anyone who dared to touch a Lord of the Sith.

Maul allowed himself a brief smile at the thought. The warrior was already dead. He just didn't know it yet.

Maul entered the tent and found Vizsla sitting on a stool, with warriors standing behind him. Before the Mandalorian leader sat a pot and two cups.

"In time for tea," Vizsla said. "Come join me."

Maul sat on a stool. Vizsla poured tea into two cups and offered one to Maul.

"Made with the florets of a Cassius tree," Vizsla said. "It's good for your health."

Maul took the cup, sniffed at the steam curling above it, then drank.

Tea with a Mandalorian, he thought. *The galaxy is certainly full of surprises.*

The Sith warrior eyed the symbol on Vizsla's armor.

"Your mark?" Maul asked.

"The sign of Clan Vizsla," the other man replied. "I am Pre Vizsla. We are the Death Watch, descendents of the true warrior faith all Mandalorians once knew."

Vizsla nodded at the watching Mandalorians.

"Now my people are living in exile because we will not abandon our heritage," he said. "Our people were warriors. Strong. Feared. Now they're ruled by the New Mandalorians, who think that being a pacifist is a good thing. They've given away our honor and tradition for peace."

Agitated, Vizsla began striding around the tent, helmet in hand.

"Duchess Satine and her corrupt leadership are crushing our souls, destroying our identity," he said. "*That* is our struggle."

Vizsla slammed down his helmet, looking around at the other warriors.

Maul sipped his tea.

"If they are weak, why do you wait?" he asked.

Vizsla refused to take the bait.

"The Duchess has powerful allies," he said. "Including your Jedi friend Kenobi. He is also responsible for our exile. Perhaps fortune brought us together."

Maul looked the warriors over. They were Mandalorians, but more than common mercenaries. They had a purpose. A plan. And their enemy, this Duchess Satine, was someone Obi-Wan valued, perhaps would even defend with his life.

If so, it would be the Jedi's undoing.

Maul nodded at Vizsla.

"It is the will of the Force," he said. "We can help you reclaim Mandalore—"

"—and punish Kenobi for his trespasses," Vizsla finished.

Maul could feel the warriors' hatred of their enemies pulsing in the Force, as well as their excitement at the idea of seeing those enemies brought down and ruined. But Bo-Katan remained calm, her face skeptical.

"We allied ourselves with Sith before," she reminded her comrades. "Count Dooku. He also betrayed us. Sith are no better than Jedi. They claim to be powerful, but we put these two back together after the Jedi gutted them."

Maul stared through the steam of his tea at the Mandalorian

woman. This was not a shove in the back, witnessed by no one. This was a public challenge, and to suffer it in silence would be a fatal display of weakness. He twitched his hand, feeling the Force awaiting his command.

Bo-Katan began to gag.

"Doubt will only lead to failure," Maul said.

The Mandalorians drew their weapons with a clatter and aimed them at Maul. But Vizsla calmly ordered them to hold their fire as Bo-Katan continued to struggle for air.

"Our combined strength will be rewarded," Maul said. "Mandalore will be yours—and Kenobi, this Sith pretender Dooku, and all our enemies will fall."

He released his grip on Bo-Katan with a contemptuous flip of his fingers. She fell to the ground, gasping for breath.

"Check on your brother," Vizsla told Maul. "We'll put it to a vote."

Maul got to his feet and pushed his way out of the tent. A moment later, Bo-Katan rose as well. She grinned at Vizsla. The Sith warrior had passed the test.

CHAPTER ELEVEN

Savage awoke to find a medical droid prodding at him with its needle-like metal arms. Surprised, he smashed the offending machine with his fist, toppling it. He didn't know where he was, and suddenly his mind jumped back to when he had found himself on a table, surrounded by the Nightsisters of his homeworld, Dathomir. He had felt their spells invading his body while he lay there helpless. Their sorcery had crawled through him like a worm, gnawing at his innards, changing his body and then his mind.

Savage raised his fist again, rage ripping through him and demanding release—but before he could do further damage, someone grabbed his arm in a powerful grip and he looked up to see his brother's face.

"Rest, apprentice," Maul said. "We're safe. Our crash was discovered by enemies of the Jedi, and we are in their care."

Savage shook the memories away. This was his brother—his Master. He realized his severed arm had been replaced with a mechanical one while he slept—a collection of silver rods and plates and pistons, interlaced with multi-colored wires. He stared at the machinery in wonder, opening and closing his artificial fingers.

"Are we prisoners?" Savage asked Maul.

"No—allies," Maul said. "They have much to offer, including their planet. They are strong—and unlike pirates, they possess honor."

"Another weakness," Savage rumbled.

Maul allowed himself a moment of satisfaction. His apprentice was shedding the weak emotions from his upbringing among the Nightbrothers of Dathomir, the feelings even Mother Talzin's sorcery hadn't been able to entirely burn away. That was best. Savage was stronger without such foolish limitations.

"They know nothing of our intentions," Maul said. "Those revelations will come too late."

The brothers heard approaching footsteps. Savage nodded at Maul as Vizsla entered the medical tent, followed by Bo-Katan. The Mandalorian looked at the pathetic heap that had once been a medical droid.

"I see you have your strength back," Vizsla said.

Savage rose, standing next to his brother. During her service to the Death Watch, Bo-Katan had seen many alien species and no shortage of imposing warriors, but the figure standing before her was impressive nonetheless. The yellow-and-black Zabrak was enormous. The red-and-black one—his brother, she had heard—wasn't as large, but his eyes were watchful and glittered with malice, and even on mechanical legs he had the grace of a jungle cat.

And of course there was his power with the Force, Bo-Katan reminded herself, remembering the invisible grip that had crushed her airway, leaving her powerless to defend herself.

"I never got your names," Vizsla said.

"I am Maul," the red-and-black Zabrak said. "This is Savage."

Vizsla nodded.

"Our brothers are in favor of an alliance to liberate Mandalore," he said.

Maul could feel the man's satisfaction. It mirrored his own.

"This Duchess of yours will soon discover the true burden of peace," he told the two Mandalorians.

CHAPTER TWELVE

Now that they were allies, Pre Vizsla decided Maul and Savage deserved a tour of the camp that the Death Watch had set up on Zanbar. As Vizsla showed them around, Maul noted how well the fighters were organized and their skill at arms. But organization and skill, while vital, weren't everything when it came to war.

"Your people are strong and skilled," he told Vizsla, as they strolled beneath the dreary gray skies. "But you will need an army to free Mandalore."

"There are more on Mandalore who will join us," Vizsla said dismissively.

Maul had heard such talk before, typically from leaders who'd been told they were great so often that they'd started believing it. That was foolish, and it was dangerous. So was any plan that assumed something would happen, instead of ensuring that it would happen.

"Their help would come too late," Maul said. "We can assemble an army—beginning with Black Sun."

Vizsla looked shocked.

"They're a crime syndicate—hardly a force to rally with," he said.

"They can provide us with the resources we need to sustain a war without the scrutiny of the Republic," Maul said.

The *Gauntlet* emerged from hyperspace near the glowing red sphere that was the volcanic planet Mustafar. Moments later, other *Kom'rk* transports and Mandalorian craft winked into existence around her. Maul nodded, appreciating the precision of the Mandalorians' maneuvers. Years of practice had made the Death Watch's warriors excellent at coordination, whether they were flying starships or storming an enemy position on the surface of a planet. They would need such coordination soon.

Maul stared at Mustafar as the task force approached the planet, which now filled the *Gauntlet*'s viewports. Their destination was down there, amid the black basalt cliffs and glowing lava flows—a fortress belonging to the underworld organization known as Black Sun.

When Savage had rescued him from exile on Lotho Minor, Maul had been startled to discover that the Force was tipped out of balance and the galaxy was at war. Darth Sidious had never told Maul the full dimensions of his plot to reclaim the galaxy for the Sith, but he had known that Naboo was one of the opening gambits in his Master's plan, just as he had known that that plan ultimately called for plunging the galaxy into a terrible conflict. That conflict had apparently started without him, pitting the Republic's human clones against the Separatists' mechanical soldiers on thousands and thousands of worlds.

But Maul cared little about the so-called Clone Wars, or the machinations Sidious had employed to set them in motion. Rather than serve the schemes of another, he had his own vision, and its success depended on other players—not admirals or generals, but criminals who had always sought to avoid the eyes of the galactic authorities, and were thriving now that those authorities' eyes were focused elsewhere.

Black Sun had existed for centuries by controlling and profiting from an enormous number of galactic crimes. The crime syndicate ran pirate gangs, smuggling rings, gambling houses, and slaver bands, among other things. Through promises of reward and threats of ruin, it commanded the loyalty of billions of beings, from small-time hustlers on backwater worlds to important government ministers on the Republic's richest planets. Some obeyed Black Sun because they wanted to gain power. Others did so because they feared to lose it. Either way, Black Sun owned them.

Black Sun's power was mostly invisible—credits diverted to mysterious bank accounts and messages that arrived from anonymous senders, then self-destructed. But the syndicate had members whose affiliation was more open. It had tens of thousands of foot soldiers, and hundreds of leaders, and sometimes leaders and foot soldiers could be found together in rich safe houses and remote fortresses.

Maul had been in one of those safe houses once—years ago, Sidious had sent him to the Core World of Ralltiir, with orders to throw Black Sun into confusion by killing many of its leaders. Maul smiled at the memories—his lightsaber had been like a wheel of fire, leaving death and terror in its wake, funneling the power of the dark side into him until the power he held within himself was intoxicating.

Black Sun had survived the attack—Sidious had only wished to hamper it for a time, not to destroy it. The criminal organization had then rebuilt itself quickly, with new would-be leaders fighting for dominance and claiming the positions of those who had been slain, until the group was as strong as it had been before. Now, one of those new leaders maintained a fortress here, on Mustafar.

Mustafar, Maul thought as the *Kom'rks* spiraled down toward the black bluffs below. He had been here before, too—Black Sun was not the only group with facilities on the lava world. Darth Sidious himself had maintained a secret redoubt elsewhere on the planet, and perhaps still did. Maul had been a child there—his earliest memories were of battling droids, of being tested, of fear and loneliness before he had learned to purge himself of those weak emotions and fill the holes left behind with anger.

The *Gauntlet* landed with a bump, and Maul shoved all thoughts of Mustafar out of his head. It was almost time for the next task he needed to accomplish to make his vision into a reality. To succeed, he would need his focus on the here and now, not on the useless, discarded past.

Maul rose from his seat. He was ready.

The Death Watch soldiers chosen for the mission marched along behind Maul, Savage, Vizsla, and Bo-Katan, the four *Kom'rks* waiting behind them on a rocky outcropping surrounded by bright lava. The Mandalorians were encased in jumpsuits and armor, but gave no indication that the scorching temperatures bothered them.

"A battalion, brother," Savage said admiringly.

"They will serve us well," Maul said.

He raised his voice to address Vizsla.

"You will now follow my lead," Maul said.

Ahead of them, a narrow bridge crossed a river of lava. Beyond it, gun emplacements protected a fortress that had been carved into the side of a cliff. The entrance was swarming with warriors—the soldiers of Black Sun. Their helmets had gold faceplates in which the eyepieces glowed like jewels.

The soldiers were Falleen, Maul saw—a green-skinned, reptilian species from the planet of the same name, in the Mid Rim. The spines on their backs emerged from their leather armor, giving them a sinister look.

Through the Force, Maul could sense the unease of the Death Watch fighters behind him. They were alarmed by the number of soldiers awaiting them.

Vizsla could sense it, too—he had no talent with the Force, but he knew his troops. He turned his gargoyle helmet to look at his men. They couldn't see his eyes behind the Mandalorian mask, but they got the message and the muttering and shifting of feet ceased as quickly as it had begun.

One of the Black Sun soldiers strode forward, with the arrogant stride of a man used to being obeyed. He was a Falleen in rich robes of purple, with a topknot and a black goatee.

"We request an audience with your leaders," Maul said, his tone formal, even polite.

The Falleen in the fancy robes looked amused.

"It'll be your funeral," he said, then grunted and led them inside.

***

The lieutenant, whose name was Ziton Moj, led them deep into the fortress. At the building's heart sat a throne room with a tall window running from floor to ceiling, looking out over the bright red lava flows beyond. In the center of the throne room sat a circle of five elevated thrones around a table. In the thrones sat five Falleen in long purple robes, wearing golden headgear—the leaders of this branch of Black Sun.

The five Falleen looked down at the two Sith and the Mandalorians with a mixture of curiosity and amusement. Standing in the center of the circle, Maul reached out in the

Force, like a nashtah sniffing at a potential meal. He could feel that the Black Sun leaders were cruel and corrupt, beings who thought they could fill the emptiness in their souls with credits or pleasures or power. But they had also grown careless, arrogant enough to let a band of warriors inside their stronghold without knowing their capabilities.

Maul knew—as the five Falleen did not—that what happened in the next few minutes would determine whether that carelessness and arrogance killed them.

"Why do you come here?" asked Xomit Grunseit, the Falleen seated at the head of the table.

"We seek an army," Maul said simply.

"Fools," Xomit spat. "We are not mercenaries."

Maul smiled. The Black Sun leaders apparently didn't recognize him, or connect him with the long-ago massacre on Ralltiir. But then Maul had guessed as much earlier. If they'd had any inkling of who he was or what he'd done, they would have fought him outside their fortress.

Xomit turned to Moj.

"Dispose of them," he ordered. "Keep their ships and weapons."

Maul saw Moj swallow. The Black Sun lieutenant knew the order meant a fight to the death, and while he wasn't afraid to begin such a battle, he knew it would be a bloody business.

Maul filed the observation away. Unlike the beings he served, Moj wasn't a fool. He might prove useful.

Before Moj could give an order, another of the Falleen crime lords spoke; his eyes fixed greedily on the hilt of Vizsla's darksaber.

"Give me that one's sword," he said.

Moj reached out his long green fingers to take the darksaber, but found Vizsla's blaster pointed at his face.

A guard approached Savage with his blaster drawn. The Sith grabbed his wrist and Maul heard the bones break, the weapon falling to the floor as the Falleen screamed. Savage grabbed the green head, twisting the Falleen's neck until it broke, then slammed the luckless soldier down to the floor.

Maul looked up from the soldier's body and regarded Xomit.

"This is your last opportunity to join us," he said.

"Quiet!" bellowed Xomit. "We are Black Sun!"

The five leaders rose from their thrones. Maul reached out to feel the Force's ripples and currents, considering the directions events might take. Everything pointed the same way.

"Very well, then," Maul said.

He glanced back at Savage, then lowered his head. Before anyone could react, Savage had ignited both blades of his saber and hurled the weapon, sending a spinning sheet of scarlet plasma knifing through the gloomy hall. The lightsaber returned to Savage's hand, its circuit of the room complete, and he deactivated the blades. The soldiers of Black Sun and the Death Watch stood there, momentarily stunned. Then all heard five thumps from behind the thrones, and the five headless bodies of the Black Sun leaders collapsed where they had stood.

Maul gave Savage an approving smile. His apprentice had performed perfectly. Then he turned to Moj, eyes blazing.

"It would seem that the decision to join us is now yours," Maul said.

Moj's eyes jumped to the tangle of dead Falleen, then back to Maul and Savage.

"After careful consideration, we will join you," he said.

CHAPTER THIRTEEN

Within an hour, Ziton Moj had squads of foot soldiers loading crates of supplies into Black Sun's frigates and the Death Watch's transports while Maul stood by the *Gauntlet*'s landing ramp and watched. The Black Sun lieutenant had excellent organizational skills, Maul thought.

It was time to return to Zanbar and go over the next phase of the plan. But Vizsla seemed to have other ideas.

"We have our army now," the Death Watch commander said. "I have a plan to undermine Satine—"

Maul cut him off, irritated.

"The army is weak," Maul said. "We are not ready for the Duchess."

"With my plan, we won't need a bigger force," Vizsla insisted. Maul could hear the anger and impatience in his voice.

Enough of this, Maul thought. *Things will go better when this Mandalorian knows his place.*

"There is only one plan," he told Vizsla. "One vision."

"And it belongs to the Death Watch," Vizsla said.

Maul allowed himself a moment in which he imagined Pre Vizsla's helmet clattering across the black rock of Mustafar with his head inside of it, after which a well-aimed kick would send both helmet and head into the river of molten lava. But unfortunately, Maul's plan required Vizsla for a while longer— the Death Watch commander would be needed when they reached Mandalore.

"Your vision lacks clarity," Maul said, keeping his anger in check. "Without us, you have no army and no reason to replace the Duchess."

Savage had felt his Master's frustration in the Force and approached Maul and Vizsla, glaring at the Mandalorian. Maul let him draw near, near enough for Vizsla to wonder if the giant Zabrak might keep coming and snap his neck, as he'd done to the luckless Falleen inside the fortress. When he saw Vizsla's back and shoulders stiffen, Maul knew the point had been taken, and stepped forward to stop Savage.

"The depth of this opportunity eludes you," Maul told Vizsla, grinning like a skull. "You shall watch and learn."

The camp on Zanbar was now larger and more crowded, swelled by the arrival of Black Sun's army of Falleen. Standing beside Vizsla and Bo-Katan, Maul watched the Death Watch and Black Sun soldiers as they waited in a chow line for the cooks to ladle out the midday meal. Maul knew they didn't like each other — the Mandalorians thought Black Sun soldiers were dishonorable criminals, while the Falleen thugs thought the Mandalorians were fanatics. But both sides were keeping their hostilities in check. For now, Maul knew, they refrained from violence because they were afraid of punishment. Later, when they understood the opportunity they had, they would cooperate more willingly. By then, both sides' drill sergeants would have taught them how to fight alongside each other.

Maul, Vizsla, and Bo-Katan looked up as several *Sarisa*-class gunships flew low over the camp, slowing for a landing nearby. The gunships were winged, with a station for two gunners located amidships.

"More criminals," Bo-Katan said disgustedly.

"Spice dealers connected to all the crime families of Coruscant," Vizsla said.

Maul nodded.

"The Pykes," he said. "They will be the next to join us."

Indeed, Lom Pyke was soon striding across the camp, followed by his family's guards and accompanied by wary Death Watch warriors. Pyke was the name of both family and species: The Pykes had small faces set on gigantic skulls, long arms and feet, and goggles covering their eyes. Their homeworld, Maul recalled, was Oba Diah, near Kessel and its infamous spice mines.

Lom Pyke got right down to business. "We know you've been forming an army," he said.

"Were you expecting us?" Maul asked.

Lom Pyke nodded, the back of his oversized head bobbing like a counterweight.

"Underworld's a small community," he said. "I have no desire to oppose you. We come to join you."

"Very good," said Vizsla. "Then ready our troops. We leave for Nal Hutta immediately."

The sluglike Hutts had ruled thousands upon thousands of worlds in the Outer Rim since the dawn of galactic history.

The Hutt clans constantly quarreled and fought, making and breaking alliances as it suited them — to a Hutt, betrayals were daily occurrences, and a good double cross was appreciated like any other form of art.

But the Hutts were always careful not to let the back-stabbing and double-dealing get too out of hand. Important Hutts from the leading clans took turns serving on the Hutt Grand Council, which had the authority to settle disputes, declare an end to feuds, and take action on behalf of the entire species.

The Grand Council met on Nal Hutta, in the heart of the galactic region known as Hutt Space. Nal Hutta was hot and sticky, notable for dreary spitting rain, the stench of rotting vegetation, and ever-present clouds of insects — all the ingredients of a Hutt paradise, in other words.

Guards in the motley livery of the Hutt clans escorted Maul, Savage, and Vizsla through a wealthy compound and into the gloomy council chamber. It was some kind of extended Hutt holiday, during which the slugs retreated to hidden Clan-worlds forbidden to outsiders. That meant only three Hutts were attending the meeting — and not all were there in the considerable flesh.

Oruba the Hutt was ghostly pale and wore a chapeau and a loose shirt made out of meters of expensive dark fabric. Gorga the Hutt peered at the visitors through a massive monocle that left his eye looking gigantic and distorted. Jabba the Hutt, a flickering blue hologram, stared at the Sith with a canny gaze and a knowing smirk.

"Da wanga oo Stuka Crispo, pa ranna hi dopa," Jabba rumbled.

Maul knew Huttese. Jabba was acknowledging that he had heard of the Death Watch, and demanding to know what they wanted.

"There are many things the Hutts influence and possess that would be useful to us," Maul said.

For a non-Hutt to speak of ways a Hutt could be *useful* was insolent, to say the least—visitors to the Hutt Council had died for far less. But Maul didn't care. The galaxy was changing, and he was the agent of that change. The Hutts could profit from this, or be destroyed.

Besides, Maul knew that Jabba was far too shrewd to let a momentary lapse of etiquette get between him and a potential windfall.

"For the right price," Jabba said in Huttese.

"We have no credits," Maul said simply.

That was going beyond insolent to downright rude, and Oruba and Gorga looked offended.

"Well, do you have something to trade?" the pale Hutt demanded.

Maul looked up at the trio of gangsters.

"Your lives," he said. "In exchange for Hutt Space and everything in its borders."

The three Hutts chortled. The insult was so obvious, and so astonishing, that it didn't matter. They would laugh for years about the two tattooed Zabraks and the Mandalorian, and the amazing thing one of them had said before the Hutts seized them all and sent them to Nal Hutta's deepest dungeons, to test their best torturers' creativity.

"A foolish move," Jabba said as a quartet of bounty hunters emerged from the shadows, blasters drawn.

The Hutts expected the firefight to be over quickly, with the insolent visitors motionless on the floor. That was why they employed these four hunters—Embo, Sugi, Latts Razzi, and Dengar—and paid them enough credits to keep them nearby.

But the newcomers showed further insolence by refusing to fall. In an eyeblink, Maul and Savage had their lightsabers drawn and ignited, and were sending laser blasts ricocheting all around the chamber, while Vizsla had his twin blasters out of their holsters and was firing as quickly as he could. Oruba howled in anger, then ducked out of sight as he realized he and Gorga were in actual danger.

Maul had enjoyed the look of outrage on the Hutts' fat faces, but the bounty hunters hired by the slugs were actually quite capable—and they were fighting in surroundings they knew well. Next to Latts—a pink-skinned Theelin with pigtails—stood Dengar, a pudgy human whose head was wrapped in white coverings. Dengar grinned as he blasted away at them.

The Sith brothers and Vizsla began to back toward the chamber door. As they did so, the green-skinned Kyuzo hunter named Embo flung his hat—a wide-brimmed, circular disk of metal—at Maul.

Darth Maul had never imagined that someone might attack him with a hat, let alone have it actually happen. The whirling metal disk took him by surprise, striking his mechanical legs and knocking him down. Savage reached for his brother, letting out a yell as the Kyuzo fired his bowcaster, grazing the black-and-yellow Nightbrother's arm.

Vizsla ducked behind the two Sith and yanked open the doors leading out of the Grand Council chamber. Two guards on the other side stared at him in disbelief. Vizsla shot them both, then turned back and activated his flamethrower, sending a huge gout of fire washing across the room. The bounty hunters fell back before the wall of heat as the three invaders fled.

"Killya hooha!" roared the hologram of Jabba, still watching the scene through the flames.

The four hunters knew Huttese, but even if they hadn't, they probably could have figured out Jabba's command.

Kill them!

CHAPTER FOURTEEN

The *Gauntlet* was parked on a landing platform near the Grand Council chamber. It had seemed quite close when they had set down for their meeting with the Hutts, but now the ship struck Pre Vizsla as entirely too far away. He kept firing his blasters at the pursuing bounty hunters, who were leading a horde of Hutt servants armed with blasters, electro-jabbers, and other weapons.

Maul and Savage continued to spin their red lightsabers with astonishing skill, batting every laser bolt that came near them back into the crowd. But there were too many pursuers—aliens and mangy-looking humans were pouring onto the platform. First there were a few thugs between them and the *Gauntlet*, then more than a few, and then they were surrounded.

You better not be late, Bo-Katan, Vizsla thought.

Fortunately, she wasn't.

A massive explosion ripped through the crowd of Hutt roughnecks, flinging bodies in all directions. The thugs hesitated, staring up into the sky in bewilderment.

Over his helmet's comlink, Vizsla heard Bo-Katan chuckling.

"I see negotiations have gone as planned," she said.

His lieutenant flew overhead, fire blasting out of her rocket jetpack, followed by the handpicked fighters she called her Nite Owls. They fired rockets into the Hutt thugs, sending them scattering.

"Secure this platform," Vizsla ordered over his comlink.

Moments later, it was the bounty hunters and Hutt soldiers who were in desperate retreat, running from the Nite Owls' missiles and the blasters of the Death Watch warriors. The Mandalorians established a perimeter, then started pushing into the Hutt compound, laying down a wall of rocket fire and blaster bolts ahead of them. The gangsters yowled as they fled headlong down the dark corridors.

Suddenly, a pale shape dropped out of the shadows near the ceiling, knocking Maul off his feet. Vizsla turned, just in time to see the butt of a rifle coming right at his eyes. It smashed him in the helmet, knocking him backward with his ears ringing.

Savage saw the attacker was a female Zabrak—Sugi, the leader of the bounty hunters who had driven them out of the council chamber. He swung his saber at her, missing, then was knocked sprawling by the Kyuzo's metal hat.

Maul aimed a blow at Sugi, who crashed to the floor. He slashed at her with his saber, expecting to cut her in two, but she dodged and the red blade merely left a rip in the ground. He continued hacking away at the bounty hunter, growling in anger as she dodged each slash. Then a white-furred anooba leapt on Maul, clawed feet a blur, and Maul's saber tumbled out of his grasp.

Vizsla got to his feet, shaking his head in an effort to clear his senses, and found Savage struggling with the green-skinned bounty hunter while Maul tried to tear the anooba off himself. It was too cramped for blasters to be of much use, and so Vizsla reached behind his shoulder for the darksaber. He activated it and the black blade screamed and wailed as he cut down the Hutt thugs trying to join the fight.

Maul hurled the anooba away and reached out with

the Force. Sugi's hands leapt to her throat as he began to strangle her.

Suddenly, the corridor was filled with blinding light, and everybody in the fight reeled, momentarily blinded and stunned. It was Latts Razzi, the female Theelin. Trying to clear his vision, Maul realized she'd thrown flash grenades into the fight.

"Come on—let's get out of here!" Latts yelled to her fellow bounty hunters.

Sugi and Embo rushed after Latts, the anooba bounding along beside them. Savage and Vizsla started to give chase, but Maul raised his hand. The bounty hunters didn't matter. With any luck, their real targets would still be in the Grand Council chamber.

Gorga had escaped, but Bo-Katan and the warriors had cornered the injured Oruba. The pale Hutt stared at Vizsla and the Sith in terror.

"Where are the others?" Maul demanded.

Oruba screamed for help in Huttese. Maul waved his hand in contempt.

"Kill him," he ordered.

Savage took a step forward and Oruba began babbling for them to wait.

"Give me a location," Maul said.

"Tatooine," Oruba gasped. "Tatooine."

"Jabba's palace," Vizsla said with satisfaction.

"Thank you for your cooperation," Maul said, nodding at his brother.

Savage stepped forward, saber raised, and brought it down.

Tatooine's twin suns—known as *Gi Dopa Gasha* in Huttese—were high in the sky when the invaders arrived.

Jabba the Hutt sat in his throne room next to Gorga, listening to the sound of fighting growing closer. The whine of blaster fire was continuous, as was the thrum of lightsabers and the screams of the wounded and dying.

As always, Jabba's throne room was filled with slaves, guards, and intergalactic lowlifes. Some were hoping for work, while others were sponging off his hospitality, emptying his larder and liquor cabinet and annoying his dancers. When the intruders first entered Jabba's palace, the Hutt's courtiers had been amused by the break in routine, expecting that the guards would kill them quickly enough. But as the sounds of fighting grew closer, the courtiers became frozen with fear. Now they were looking for a way to escape, only to find that there wasn't one.

Jabba just sat on his throne and waited, curious to see what would happen.

The sounds of guns and sabers finally stopped. A moment later, two burning-eyed Sith strode into the throne room, sabers lit, followed by a pair of Mandalorian warriors.

Jabba knew who the intruders were. He'd known even before their audacious raid on Nal Hutta, because it was his job to know such things. Pre Vizsla and Bo-Katan, two leaders of the Death Watch. Savage Opress, Count Dooku's creature—whom he suspected was really a pawn of the witch Mother Talzin. And, most intriguingly, Darth Maul—the Sith warrior supposedly slain by Obi-Wan Kenobi all those years ago on Naboo.

Interesting, Jabba thought. *Very interesting.*

One of Jabba's Gamorrean guards lumbered to put his body and ax between the intruders and his master. The piglike guard was either braver than most of his species or stupider, though the latter was hard to believe. Savage cut him down in an instant and Maul stepped forward as the members of Jabba's court tried to burrow into the throne room's walls.

Jabba laughed.

"Your reputations precede you," he said in Huttese. His latest talkdroid, a blue-and-white model with a cylindrical head, hesitantly translated the words into Basic.

"Give up, Jabba!" said Vizsla. "You're the only one left."

"Submit or suffer," Maul said.

Jabba looked at Gorga, who shrugged and nodded. They'd discussed this before, when they decided to simply wait for the raiders to follow Gorga to Tatooine, though Jabba had sent his son Rotta away to make sure the Huttlet would be safe. The two Sith and the Death Watch had thrown the galactic underworld into turmoil. If the Hutts were patient, they would be able to reassert their dominance after this storm had blown itself out, taking possession of the markets and criminal enterprises that would be up for grabs. The Hutt clans would be even more powerful than they had been. What were a few insults, compared with an opportunity like that?

"I think we've reached a majority," Jabba said in Huttese, nodding to the droid. It stepped forward tentatively, obviously nervous about its safety.

"The mighty Jabba and the Hutt families have decided to join you," the droid told Maul.

CHAPTER FIFTEEN

Maul and Vizsla strode through Jabba's palace, given a wide berth by the Hutt crime lord's red-skinned Nikto guards and his other servants—all of whom were now theirs to command.

"Between the Hutts, Black Sun, and the Pykes, we'll have a large reserve of muscle and supplies," Vizsla said.

"Yes," Maul said.

"Then Mandalore and Kenobi are still our priority?" Vizsla asked.

"They are vital," Maul said.

"I'm curious to hear the rest of your plan," Vizsla said.

Maul stopped, staring into the Mandalorian leader's cold blue eyes.

"The vision has expanded," he said. "You will still rule Mandalore—and under your protection, I will command a new galactic underworld."

Vizsla looked stunned for a moment, but kept his composure. After a long pause, he nodded.

"Mandalore influences a league of two thousand neutral systems," the Mandalorian said. "It gives you a great deal of options for your enterprise."

"You have learned from your previous oversights," Maul said. "With their combined forces, the Republic and Separatists will be irrelevant."

"Then we are ready?" Vizsla asked.

"Mobilize the army," Maul said. "Send an advance guard to the capital. I want a list of targets vital to Mandalore's security."

Maul could feel the eagerness swelling in Vizsla, the wild joy and lust for revenge. He gave the Death Watch commander a stern look of warning.

"Choose wisely," Maul said. "There will be no second chances."

Maul strode away. Vizsla watched him go for a moment,

then turned, joining Bo-Katan where she'd been waiting for him a short distance away.

"Stay focused," he told his lieutenant. "Mandalore will soon be ours, and Maul and his brother will be dead— alongside the Duchess."

PART THREE:
SHADES OF REASON

CHAPTER SIXTEEN

Not so long ago, the camp on Zanbar had been a small collection of tents housing the Death Watch soldiers. Now, starships ringed the camp—the Death Watch's *Kom'rk* transports waited next to Gozanti cruisers, spice freighters, and smuggler craft. Inside the ring, the encampment had grown into a sprawling collection of tents, training grounds, and equipment depots. Mandalorian warriors barked orders at mixed groups of the Death Watch soldiers, Black Sun soldiers, Pyke retainers, and Hutt thugs. These various groups now answered to a single name—the Shadow Collective.

In the camp's main tent, the Shadow Collective's leaders were gathered around a holographic map of the planet Mandalore. Pre Vizsla, commander of the Death Watch, stood with his lieutenant, Bo-Katan. The Falleen Ziton Moj, the Captain of the Guard for Black Sun, exchanged glances with the spice dealer Lom Pyke. Nikto enforcers employed by the Hutts had crowded into the tent, muttering to themselves in Huttese. All gave a respectful amount of space to the Zabrak warrior Savage Opress. But the man all eyes were drawn to was Savage's Master—the Sith Lord Darth Maul.

Maul stared at the planet shimmering before them: Mandalore, capital of Mandalorian Space and domain of Duchess Satine, the leader of the New Mandalorians and spokeswoman for a group of some two thousand systems determined to stay neutral in the civil war between the Republic and the Separatists. Mandalore was mottled with forests and jungles and hills, but much of the planet had been reduced to lonely drifts of white sand—the remnant of a terrible war with the Republic and a later conflict among the system's quarrelsome clans. The New Mandalorians dwelled in great domed cities that rose from the wastes—showcases for their mastery of technology and their dedication to peace.

At a command from Vizsla, the map froze. One of those

domed cities was flashing. It then expanded until it filled the map. This was Sundari, the New Mandalorian capital — and the key to the next part of Maul's plan for establishing his criminal empire.

"Where are my targets?" Maul asked, staring at the miniature city in front of him.

"We've identified them at these locations," Vizsla said, pointing at the map. "However, as I've said before, if we try to take Mandalore by force, our people will turn against us."

Maul considered the city and the circles that indicated the Shadow Collective's targets. He could feel the eyes of the room on him, waiting for him to speak.

"I will use my army to attack different targets across Sundari, and sow chaos to undermine the Duchess's rule," Maul said. "We will make them look too weak to maintain control. Then the Death Watch will bring peace where the peacemaker Satine cannot."

"We'll be saviors," Vizsla said.

"Exactly," Maul said.

The meeting broke up, and Bo-Katan started across the camp to prepare the troops, striding alongside Vizsla. She looked around to make sure none of the Sith or other Shadow

Collective leaders were nearby, then spoke urgently to her fellow Mandalorian.

"It's a risk to trust those monsters," Bo-Katan said. "How do we know they'll keep their end of the bargain?"

"We need the Sith to cause some pain and show how weak Satine really is," Vizsla said. "After this is done, no one will doubt why we're in power. Most will welcome us."

"Then what?" Bo-Katan asked doubtfully.

"Then we execute Maul and his brother," Vizsla said. "Their army will scatter, and Mandalore will be ours."

Behind them, in the tent, Maul and Savage were studying the map. Maul stared at the red circles of targets, mind working, but his apprentice was troubled. Finally, Savage could no longer keep silent.

"I believe Vizsla will betray us," he said.

Savage had wondered if Maul would be surprised, if he would argue with him. But his Master's expression barely changed.

"We have no other choice," Maul said. "We cannot rule openly without drawing the attention of the Jedi. We need Vizsla as the face of our rule for now."

Savage considered that.

"The promise of wealth will find us a new face on Mandalore," he said.

Maul looked approvingly at Savage.

"You have learned well, my apprentice," he said. "Greed never fails to motivate."

CHAPTER SEVENTEEN

The ancient clan poets of Mandalore had once written odes to sunlight on the planet's rolling hills, but such songs were now long forgotten. The vast white wastes reflected the sunlight and turned it harsh and blinding. The dome of the capital city of Sundari filtered and softened the light, but outside on the loading docks there was no dome to protect the eyes. It was a place of sharp shadows and eerie quiet, one that put police officers and customs officials in bad moods and made starship captains hurry through their delivery checklists, eager to be elsewhere.

A bug-eyed RA-series droid and a police officer in a green

uniform approached one of the many cargo containers that had been off-loaded recently and now waited to be approved for import, then transferred to a warehouse on the docks or shipped into Sundari itself. While the officer waited impatiently, the droid glanced at the handheld scanner, shook it, and scanned the container again.

"What's the matter?" asked the officer, mouth turned down below the eyepieces of his helmet.

"I am scanning life-forms," the droid said. "I believe this spice shipment is infested."

"Step back," the officer said, irritated with the unhappy turn his day had just taken.

Suddenly, the container door exploded outward and blaster fire erupted from inside. The droid collapsed, perforated by a laser blast. The police officer managed to return fire before Lom Pyke aimed a forearm cross at his chin, knocking him unconscious.

"Find me someone in charge," Lom Pyke barked to the other smugglers as they hurried out of the container and fanned out across the docks.

In Sundari's Peace Park, a silver RIC-series droid led a group of tourists toward the Memorial Shrine, past the manicured shrubs and carefully placed rocks. Police officers stood on either side of the Memorial Shrine, with others stationed at their post. They stood idly, watching the lines of airspeeders humming by in Sundari's always-crowded traffic lanes and the crowds of blond and red-haired Mandalorians enjoying the day.

"The Memorial Shrine was attacked by terrorists," the tour droid explained, pointing out the blackened section of flooring while a screen mounted on its head replayed scenes of the park as it had looked before the attack. "The Duchess has left it broken as a reminder of aggressive action."

The tour droid let out an electronic groan and toppled forward, its metal head smoking.

"We will try to be more careful," Ziton Moj said as he lifted his blaster for another shot. Suddenly, cloaked figures seemed to be everywhere in the park, displaying blasters they'd kept hidden. Blasters barked and laser beams zipped through the crowd, finding targets. The two officers guarding the memorial fell and the Mandalorians in the park began to scream.

The Shadow Collective's thugs were firing at the police from all directions, not caring about civilians with the poor luck to be caught in the crossfire. Moj saw an officer with a captain's insignia trying to organize the remaining officers. He was yelling for them to fall back. Moj sent a blaster bolt in his direction to hurry him along, then nodded at his soldiers as the police abandoned the park.

The Mandalorians were a big, sturdy people who still looked like the warriors they once had been. But Moj saw panic in their eyes and in the way they flapped their arms uselessly at the sight of outsiders with weapons. They were like a herd of frightened nerfs, and now there was a boar-wolf loose among them.

A whole pack *of boar-wolves,* Moj thought as his thugs began grabbing random civilians to rob or beat. The Shadow Collective had its orders: cause as much panic and chaos as possible. And after long days being drilled by humorless Death Watch warriors, they were itching for the opportunity to do just that.

The police were soon overwhelmed by the reports flooding in. Almost instantaneously, a tranquil day in Sundari had turned into a nightmare, with gangs of armed bandits terrorizing people at points all over the city. Police speeders raced through the traffic lanes with alarms blaring and lights flashing as commanders struggled to find a pattern to the mayhem and come up with a plan to stop it.

In the main square, below the battlements of the Sundari

Royal Palace, a crowd was gathering. Duchess Satine Kryze, ruler of the planet and leader of the New Mandalorians, strode out onto a balcony overlooking the square, followed by Prime Minister Armatan and her advisors.

The crowd was shouting. Satine raised her arms in appeal, her regal face framed by her carefully coiffed blond hair and jeweled headband, and began to speak.

"I need you all to remain calm," the Duchess said. "Holding on to our ideals is the only way we'll prevail. These attackers are just thugs brought on by the lowest element."

But reports true, exaggerated, and false continued to circulate through the crowd, and the angry shouts only grew louder.

"Listen to me," Satine pleaded. "Violence is not the way! That is what leads us closer to ruin."

Some of the Mandalorians below were pointing up, into Sundari's skies, beneath the sheltering dome. They weren't pointing at her, Satine realized—something else had attracted their attention. She craned her head to look, wondering what new horror the day had in store for her planet and her people.

Lom Pyke and his followers stopped their speeder sled in front of one of Sundari's banking centers. Lom Pyke grinned as police ran forward to intercept them.

"We're here to make a withdrawal," he announced.

"Now!" an officer yelled, pressing a button on his wrist comlink. The doors to the bank flung outward and more police rushed out, holding blasters and shields thick enough to deflect incoming laser fire. The guards aimed their guns at the Pyke band.

"Your assault on Mandalore ends here," the lead officer said. "We are ready for you."

Lom Pyke just laughed.

The officers watched as the ranks of Pyke thugs stirred, then parted. A figure with huge shoulders pushed his way to the front of the gang, facing the officers. Their eyes skittered nervously across his massive chest, taking in his yellow tattoos, his mechanical arm, his horns, and his burning eyes before settling on the double-bladed lightsaber he ignited and began to wave back and forth.

Savage Opress let out a low, rumbling growl.

The police raised their weapons.

"Take him!" yelled the lead officer, sensing that his men were nervous and fearing they might not hold their ground if the huge Zabrak attacked first.

The police opened fire, brilliant shafts of laser light zipping at the huge Sith warrior. Savage's saber spun and sang, aiming the laser bolts back at the men who had fired them. A moment later the firing stopped. Only two officers were still standing.

Savage strode forward, a terrible smile on his face.

As Satine watched, warriors in blue and gray armor descended from the sky, flames spitting from their jetpacks, to land in formation in the square between the crowd and her royal balcony.

It was the Death Watch, Satine realized.

The Duchess found herself wondering exactly how many times the terrorists of the Death Watch had tried to kill her. She'd lost count, but at some point she'd accepted that the attempts would never stop. The misguided fanatics had tried to end her life here in Sundari, and on Concordia, and had hunted her all the way to Coruscant, and now here they were again.

She had never given up hope that she might reach them, might get them to listen. But the idea of a Mandalore who believed in peace and progress was too infuriating for them to accept. To them, it mattered not at all that the New Mandalorians had built this city and others across Mandalore, or that they had made Mandalore's cunningly built ships and speeders the envy of thousands of worlds. They didn't care that a great warlord like Satine's own father had eventually rejected war and accepted that only peace could be Mandalore's salvation. Rather than accept a civilization built on peace, the Death Watch would burn everything Satine and her predecessors had created. They would prefer to dwell in poverty in the trackless wastes that were a reminder of where foolish warrior codes had brought Mandalore before.

Satine had accepted long ago that she might have to die for her beliefs. But she had never accepted that her people might have to do the same. She wouldn't let them die for the Republic or the Separatists, trapped amid the madness of their current war, and she certainly wouldn't sacrifice them because a few fanatics wanted to return to the madness of the Great Clan Wars.

Satine stepped forward to try to break the spell, but the Death Watch leader had spoken first.

"People of Mandalore, I'm Pre Vizsla of Clan Vizsla," he said, and Satine shook her head grimly. Satine had known Vizsla her entire life—Vizsla had served her as governor of Concordia, while secretly turning the moon into the Death Watch's armed camp. Now he was her most determined enemy.

Satine wondered when the blaster fire would come her way and end her life. But Vizsla kept talking.

"I've carried on our ancient ways, and it's time we rise and reclaim our birthright as warriors," Vizsla said. "It is time to reclaim our hearts!"

The crowd erupted in cheers.

"Join me and let us defend Mandalore against the criminals," Vizsla urged. "The Duchess can't answer their violence with her passive beliefs! We need action, not pacifism—"

Satine stepped forward, desperate.

"Do not listen to him!" she urged. "This will cause the end of Mandalore as you know it!"

"This isn't a Mandalore we want to know!" Vizsla shouted. "Our very name should send fear across the galaxy!"

Cheers rolled through the crowd once more. And then the chant began, at first from a few, then taken up until it was a continuous roar.

"VIZSLA! VIZSLA! VIZSLA!"

Vizsla stared at Satine, his blue eyes icy and triumphant, and suddenly the Duchess realized there was no need for him to kill her. He had already won.

CHAPTER EIGHTEEN

At the shipping docks, several disarmed police officers, dock-workers, and droids found themselves ushered by thugs into an empty cargo container. The doors shut behind them and they heard them being locked.

"What should we do?" asked a droid.

"There's nothing we can do," a police officer replied. "The Duchess's forces are being overrun across the entire planet."

Suddenly, the cough of laser blasts sounded all around the container, followed by the grunts and thuds of a ferocious fight. All inside the container listened anxiously. Then there was silence.

The doors opened and the captives emerged tentatively into the harsh sunlight once again. The thugs were disarmed, standing motionless. They glumly regarded a group of warriors wearing Mandalorian armor, blasters in their hands.

"What's going on?" stammered the police officer.

"This port is now secured," a warrior replied, his voice filtered by his helmet.

"You have my thanks, soldier," the officer said.

"No," the man replied. "Thank Pre Vizsla."

In Peace Park, the outnumbered and outgunned Mandalorian police could do little to stop the Shadow Collective's reign of terror. But suddenly, the underworld thugs were kicking and jerking, arms pinned to their sides by lassos that had appeared out of the air, fired by the wrist rockets of the Death Watch's warriors swooping in from above.

The soldiers touched down and shut off their jetpacks. A cluster of frightened children gazed up at Bo-Katan as her Nite Owls led the Shadow Collective's operatives away.

Bo-Katan offered her hand to a child who had fallen.

"You're safe now," she said soothingly.

Lom Pyke's crew rushed away from the looted banking center, metal cases thrown over their shoulders. Police officers who'd responded to the urgent calls for help chased after them, eyes on the giant figure of Savage Opress. Mandalorians gaped at the onrushing thugs, trying to figure out which way to run.

One woman found herself in Savage's path. Barely breaking stride, the huge Zabrak flung her aside, throwing her hard enough that she sailed over the edge of the rooftop. She shrieked, barely catching a railing and saving herself from a fatal fall.

The police officers stopped chasing the Pykes long enough to pull the terrified woman to safety. Continuing their pursuit, they rounded the corner to find that the Death Watch had arrived, led by Pre Vizsla himself. The Mandalorian commander had drawn his black blade and was staring down Savage, who circled him warily, double-bladed saber at the ready.

The two came together with a crash of sabers and grunts of effort. The police winced, fearful that Vizsla would be cut down, as so many of their colleagues had been. But Vizsla parried Savage's thrusts and wild swings, waiting until he saw an opening and countering with an attack of his own. Mandalorian and Zabrak kicked and ducked and swung and dodged, sabers whining, as the Pykes and the Death Watch looked on in fascination and Sundari's citizens peered around them from a safer distance.

Vizsla wasn't just holding his own, the police realized—he was *winning*.

Vizsla flicked his wrists deftly and spun Savage's lightsaber out of his hands, then kicked the Sith warrior to the ground and stood over him. Beaten, Savage offered no resistance. The Pykes dropped their cases of stolen credits and raised their arms as the Death Watch's warriors advanced with their blasters drawn.

"This monster will not trouble the people of Mandalore any longer," Vizsla said, making sure the gathering crowd could hear him. "Take him away, Captain."

Satine sat numbly on her throne in Sundari's royal palace, gazing at the geometric shadows cast by the afternoon sun and listening to the crowd outside chanting for Vizsla and the Death Watch.

"Duchess, Pre Vizsla and his men have entered the palace," Prime Minister Armatan said. "Should we stop them?"

Satine wondered if she looked as stricken as her advisors and royal guards did.

"How can we?" she asked. "The people are on their side now."

The doors opened, revealing a line of the Death Watch warriors. Vizsla led them into the royal chamber, eyes locked on the Duchess where she sat waiting for him. Her guards moved to intercept Vizsla, weapons raised.

"No!" Satine said sharply. "There will be no bloodshed."

"But, Duchess—" protested Armatan.

Satine looked at him sadly. He was a good man, and she feared to think how the Death Watch might repay him for his service to the New Mandalorian cause. But she would not allow Armatan to die for her—nor would anyone else in the royal chamber do so.

"I will not be provoked to violence by these terrorists," Satine said grimly, glaring at Vizsla.

Vizsla didn't bother acknowledging the insult. It was hollow and they both knew it. He strode across the chamber, listening to the chants outside, savoring the moment he had worked toward for so long.

"Listen, Duchess," Vizsla said. "Do you hear the people? They cry out for change. Your weak-minded rule of Mandalore is at an end. The resurrection of our warrior past is about to begin."

Once they had taken control of the royal chamber, the Death Watch led Savage, Ziton Moj, and Lom Pyke out onto the balcony overlooking Sundari's main square, their wrists immobilized by glowing energy binders. Bo-Katan strode past them, heavy blaster slung over one shoulder, and gazed out over the crowd.

"Duchess Satine and the New Mandalorian leaders have fled in cowardice, while the Death Watch brought these criminals to justice," she announced.

The assembled Mandalorians booed the Shadow Collective members. Then the shouts turned to cheers as Vizsla stepped out on the balcony. Bo-Katan let the cheers gather and build, then addressed the crowd again.

"Your new Prime Minister, Pre Vizsla—leader of the Death Watch, exiled governor of Concordia, true son of Mandalore—presents you with the lords of the most-feared crime families in the galaxy," she said.

The crowd roared its approval. Vizsla, the new Mandalore, stood at the center of the shouts and applause and soaked it all in.

CHAPTER NINETEEN

They led Satine to a prison cell in her own palace, shutting her in a little room with a cot, desk, and chair, behind a door made of Mandalorian iron. She paced back and forth until her agitation became too much to bear.

"You cannot hold me here!" Satine called, voice pinched with fury. "I am the Duchess of Mandalore! Your actions will bring our civilization to ruin!"

The guards didn't respond. But someone else did.

"Is that you, Satine?" came a voice from the next cell.

Satine stopped pacing. The voice was familiar.

"Almec?" she asked in amazement.

That was exactly who it was—Almec, her former Prime Minister. He had served her faithfully for years, but the war between the Republic and the Separatists had proved his undoing. When wartime restrictions on trade interrupted the flow of goods from the galaxy to Mandalore's cities, Almec had conspired with Mandalorian criminals to strengthen the black market. He had done so, he claimed, because smuggling was the only way to keep Mandalore from going hungry. But the illicit trade had also put credits in his own pockets, while fewer and fewer shipments reached the people he claimed to be helping. Soon the only ones who profited were Almec, the smugglers, and the corrupt officials paid to look the other way.

At least that was what Sundari's courts had decided. Or perhaps Almec had been crooked from the start—Satine didn't know what to believe anymore. Almec had bought off members of her royal guard, imprisoned her, and tried to force her to sign a confession. But his plot had failed, and he had languished in jail ever since.

"Here for a visit?" Almec asked, and Satine could hear him sneering. "Or has peace betrayed you, too, Duchess?"

"Peace exists only in the minds of the faithful," Satine replied.

"And faith has been the greatest disappointment," Almec shot back.

"Only when it is broken," Satine said. "What you did for the people betrayed their trust."

"And you betrayed mine," Almec said. "Destitution leaves little room for faith. My actions allowed the people hope in your leadership. The supplies I bought on the black market kept you in power."

"Another error in judgment," Satine said. "The people made willing sacrifices for their freedom. Corruption is not the answer."

Almec began to laugh. The Duchess had not lost her capacity for lofty speeches — not even from the rather diminished throne of a cheap chair in a cell where she'd spend the rest of her life, however long the Death Watch decided that life should be.

"Then enjoy your freedom, Duchess," Almec said mockingly. "You'll have plenty of time to tell me all about it."

Darth Maul found Sundari a curious place.

The space beneath the city's dome was honeycombed with buildings made out of great blocks of permacrete and transparisteel and Mandalorian iron, crisscrossed by traffic lanes thick with airspeeders, power sleds, and swoops. The Mandalorian machines were sleek and powerful—not made for war, but easily converted to it. The city was beautiful and green, but every centimeter of that greenery was meticulously manicured, with even the trees and shrubs in the rooftop gardens and plazas cut into geometric shapes.

Maul could feel the potential of the Mandalorians in everything they did, and he could also feel how that potential had been rigidly redirected and kept throttled. When it was unleashed once again, he thought, they would make fine servants for his new Sith.

Bo-Katan and a squad of soldiers led Maul through the palace and into the royal chamber. Pre Vizsla lounged on the throne, a backdrop of stained transparisteel softly glowing behind him.

"The transition of power will be seamless," Vizsla said. "We now have the support of the people, and Satine to bait Kenobi. With his demise, our deal will be complete."

Maul stepped forward.

"Your oversight requires correction," he told Vizsla. "We now have a base, an army, and the means to expand to other neutral systems."

Vizsla waved that away.

"It wasn't an oversight," he said. "It was intentional. I

don't have an interest in the other systems."

Vizsla leaned forward, fixing Maul with his gaze.

"Your vision no longer matters," he said.

Bo-Katan and another enforcer held their blasters to Maul's head. A soldier stripped the Sith warrior of his saber and locked his wrists behind his back with energy binders.

Maul said nothing. He was relieved that Vizsla had managed to wait this long, that he had kept his impatience in check. If the Death Watch leader had moved against him earlier, the plan would have been ruined.

Now, Vizsla only had one role left to play—and soon it would be time for him to play it.

"Oh, don't fret," Vizsla assured him. "I'll still honor our deal. Kenobi will be dealt with. But now you'll do as *I* say."

The crowd outside in the square had already seen a number of extraordinary things that day. But now Pre Vizsla—their new Prime Minister and Mandalore—had come to address them again. This time, his soldiers were guarding a Zabrak with red and black tattoos. The captive warrior practically radiated coiled menace and danger, and the crowd was relieved to see his arms trussed behind his back.

"The violence is over!" Vizsla assured them. "The last of

the parasites infecting Mandalore has been caught!"

Vizsla grinned as Bo-Katan and her enforcers forced Maul forward, displaying him to the mob below.

"The Duchess has abandoned her duty to protect Mandalore," Vizsla told them. "Her political dream only encourages aggression against our planet."

Bo-Katan hefted her rifle and smashed Maul in the head with it, bringing a roar of approval from the crowd. Maul wondered how long she had been waiting to do that, and if she had any idea that she had just guaranteed herself a particularly ugly death.

"We have learned from this beast the consequences of pacifist principles," Vizsla said. "It's now time to restore the traditions of Mandalore. No one will ever threaten us again!"

The Death Watch marched Maul away to choruses of cheers.

CHAPTER TWENTY

They locked Maul in a cell with his brother. Savage, agitated, paced back and forth as best he could in the tiny cell. Maul chose to meditate, letting his mind drift among the currents and eddies of the Force, testing the probabilities that lay ahead to see how they had changed. In the majority of them, he saw, his plan still worked out as he had seen in his visions.

Savage continued to pace. Maul decided to try to calm his apprentice. Savage's emotions were powerful, and it was wasteful for him to let anger and frustration bleed out in a cell instead of using them to destroy their enemies.

"Vizsla has captured the support of his people, just as we planned," Maul said. "However, he is not their anointed leader yet. There is still time for us to put in place a leader under our control."

"Then let us escape and we shall find one," Savage said, seething.

Maul glanced at the guard stationed outside the cell door.

"Patience," Maul said. "We must move cautiously. By placing us in prison, Vizsla has unwittingly put us within reach of several candidates for his successor."

That made Savage stop pacing. He looked at Maul, curious.

"What do you mean, brother?" he asked.

"Vizsla has imprisoned the Duchess here," Maul said. "Other political advisors of hers will be within these walls. They will suit our purposes well."

The guard overheard their conversation and turned.

"Hey!" he yelled. "Quiet, you two!"

Maul and Savage stared at the guard with freezing contempt, then looked at each other.

Maul smiled faintly.

"Apprentice, I wish to tour this facility," he said.

A moment later, the door to their cell exploded outward, ripped away by a tremendous surge in the Force. Stunned by the blast, the guard stumbled forward and toppled over the railing, screaming uselessly as he fell.

Maul and Savage made their way down the cellblock, peering in at the prisoners. They stopped before a cell occupied by a striking woman with blond hair.

"You are the now-former Duchess Satine, are you not?" asked Maul.

Fear showed in the woman's eyes for a moment, but then she pushed it away and glared out at the two Zabraks.

"What do you want, you monster?" she demanded.

Definitely the Duchess, Maul thought, admiring her spirit.

"Nothing yet," Maul said. "But I will have a use for you in time. Where are the other leaders of your people?"

"You should know already," Satine said bitterly. "They've either sided with Vizsla or have been killed. There's no one left now but Almec and me—but he's as corrupt and vile as you."

"Really?" Maul grinned. "Thank you for being so cooperative."

A man with a strong chin and nose sat in the next cell. Maul unlocked the door and he and Savage entered the cramped space. Almec got to his feet, then backed up, bumping into the wall. There was nowhere to run.

"Almec?" Maul asked.

"Yes," Almec said, obviously frightened.

"I can deliver you from this prison," Maul said. "What was your position in this government?"

Now that he knew his death wasn't imminent, Almec managed to control his fear. *Good,* thought Maul. Maybe the man wouldn't be as useless as he'd first seemed.

"I am the former Prime Minister," Almec said with as much dignity as he could manage. "Satine imprisoned me on charges of corruption and conspiracy for using the black market."

Maul smiled. The man was perfect for his designs — so much better than Pre Vizsla, in fact.

Satine had been listening from her cell. Now, she could no longer stand it.

"He's a murderer!" Satine objected. "He caused the death of children!"

Savage turned in the direction of her cell, his eyes blazing orange and red.

"Quiet!" he bellowed.

A guard on the next level down heard the ruckus and spotted the two Zabraks out of their cell. He fired, the blaster bolt going wide. Savage reached down with the Force and dragged the man into the air, choking him. The guard's legs kicked desperately as he struggled for breath.

Maul stepped closer to Almec.

"What do you want from me?" the former Prime Minister asked.

"Mandalore is in need of a Prime Minister," Maul said.

"I thought you were in league with Pre Vizsla," Almec said, confused.

"We were," Maul said.

Savage tired of tormenting the guard and broke his neck with the Force. He released the man and his body plummeted out of sight as Satine looked on in horror.

"Clearly you are powerful," Almec said, trying to placate the two deadly warriors. "But how can two of you overthrow Vizsla and his supporters?"

"Vizsla is a soldier, and like all soldiers he is bound by honor," Maul said. "I will challenge him to single combat in front of his men. He cannot deny me."

Almec nodded.

"If you defeat him, according to the ancient laws of Mandalore his soldiers will be honor-bound to follow you," he said.

"Exactly," Maul said.

CHAPTER TWENTY-ONE

Uizsla was sitting with Bo-Katan and a group of warriors when the commotion began outside the royal chamber. A hologram materialized from the transmitter in the floor and a Death Watch enforcer stood before them.

"Sir, they're attacking—" he warned, then began to choke.

The hologram cut out and the doors at the far end of the royal chamber swung open. Vizsla scrambled to his feet in disbelief as Maul strode down the length of the chamber, followed by Savage and—of all people—Almec.

"I challenge you, one warrior to another," Maul said. "And only the strongest shall rule Mandalore."

"So be it," Vizsla said.

He gestured to the Death Watch fighters.

"Give him his weapon," Vizsla said.

Vizsla ignited the darksaber, which whined in his fist, the blade like a slice of deep space. It seemed to pulse with a terrible hunger. Maul stared at Vizsla over his humming scarlet blade. The Mandalorians looked on in fascination.

Watching from where he stood next to Savage, Almec smiled at the trap Vizsla had set for himself. The Death Watch commander had spent years dreaming of restoring the pitiless old warrior codes that had bound Mandalore's clans for thousands of years. Now that he had succeeded, he would have to live by them—or die.

As for himself, Almec had grown up a New Mandalorian, despising the old ways, the feuds and bloodlust and lives thrown away in barbaric contests of supposed honor. But now the throne of Mandalore belonged to the Death Watch, and Sundari's royal chamber was a dueling ground. The old ways were dead—and Almec would bury his past along with them.

"For Mandalore!" Vizsla shouted, slashing at Maul with murderous fury. The Sith warrior parried the attack and swung his blade in a humming arc. The Mandalorian countered the blow. They circled each other warily, looking for a gap in each other's defenses, then came together with blades crossed, sparks and spatters of light marking the places the deadly plasma of darksaber and lightsaber contacted each other.

Maul shoved Vizsla back, the darksaber keening as it whistled through the air, and stared at the Death Watch commander. Vizsla was an excellent duelist — strong, graceful, and able to sense what an opponent's smallest movement indicated would happen next. But for all that, Vizsla could not sense the Force. He would never be able to see things before they happened, or command the laws of the universe to bend for him.

Savage knew it, too — Maul caught sight of his apprentice's slight smile where he stood, watching Master and Mandalorian continue their deadly dance. The two dodged and weaved as their blades buzzed and whined, meeting and parting in blurred arcs as Maul and Vizsla grunted with effort.

Suddenly, Vizsla's hand dipped for his holster. He drew his blaster and fired in one motion. The quick draw would have left most enemies lying on the polished floor with a smoking hole in their chests, and it took Maul by surprise. But the Force saved him, lending him the speed to sense the attack, raise his saber, and intercept the bolt before it killed him. Still, the shot knocked the saber out of his hands. Vizsla rushed in for the kill, darksaber raised to cut Maul in two.

The killing stroke never came. Maul stood his ground, his hands locking onto Vizsla's wrists. The darksaber flew out of the Mandalorian's hands and skated across the polished marble as Maul flung Vizsla to the floor.

Vizsla managed to rise to his knees, but couldn't get up. Savage grinned. Bo-Katan took a step forward, reaching for her weapons, but one of the soldiers stopped her. The warrior code forbade her from interfering. She watched in frustration as Maul leapt on Vizsla with his fists flying, battering the Death Watch commander again and again.

Maul stretched out his hand and the darksaber flew into his grasp.

Vizsla, swaying slightly on his knees, stared at the black blade in Maul's hand. It was beautiful.

"Like you said, only the strongest should rule," Vizsla said.

The darksaber howled and Vizsla's headless body slumped to the floor.

Maul raised the black blade, his gaze pinning each warrior in turn.

"I claim this sword—and my rightful place as ruler of the Death Watch," he proclaimed.

One by one, the Mandalorians dropped to one knee, obeying the code and acknowledging Maul's claim. But Bo-Katan remained on her feet. So did seven other of the Death Watch's warriors. Maul turned his blazing eyes on her, making sure she could read the message there.

Submit—or pay the price.

"Never!" Bo-Katan yelled. "No outsider will ever rule Mandalore!"

"If you will not join me, you will all die," Maul warned.

The warriors who had kneeled now got up slowly, turning until they were facing Bo-Katan and the soldiers who had refused to acknowledge Maul. Both sides raised their weapons.

"You're all traitors!" Bo-Katan yelled.

"Unfortunately, history won't see it that way," Maul said. "Execute them."

But Bo-Katan's warriors fired first, forcing their former comrades to duck. Bo-Katan fired her blaster furiously at Maul and Savage. They dodged, and the eight rebellious Mandalorians fought their way across the royal chamber. Bo-Katan flicked her wrists and sent a trio of thermal detonators bouncing across the floor. Then she and her followers ignited their jetpacks and streaked across the sky.

Picking himself off the floor of the throne room after the detonators' impact, Maul stared after the fleeing Mandalorians for a moment, then turned away. They were an annoyance— no more.

The Death Watch was his to command.

He was the new Mandalore.

CHAPTER TWENTY-TWO

Almec walked out onto the royal balcony and found Sundari's main square filled with Mandalorians, gazing up at the palace with wildly mingled fear and anxiety and confusion.

"Silence, please—silence!" he called. "Hear me now!"

The crowd slowly subsided. Almec saw people looking up at him in disbelief and disdain, remembering the circumstances of his arrest and his now-interrupted prison sentence. He would address that particular point in a moment. First, he had something else to tell them.

"Duchess Satine, the so-called pacifist, who could not

protect you when your lives were at stake, has murdered Pre Vizsla, the true hero of Mandalore," Almec said.

There were gasps and cries below. Almec waited for the crowd to quiet a bit, to get over the shock of the news.

"Satine is now under arrest," he said. "And it was Pre Vizsla's last command that I be reinstated as Prime Minister."

A few cheered. But many more clearly doubted him.

"I know my past is checkered," Almec said. "But I promise you, I take full responsibility for my people, and my heart now bleeds for your pain. However, from this point on, Mandalore will be strong and we will be known as the warriors we were always meant to be."

Cheers rang out here and there, then began to spread. He stood and waited as the sound slowly built, reaching a crescendo as a unit of heavily armed warriors marched out onto the balcony and flanked their Prime Minister on either side.

Almec could still hear the cheers after he reentered the royal chamber. He found Maul seated on the Mandalorian throne, its transparisteel panels glowing behind him. Maul gazed at him for a long moment, until Almec began to shift his feet uneasily.

Finally, the Sith warrior spoke.

"You have done well, Prime Minister," Maul said.

Almec tried not to let his relief show.

"I shall waste no time in building my administration," he told Maul.

"Choose wisely," Maul said. "I will hold you personally responsible for their failures."

Almec swallowed nervously.

"Yes, Master," he said. "Uh, is there anything more you require?"

Maul waved one hand carelessly.

"Go—rule my people," he said.

Almec bowed and removed himself from Maul's presence as quickly as his dignity allowed. Maul sat for a while, considering all that had occurred. Mandalore was his. Now, more worlds would follow.

Darth Maul rearranged himself on the throne of Mandalore, steepled his fingers, and smiled.

PART FOUR:
THE LAWLESS

CHAPTER TWENTY-THREE

Beneath Sundari's royal palace, now occupied by Darth Maul, Duchess Satine Kryze sat in her cell and waited for something to change.

The guards had told her of the astonishing events as they'd unfolded, eager to boast of each new defeat for the pacifist cause. In the weeks since Vizsla's death, Maul and Almec had gotten rid of anyone who might still be loyal to Satine's regime and filled Mandalore's ministries with their own followers. They had been busy, but sooner or later their attention would return to the Duchess, left to rot in her own prison.

They would kill her, of course. Satine was sure of that. The only question was whether they'd publicly disgrace her first. Almec would enjoy a show trial, seeing it as a chance to settle the score for his own arrest and sentence for corruption and conspiracy. But what of the Sith? Satine doubted that Maul was much of a believer in judicial proceedings.

Satine breathed in and out slowly, calming herself as best she could. Whatever came, she promised herself, she would meet it with as much grace and dignity as she could manage. She would do so for her people and for her planet. When Mandalore first rejected war and barbarism, more than seven centuries of peace had followed. Then the planet had turned its back on violence again after the Great Clan Wars. When the current spasm of madness had passed, Mandalore would find a way to choose peace again.

And when that happened, perhaps someone might remember the name of Duchess Satine.

The thought gave her some small comfort, where she had no other hope, and she sat down to wait.

As it turned out, she didn't have to wait for long.

At first Satine ignored the footsteps coming down the cellblock. But when they drew near to her own cell, she looked up. A Mandalorian commando was looking through the transparisteel at her. His helmet and armor had been repainted red and black—the colors of Darth Maul.

Perhaps she'd been wrong, Satine thought grimly. Perhaps they'd decided to execute her now, to make a clean break with the past.

The door slid open.

"What do you want, traitor?" Satine spat.

The commando swayed slightly and then fell forward, helmet bouncing off the floor of the cell with a ring of metal on metal. Satine looked at the fallen Mandalorian in disbelief for a moment before it occurred to her to look behind him.

Her eyes widened in astonishment.

Standing in the cell's doorway was her nephew, Korkie Kryze. A student at Sundari's Royal Academy of Government, he was in his late teens—nearly a man, with red-gold hair and a long, aristocratic-looking nose.

"I would never betray you, Auntie Satine," Korkie said. "I'm here to rescue you."

"Korkie!" Satine rushed out and embraced him, but their reunion was almost instantly ruined—one of Maul's commandos marched down the cellblock toward them, blaster raised.

"Freeze!" the commando ordered. "Hold it there!"

Satine and Korkie raised their arms in surrender—only

to hear a blaster cough and watch the commando drop to the deck. Satine turned and saw another warrior approaching from the opposite direction, gun still drawn. The armored figure was slim and lethal-looking—a woman wearing traditional Mandalorian gear, Satine realized. Her helmet was gracefully curved, with a white faceplate. The hard T of the visor was indented and angled to suggest eyes and a beak, like those of the night birds that still hunted in Mandalore's few remaining forests.

"The Death Watch!" Satine said. "Why are you helping?"

Then she realized Korkie was grinning.

"It's OK, Auntie," the boy said. "She's on our side now."

Bo-Katan came to stand beside the boy and the Duchess, eyes searching the cellblock for enemies. For the moment, they were alone. Bo-Katan stared at the Duchess, lost for a moment in the long history that linked them. She had spent years working to ensure Satine's downfall. Now, she was risking her life to break her out of jail. The galaxy, Bo-Katan thought, was stranger than anyone could possibly imagine.

Yet here they were. And in an unpredictable galaxy, you fell back on the wisdom of those who had come before you.

"The enemy of my enemy is my friend," Bo-Katan said.

Satine had spent her life rejecting such simple talk, urging Mandalorians to look beyond philosophy that grew out of the barrel of a gun. But now she nodded at Bo-Katan.

"I can agree with that," Satine said. "Come on, let's go."

The unlikely trio—a teenage cadet, a Death Watch warrior, and a pacifist former Duchess—emerged on the landing platform that served the prison. Two of Bo-Katan's Nite Owls were waiting for them, as well as three of Korkie's fellow cadets from the academy—Amis, Soniee, and Lagos. A speeder hovered on the platform, ready for passengers, with smaller speeders waiting nearby.

Looking at the four teenagers, Satine felt something grab at her heart. They should have been at the academy, preparing for graduation and jobs creating a better Mandalore. Instead they were risking their lives as part of a prison break in a war-torn city.

She pushed the thought away. Much worse things awaited Mandalore's children under the rule of Darth Maul. And besides, she remembered with a smile, these four cadets had broken her out of prison once before. Two years ago, they had been the ones who foiled Almec's plans to seize power and frame her for corruption.

Perhaps that was a good omen for their planet.

"It's all clear," Amis said. "Come on!"

Of course, thought Satine, *last time the cadets had had a Jedi helping them—without Anakin Skywalker's apprentice Ahsoka Tano, things might not have gone as well as they had.*

Speaking of the Jedi . . .

"We need to contact the Jedi Council," Satine said. "Korkie, give me your comlink."

"It won't be any good unless we get you outside the city," Korkie warned. "All other frequencies are jammed."

Satine frowned. She'd been hoping Maul and Almec might have been too busy to shut down communications, but no such luck.

"You are all taking a terrible risk by helping me," Satine said.

Korkie grinned.

"Nothing we haven't done before, right, Auntie?" he said.

Bo-Katan shook her head, gesturing for Satine to get in the lead speeder. At least they'd sent the Duchess to prison in one of her sensible outfits, instead of some ridiculous formal dress dripping with jewels.

"Let's get going," Bo-Katan said gruffly.

Korkie handed Satine his comlink and joined her in the lead speeder as his fellow cadets found places in the other speeders. As they started the engines, Satine heard a hiss of propellant and looked up to see commandos in red-and-black armor racing toward them, fire blasting out of their jetpacks. Bo-Katan heard them coming, too, and gestured for her warriors to take off.

The speeders flew off between Sundari's skyscrapers. Bo-Katan's warriors followed, jetpacks blazing. Sundari's city-block ladders and towers were a blur as they raced past, heading for the landing platforms that extended like fingers from the perimeter of Sundari's dome. The commandos loyal to Maul settled in behind them, human missiles streaking across the city. Their jetpacks burned like torches. Satine felt her stomach protest as the speeder cut a corner at perilous speed.

Laser blasts streaked past the speeders as Maul's commandos opened fire, trying to cut them off before they could reach the landing platforms. Satine winced, trying to will the speeders to go faster. Lasers were sizzling all around them, their brilliance leaving spots on her vision.

Behind the former Duchess, Bo-Katan tried to calculate the remaining distance to the landing platform, weighing it against the speed and skill of the commandos chasing them.

She didn't like what those calculations told her.

Bo-Katan gestured urgently to her two warriors.

"Take 'em out!" she yelled. "Get the Duchess clear!"

The two warriors zoomed upward and arched their backs, rocketing backward in a neat loop to intercept the incoming commandos, whom they tackled in midair. Locked in a deadly embrace, the four Mandalorians pinwheeled across the sky, limbs kicking.

One of Maul's commandos was still chasing them. Bo-Katan fired her grappling line, lassoing him neatly. Holding on to the line, she whipped the commando around in an arc that ended with a sickening impact against a building.

For a moment Bo-Katan wondered which former comrade of hers it had been, then pushed the thought out of her mind. This was no day to be sentimental about the fate of traitors.

They had almost reached the landing platform. Bo-Katan started to relax, but went rigid when she heard the roar of more jetpacks behind her.

Six more of Maul's commandos had joined the chase.

The speeders reached the landing platform and Bo-Katan and her warriors touched down behind them, urging Satine and the cadets to take shelter as they turned to fire at their airborne pursuers.

Satine checked her comlink.

"The transmission is still blocked," she told Korkie, voice tight with frustration.

Laser bolts sang through the air as the two teams of warriors blasted away at each other. Satine jumped to her feet, heedless of the danger. Korkie ran right behind her, firing at

Maul's commandos to give his aunt cover. Bo-Katan watched in amazement as the former Duchess ran across the platform, trying to find a place where she could get a signal.

Finally, the comlink indicated it had connected with the HoloNet transmitters in orbit above Mandalore.

"This is a message for Obi-Wan Kenobi," Satine said urgently, raising her voice to be heard above the crackle of blaster fire. "I've lost Mandalore. My people have been massacred. . . ."

A commando knocked Korkie sprawling. Satine looked up and saw more of Maul's loyalists touching down around her. The battle had been lost.

"Obi-Wan," Satine said into the comlink, "I need your help."

Maul's commandos had her surrounded. Satine raised her chin, eyes flashing with defiance, as they reached for her.

CHAPTER TWENTY- FOUR

On Coruscant, Obi-Wan Kenobi entered the Jedi Temple's war room, where Yoda and Ki-Adi-Mundi were waiting for him.

"You summoned me, Masters?" he asked politely.

The look on their faces told him he wouldn't like the news.

Ki-Adi-Mundi reached for the controls to the holo-projector, then stepped back as the message began to play. A hologram sprang into being and a three-dimensional portrait of Duchess Satine stood before him. She looked determined, as she always did. But she also looked exhausted and deeply worried, and Obi-Wan knew something was very wrong.

"This is a message for Obi-Wan Kenobi," Satine said. *"I've lost Mandalore. My people have been massacred. And Almec is now the Prime Minister. I can't explain everything now, but Almec has the support of the crime families. Obi-Wan . . . I need your help."*

Mandalorian commandos in red-and-black armor stepped in front of Satine and a moment later the hologram cut off. Obi-Wan stared into the gloom of the war room, hoping the message might somehow resume, that the foreboding image wouldn't be the end of the communication.

"Your thoughts on this, Master Kenobi?" asked Yoda.

Obi-Wan stared down at the deactivated holoprojector.

When Obi-Wan was still a Padawan, Mandalore had been engulfed by endless battles between its clan leaders. Satine's father, the greatest warlord of Clan Kryze, had sent his daughter to Coruscant for training in statecraft and diplomacy. After he died, Satine was his clan's brightest hope. The Jedi Council had ordered Obi-Wan and his Master, Qui-Gon Jinn, to bring her back to Mandalore and keep her safe.

That had proved difficult. The three had spent months on the run, with the two Jedi protecting Satine from seemingly endless enemies. Once the danger had passed, Qui-Gon and Obi-Wan had stayed to monitor the situation for the Republic, watching as the charismatic young Duchess rallied the weary warlords to the New Mandalorian cause.

To Qui-Gon's amusement, Satine and Obi-Wan had quarreled about nearly everything. They had also fallen deeply in love, despite their vows to avoid doing so — or maybe because of them. When Satine was safe again, Obi-Wan had simultaneously hoped she would ask him to stay with her and dreaded that she might do so. Emotional attachments were forbidden for Jedi, to say nothing of marrying Mandalorian noblewomen. He would have been expelled from the Jedi Order — and that was a fate he had been willing to accept.

But Satine had not asked him. Obi-Wan had continued his Jedi training, and shoved the thought of Satine down so deep in his memory that the regrets came rarely. For the most part, he was grateful for the life of service he had pursued.

For the most part, but not entirely. All of a sudden, he felt terribly guilty. She had loved him and he had abandoned her.

He met Yoda's green-eyed gaze and knew he would tell the wizened Jedi Grandmaster none of this. Yoda could be kind and sympathetic, but Obi-Wan doubted if he really understood the human heart, or accepted its weaknesses.

Don't center on your anxieties, Obi-Wan thought. *Fear, jealousy, suffering . . . these open the doors to the dark side.*

"Satine has been at odds with the Death Watch for years," Obi-Wan said, keeping his voice carefully neutral. "And according to a report from Padawan Tano, they are no longer in league with the Separatists. If there was a takeover on Mandalore, it was most likely an independent act caused by the Death Watch alone."

Yoda nodded and looked at Ki-Adi-Mundi.

"Without involvement from the Separatists, if this is an internal affair for the Mandalorians, I'm afraid we cannot help," the cone-headed Cerean Jedi said.

Obi-Wan saw that the matter was closed as far as they were concerned—thousands of worlds were engulfed by war, and the Jedi were needed on more battlefields than they could possibly visit. But it wasn't that simple—at least not to Obi-Wan.

"We cannot just hand Mandalore over to these crime families and let Satine become a martyr," Obi-Wan insisted.

The two elder Jedi looked at him patiently.

"I'm afraid her decision to keep Mandalore neutral makes this situation difficult," Ki-Adi-Mundi said diplomatically.

Ah yes, Obi-Wan thought. *Politics, the enemy of decisive action.*

Unfortunately, Ki-Adi-Mundi was right. With help from Obi-Wan and Padmé Amidala, Satine had foiled a murky plot that would have sent Republic peacekeepers to Mandalore in force. The Republic fleet had stood down in its final hours of preparation, leaving Mandalore's neutrality unchallenged. Satine had won and the Republic had been deeply embarrassed—and because of that, no help would be forthcoming this time.

"Understand your feelings I do, Obi-Wan," Yoda said. "But to take action, support from the Senate we will need."

I very much doubt you understand my feelings, Obi-Wan thought. He shoved the thought away, locking it up with many other things that a Jedi wasn't allowed to say and wasn't supposed to feel.

"You know what the Senate will decide," Obi-Wan said. "They will not send aid to a neutral system."

"At this time, nothing more can we do," Yoda said.

There's nothing you *can do, Master Yoda,* Obi-Wan thought. *But I have an idea.*

Obi-Wan found Anakin beside his starfighter in the Jedi hangar, talking excitedly with R2-D2 and a gaggle of mechanics about the relationship between etheric rudders and acceleration compensators. Obi-Wan waited impatiently for the incomprehensible conversation to end.

It showed no signs of doing so, until Anakin saw his former Master waiting. His eyes widened when he saw Obi-Wan was wearing the armor confiscated from the bounty hunter Rako Hardeen. Anakin excused himself, leaving Artoo to beep indignantly at the mechanics about something or other.

"Not faking your own death again, are you?" Anakin asked.

Obi-Wan explained the situation quickly.

"And the Jedi Council will do nothing, of course," Anakin said disgustedly.

"It's not as simple as that," Obi-Wan said reluctantly. "The Senate—"

"The Senate will do even less," Anakin said. "But we're not the Senate or the Council, are we? Ready when you are, Obi-Wan."

Obi-Wan felt a surge of gratitude. Anakin was loyal, and a good friend. But that wasn't what he wanted from his former Padawan.

"I'll hear quite enough from Master Yoda without involving you," Obi-Wan said. "Let's keep the level of uproar to merely enormous, shall we?"

Anakin shook his head.

"Anakin, this is my burden to bear," Obi-Wan said. "I

appreciate your wanting to help, but I must do this alone."

Anakin gazed at Obi-Wan, saw he wouldn't change his mind, and nodded unhappily.

"I was wondering if I might borrow that old freighter of yours," Obi-Wan said.

"The *Twilight*?" Anakin asked. "Sure. Though you should know—"

"Is she spaceworthy these days?" Obi-Wan asked.

"The engines need tuning, and she's pitching more than I'd like, and there's a list of other little problems," Anakin said with a frown. "If you give me and Artoo an hour—"

"As long as she'll fly—and land," Obi-Wan said. "I'm not planning on making the Kessel Run, or trying my hand at the five Fire Rings of Fornax."

"She's all yours, then," said Anakin, amused at the idea of Obi-Wan finding himself in either one of those places. Obi-Wan's ideal space voyage would be spent meditating until a droid pilot told him they'd arrived.

Obi-Wan smiled and turned to walk across the hangar, Hardeen's helmet tucked under one arm.

"Thank you, Anakin," he called back over his shoulder. "I promise I'll return her without a scratch."

"Scratches add character," Anakin said. "Don't worry

about it, Obi-Wan. Just go rescue your girlfriend."

"I told you, Anakin, she's not my—" Obi-Wan said, then saw Anakin smiling at him.

He nodded and smiled back.

"May the Force be with you," Anakin said.

CHAPTER TWENTY-FIVE

Two of Maul's commandos led Satine into the royal chamber, with Prime Minister Almec walking at the head of the procession. Darth Maul sat in the throne that had once been Satine's, his burning eyes seeming to drill into her brain. She fought down her disgust at the sight of this amoral murderer lounging in a hall where so many had worked so hard to further the cause of peace.

"Satine's accomplices have escaped, including the renegade Death Watch soldiers, but we will find them," Almec said. "The Duchess appears to have contacted the Jedi—just as anticipated."

Satine looked at Maul in horror. The Sith Lord smiled with a terrible glee.

"Good," Maul said. "You have done well."

"What of the people?" Almec asked.

"You are the legitimate Prime Minister," Maul said. "Mandalore is a sovereign planet, and you will maintain its neutrality."

It sounded almost reasonable, particularly when said in Maul's smooth, cultured voice. But Satine knew it was a way of hiding some awful plot. If Mandalore wasn't to become part of Count Dooku's Confederacy of Independent Systems, perhaps Maul meant to hand the planet over to his criminal allies—the pirates, smugglers, and slavers who had terrorized the people of Sundari.

"And what of the Jedi?" Almec asked.

"We are prepared for Kenobi," Maul said.

Oh, Obi-Wan, Satine thought. *What have I done?*

There was nothing wrong with the *Twilight*, Obi-Wan decided, that couldn't be fixed if you gave an army of mechanics a dozen repair droids and the parts for an entirely new ship. The battered G9 Rigger shed several hull plates in Coruscant's upper atmosphere, her static discharge ports were fouled, the navicomputer insisted it was three parsecs rimward of Devaron, and the pilot's console was filled with red alert lights.

But the freighter made it to orbit around Mandalore without falling apart, and Obi-Wan set a course for Sundari. He coaxed the struggling *Twilight* over the blinding white sands, trying to keep her from pitching upward as warning lights flashed and malfunctioning instruments beeped for attention. The moon Concordia was rising, a green half circle in the bright sky.

The *Twilight* lurched on final approach to Sundari, trying to go into a spin before Obi-Wan coaxed her into a low hover above the docks instead. The freighter shuddered and a loud grinding noise began somewhere belowdecks. As she began to smoke, Obi-Wan brought her down the last few meters. It was more of a controlled fall than a landing, but they were down.

Obi-Wan persuaded the landing ramp to lower itself and strode off the ship, peering at Sundari through the bladelike lenses of Rako Hardeen's helmet. A Mandalorian commando approached, wearing red-and-black armor. The man cocked his head curiously at the smoking freighter.

"You better get your ship looked at," the commando said.

A piece of the *Twilight* fell off with a clang. Behind his helmet, Obi-Wan winced.

"Oh, it's my friend's ship," Obi-Wan said. "He told me it was perfectly fine. I'm terribly sorry about that."

"Do you have a landing permit?" the commando asked, after deciding no other malfunction was imminent.

Obi-Wan patted at the pockets of his jumpsuit.

"Um, I think I left it in the ship," he said. "Come with me and I'll get it."

The commando followed Obi-Wan back up the ramp. The sounds of a short, sharp struggle followed. A few minutes later, a figure in red-and-black Mandalorian armor walked back down the ramp, adjusting his helmet.

From a distance, Bo-Katan and the Nite Owls watched as Obi-Wan entered the occupied city of Sundari.

CHAPTER TWENTY-SIX

Satine sat alone in her cell once more, wishing there were some way for her to send her thoughts across the stars, to warn Obi-Wan that he was walking into a trap.

The door to her cell rattled, then opened. A commando stood there in red-and-black armor.

"Here to do more of your master's bidding?" Satine asked, voice thick with contempt.

The commando stepped closer.

"I do my own bidding," he said, the helmet's filtering turning the voice harsh—but also somehow familiar.

Then the commando reached up and removed his helmet.

"Obi-Wan!" Satine gasped.

Before the Jedi could move, Satine had wrapped her arms around him. Obi-Wan smiled. Then Satine looked at him, her initial joy clouding over, leaving her looking worried and frightened.

"Are you alone?" she asked.

"Yes," Obi-Wan said. "The Jedi Council and Galactic Senate will be of no help to us here."

He led her down the cellblock toward the elevators, making certain they were not being followed.

"I trust you have an escape plan, then?" Satine asked.

"As always, my dear," Obi-Wan said, putting his helmet in place once more. The elevator doors opened, revealing one of Maul's commandos. Obi-Wan pushed Satine inside in gruff silence. The commando gave them a once-over as the elevator began to descend.

"There's no record of a prison transfer here," he said.

"The orders came from upstairs," Obi-Wan explained.

Apparently satisfied, the commando looked away. Satine's shoulders sagged in relief.

Then the man turned back to Obi-Wan.

"What's the authorization code?" he asked.

Obi-Wan brought his fist up with Jedi speed. The

commando was unconscious before his body hit the floor.

Always violence, Satine thought, but didn't say anything.

The doors opened and Satine and Obi-Wan dashed across the landing platform to Obi-Wan's waiting speeder bike. Another commando chased after them, yelling for them to halt.

"It's the Duchess!" he said into his comlink. "She's getting away!"

The speeder bike had shrunk to a tiny dot amid Sundari's traffic before he could draw his blaster.

Obi-Wan sped across the city, zipping past airspeeders and delivery hovertrucks and startled swoop drivers, while Satine pressed herself against his back. Now he could hear the sound of blaster fire and the roar of jetpacks above the wind whistling past his ears.

He juked and weaved in and out of Sundari's traffic lanes, trusting the Force to maneuver him out of harm's way and wondering if that trust would be enough. The Republic's clone troopers swore you never heard the blaster bolt that killed you. Obi-Wan wasn't sure how they could be certain of this, since no one who knew for sure could share the information. He was reluctant to find out himself.

They shot through the tunnel connecting the docks to the rest of the city and came to a skidding stop, leaping off the speeder bike as blaster bolts hissed past them. Ahead of them sat the *Twilight*, waiting on her landing gear with her ramp down. Obi-Wan hurried Satine up the ramp and flung himself into the pilot's seat, toggling the freighter's laser cannons and hoping they wouldn't decide that this was a good time to malfunction.

They were working—cannon fire forced the commandos to scatter. The *Twilight* lifted off sluggishly, blasterfire thumping into her belly armor and wings.

"Is this thing going to fly?" Satine asked doubtfully.

"Of course it will fly!" Obi-Wan replied, adding a silent prayer for the battered freighter not to prove him wrong.

Two commandos ducked their heads and braced themselves, leaving the rockets on their jetpacks aimed directly at the *Twilight*. Obi-Wan paled and tried to coax more lift from the freighter. Blasters were no threat to her, but rockets could do substantial damage.

He heard the rockets whistling through the air. Then the *Twilight* shuddered. Sparks flew out of the cockpit's consoles and electricity began to crawl across the instruments. Alarms blared and the freighter began to spin.

"Brace yourself," Obi-Wan warned Satine.

He tried to wrestle the *Twilight* back onto a proper trajectory, but found the steering completely unresponsive. She was a hunk of metal, responding to no commands except those of physics.

The nose dipped and the landing platform seemed to spin crazily beneath them.

"Let's get out of here!" Obi-Wan yelled, shoving Satine ahead of him. They stumbled down the corridor connecting the cockpit with the rear cargo hold, the ship whirling around them. Satine stumbled and Obi-Wan barely managed to grab her and stop her from being thrown out of the open back of the freighter. Thick smoke was pouring through every conduit and seam in the hull now.

Obi-Wan put his arm around Satine and they jumped from the back of the *Twilight*. He had no time to call upon the Force to cushion his fall, and the impact with the landing platform knocked the air out of his lungs. The *Twilight* smashed into the deck nearby and toppled over the side of the platform with a shriek of metal. A moment later he heard the boom of an explosion below them.

Obi-Wan tried to get up. He needed to see if Satine had been badly injured. But he couldn't. His vision was blurry, and his body refused to obey him.

He strained to focus on two figures walking down the platform toward them.

"No," he muttered. "It can't be."

But it was. Darth Maul and Savage Opress were the masterminds behind Satine's downfall.

Obi-Wan opened himself to the Force, letting it flow into him and calling on it for strength. He got unsteadily to his feet, still dizzy, and ignited his lightsaber. Satine was lying on the platform nearby. There was no time to check on her.

Obi-Wan stumbled toward the two brothers, lightsaber held uncertainly in front of him, like a man with a cane.

Maul stretched out his hand and Obi-Wan gagged, feet kicking uselessly as Maul held him in midair. He tried to break Maul's Force grip, but didn't have the strength.

Savage picked up Satine's limp body and threw the unconscious former Duchess over one broad shoulder. Maul looked at Obi-Wan contemptuously, then hurled the Jedi back onto the platform. Obi-Wan landed in a heap at the feet of the Sith Lord's commandos.

"We meet again, Kenobi," Maul sneered. "Welcome to my world. Take them back to the palace."

The commandos dragged the helpless Jedi behind them. Obi-Wan tried to resist, but his vision was becoming blurry again, and there was a roaring in his ears. He bumped his head and everything went black.

By the time Obi-Wan could think and move again, Maul's commandos had put him in shackles and taken him to the royal palace. They led him to the royal chamber, where Savage stood guard over Satine. Almec stood to one side, looking wary, as Maul paced in front of Obi-Wan, his mechanical legs whirring and whining.

"Your noble flaw is a weakness shared by you and the Duchess," Maul said.

He lifted his hand and Obi-Wan waited for the invisible fingers of the dark side to close around his throat. But nothing happened.

Satine began to gag and lifted her hands to her throat, eyes wild.

Obi-Wan stared at Maul, face grown pale.

Maul smiled.

"You should have chosen the dark side, Master Jedi," he said.

Satine gasped for air. Obi-Wan's eyes found hers.

"Obi-Wan . . . " she managed to say, struggling with the effort. Maul turned his outstretched fingers into a claw and Obi-Wan saw Satine struggling to resist him.

"Your emotions betray you," Maul said. "Your fear—and yes, your anger. Let your anger deepen your hate."

"Don't listen to him, Obi," Satine said between gasps.

"Quiet," Savage growled at her.

"You can kill me, but you will never destroy me," Obi-Wan said to Maul. "It takes strength to resist the dark side. Only the weak embrace it."

"It is more powerful than you know," Maul replied, refusing to be baited.

"And those who oppose it are more powerful than you'll ever be," Obi-Wan said.

He lifted his chin and stared at Maul.

"I know where you're from," Obi-Wan said. "I've been to your village. I know the decision to join the dark side wasn't yours. The Nightsisters made it for you."

Savage turned his attention from Satine to his Master. Maul whirled on Obi-Wan, fury in his burning eyes.

"Silence!" Maul barked.

Satine fought for air.

"You think you know me?" Maul asked. "It was I who sat for years thinking of nothing but you, nothing but this moment. And now the perfect tool for my vengeance is in front of us."

His outstretched hand was now a fist. Satine was frantic, helpless.

"Maybe I won't kill you," Maul said. "But I will make you share my pain, Kenobi."

The commandos forced Obi-Wan to his knees.

Maul ignited the darksaber.

He looked at Obi-Wan for a long moment, then turned and walked slowly toward Satine. The blade of the darksaber whined eagerly in his hand.

Satine saw Maul coming. She looked past him, locking her eyes on Obi-Wan as Maul drew back the darksaber and rammed it into her body.

The commandos released Obi-Wan as Maul stepped back and Satine slumped to the bright, polished floor. Obi-Wan rushed to the Duchess's side, cradling her head in his arms. She reached up tentatively and stroked his beard.

"Satine," he managed, voice breaking.

"Remember, my dear Obi-Wan," she said quietly, eyes already dimming. "No matter what, don't let go of what you believe in. I never did."

Obi-Wan managed to nod.

Savage looked up at Maul, who was staring down at the Jedi Master and the dead Duchess.

"Do we kill him now, brother?" Savage asked.

"No," Maul said. "Imprison him below. Let him drown in his misery."

CHAPTER TWENTY- SEVEN

Mas Amedda arrived for his afternoon meeting with Supreme Chancellor Palpatine and found the Republic's leader staring out the window of his office, gnawing at his lower lip as airspeeders, shuttles, and military vehicles zipped past Coruscant's towering skyscrapers.

"My Lord?" the Chagrian Vice Chancellor asked, his blue skin darkening with worry.

"There is a disturbance in the Force," Palpatine said. "Prepare my ship."

Amedda had kept many of Palpatine's secrets for years,

and knew his moods better than anyone else on the Republic's capital planet. Whatever was troubling the Supreme Chancellor was urgent—and for a being who often thought in terms of decades or even centuries, few things qualified as urgent.

Amedda hurried from the office, already activating his comlink.

A squad of commandos led a shackled Obi-Wan into the royal palace's cellblock, dim and gloomy now that night had fallen.

Suddenly, a slim figure in Mandalorian armor appeared out of nowhere, kicking the lead commando in the face and snapping his helmet back.

"It's the rebels!" the man yelled, as steel-armored warriors swarmed the Maul loyalists.

Within seconds the guards were lying motionless on the floor. Obi-Wan looked around in surprise as the woman who'd led the attack unlocked his binders.

"Sorry, I don't believe we've met," Obi-Wan said. "You are?"

"Bo-Katan," the woman said gruffly. "I'm here to rescue you. That's all you need to know."

She handed over his lightsaber.

"Sounds good to me," Obi-Wan said, returning the weapon to its normal place on his belt.

One of the warriors held out a Mandalorian jetpack.

"You ever use one of these before?" Bo-Katan asked.

"No," Obi-Wan said. "But in this case, I'm a fast learner."

She eyed him skeptically, then nodded.

"Let's go," Bo-Katan said.

The unmarked shuttle landed on the royal palace's platform, reserved for Mandalore's rulers and their most important advisors. The ramp lowered and a hooded figure in dark robes descended. The commandos rushing to intercept him reached for their throats, gagging, and the cloaked figure swept past them without a sideways glance, gaze fixed straight ahead.

Lifting off from the palace alongside Bo-Katan and her soldiers, Obi-Wan was briefly worried he wouldn't be able to control his Mandalorian jetpack. It would be ridiculous to be broken out of prison only to immediately fly off in the wrong direction and smash into the side of a building.

Fortunately, he got the hang of it quickly enough. The trick was to angle your body slightly in the direction you wanted to go and to keep your arms and legs in the same plane, so they wouldn't create air resistance and send you tumbling or spinning through the air. In very different circumstances it might even have been fun.

But Obi-Wan's skill was nothing compared with what Bo-Katan and her warriors could do. They were true acrobats, able to turn somersaults in midair while firing back at the commandos pursuing them, with a perfect understanding of their bodies, their jetpacks, and what the smallest movement or change in position would mean. It was amazing that his Jedi forebears had fought whole planets full of Mandalorians with such weapons and training. He didn't envy them the assignment.

Bo-Katan and her soldiers dodged a fusillade of blaster bolts from a new group of Maul's commandos joining the chase, then zipped into the transportation tunnel that led to the docks, roaring past a cargo-hauler driven by a terrified Rodian. They emerged to find a pitched battle under way between Bo-Katan's fighters and Maul's loyalists.

Bo-Katan surveyed the number of commandos Maul had sent after them and shook her head in wonder.

"Maul must want you dead," she said.

"You have no idea," Obi-Wan replied.

The feeling had begun as a faint stirring in the Force, like the tiniest ripple of something moving slowly through deep water, far away but drawing steadily closer. It intensified, until it felt like the Force itself was roiling, heaving like the sea in the grip of an enormous storm.

"I sense a presence," Maul warned Savage. "A presence I haven't felt since . . . "

And then Maul knew.

"Master," he said, leaning forward on the throne.

The commandos guarding the royal chamber reached for their throats. As Maul watched, an unseen force lifted them high in the air, then slammed them to the floor, where they lay motionless in their red-and-black armor.

The doors opened, then closed behind a figure in dark robes. A deep cowl hid most of the face, leaving only a pale chin and a downturned mouth visible. To most eyes the man in those simple robes of rough cloth was unremarkable, just another being making his way in the universe. But to those who could feel the Force he was anything but ordinary. To them, he was a dark sun blazing with power that was simultaneously hypnotizing and terrifying to behold.

Darth Sidious, the reigning Dark Lord of the Sith, had come to Mandalore.

Savage stared at the new arrival in astonishment, transfixed by the sight. Maul felt himself leap from the throne, mechanical legs clacking down the steps and toward his old Master. The motion was almost automatic, involuntary. Maul's earliest memories were of that hooded figure — his tests, his teachings, and also his torments. He had been Maul's father, his protector, his torturer.

He had been everything.

Maul halted before Sidious and kneeled, bowing his head.

"Master," he said simply.

Sidious stopped. For a moment all was silent.

"I am most impressed to see you have survived your injuries," he said, the voice as rough and cracked as Maul remembered.

"I used your training, Master," Maul said. "And I have built all of this in hopes of returning to your side."

Sidious lifted his head slightly, and Maul saw his yellow eyes beneath the hood. They were as cold as space.

"How unfortunate that you are attempting to deceive me," Sidious said.

"Master?" Maul asked.

"You have become a rival," Sidious declared.

He raised his arms and both Maul and Savage flew through the air, smashing into the elegantly patterned walls of the royal chamber and crashing to the floor. Maul sprang to his feet and ignited his lightsaber. Savage did the same. The two Zabraks stared grimly at the hooded figure.

Sidious retrieved a pair of elegant-looking lightsabers from within the depths of his robes and ignited them. The blades turned his pale face a hellish red.

Maul and Savage didn't waste time seeking an advantageous position. They simply charged, blades humming, trying to overpower Sidious with the animal ferocity of their attack. Sidious caught their sabers on his, the weapons howling and crackling where they touched. Maul saw that Savage was startled by the seemingly frail man's enormous strength.

Maul stared at his Master's face. He saw the strain as Sidious called upon the Force to keep the brothers at bay. But there was something else there, too—a terrible pleasure. Sidious began to grin.

On the docks, all was chaos. Mandalorians loyal to Bo-Katan fired their blasters at their former comrades in red-and-black armor, or tried to incinerate them with blasts from their flamethrowers, or wrestled with them, knives clutched in their fists. Laserfire sang and men screamed.

A Mandalorian attack craft settled onto the platform. Its ramp lowered and more of Maul's commandos raced out to join the fight.

Bo-Katan hadn't liked the odds when they'd first reached the docks, and she liked them even less now. She had imagined she might die in a firefight—every warrior knew that was a possibility. She had even imagined it might be a necessary sacrifice, the price of seeing the New Mandalorians overthrown and her people's traditions restored. But she had never imagined those trying to kill her would be other members of the Death Watch— men and women she had trained with and fought alongside.

It was a stupid, pointless way to die, Bo-Katan thought, but it seemed increasingly likely that would be her fate—and soon after that, Mandalore would be ruled by a renegade Sith, a false Mandalore who would use the Death Watch as enforcers in his ever-expanding empire of crime and dishonor.

That wasn't what Pre Vizsla had dreamed of, or what she had fought for.

There was another way, Bo-Katan realized—one that might not save her life, but that could deny Maul his victory. It would have been unthinkable even a day ago, but now, somehow, it was the only way.

She activated her comlink and gave a short, sharp command.

When Bo-Katan heard the whine of the *Kom'rk*-class transport's engines descending from above them, she caught Obi-Wan's eye where the bearded Jedi stood deflecting blaster bolts with the blue blade of his lightsaber. She gestured at the ship as its pilot brought it down on the landing platform. Obi-Wan nodded and raised his saber. The two raced for the ramp, blaster bolts sizzling all around them.

Obi-Wan was halfway up the ramp before he realized the Mandalorian woman hadn't followed.

"Go back to your Republic and tell them what has happened," Bo-Katan yelled.

Obi-Wan cocked his head at her, surprised.

"That would likely lead to a Republic invasion of Mandalore," he said.

"Yes . . . and Maul will die," Bo-Katan said. "But Mandalore will survive. We always survive. Now go!"

Bo-Katan raced back into the fight, blasters spitting fire. She did not look back.

The three-pronged duel between Sidious, and Maul and Savage had moved, like some deadly ballet, from the throne room to the steps of the palace. Sidious's lightsabers twirled swiftly and elegantly, turning aside the furious blows Maul and

Savage rained down upon him as the three Sith leapt and spun.

Maul had fought his Master many times, starting when he was little more than a child and continuing through his apprenticeship. His body bore innumerable scars from those duels—lessons in the peril of being too slow or too quick, too weak or too distracted.

During Maul's apprenticeship he had always known that Sidious had been willing to kill him. The Sith had not survived their centuries of exile by being sentimental, and a student who couldn't stand against his Master in a mere training exercise was worse than useless—he was a waste of valuable resources better used elsewhere. But Maul had never faced his Master when he was actually *trying* to kill him.

Maul had grown more powerful since the last time he'd been in Sidious's presence, before the Neimoidian invasion of Naboo had turned disastrous and Obi-Wan had bested him inside the Theed power core. His hermitage on Lotho Minor, his lessons on Umbara, his restoration by Mother Talzin, and his training of Savage had all strengthened him, made him a more worthy vessel for the dark side to fill with its power.

But strong as he had become, Maul found himself in awe of Sidious. The Sith Lord was astonishingly fast and efficient, and the Force flowed through him effortlessly. His sabers stabbed and slashed through the smallest hole in an opponent's guard, his movements never carried him a millimeter out of position, and he could sense every attack Maul or Savage made before it developed.

Maul tried to slash past Sidious's guard, only to find his Master had given ground, causing Maul to extend his arms too far and leave himself slightly unbalanced. It was the smallest stumble, easily corrected, but Sidious saw it—and pounced before Maul could draw himself back. Snarling, he reached out with the Force and slammed Maul against the wall, leaving him lying stunned in a heap.

Savage knew the dangers of facing the Sith Lord alone, and pressed his attack before Sidious could draw his hand back from Force-shoving Maul into the wall. Teeth bared, Savage windmilled his double saber, hoping to disarm Sidious or force him to give ground. If he did, that would allow the yellow-and-black Zabrak to follow his initial attack with a lightning-quick thrust that would penetrate Sidious's defenses and wound or even kill him.

Maul tried to shake off his attack, rocketing up from the floor. Sidious neatly side-stepped Savage's assault, drawing back as the massive Zabrak raised his double-bladed saber high to try to pummel him with it.

Savage didn't think Sidious was fast enough to take advantage of the brief opening in his defenses, but he was wrong.

Sidious rammed one of his blades through Savage's black armor, the glowing crimson tip of the saber appearing between his shoulder blades. Savage gasped, his saber tumbling from his grasp. Sidious yanked his weapon back and Savage seemed to hang suspended for a moment, as if he were being levitated with the Force. Then he crashed to the ground.

Sidious stepped back as Maul rushed to his fallen brother's side.

A mist seemed to rise from Savage's body, emerging from his wounds and then from his eyes, ears, nose, and mouth. As Maul and Sidious watched, Savage's horns shrank and the massive bands of muscle melted away from his chest and shoulders. The last misty remnants of Mother Talzin's magic grew hazy and tattered, then dispersed and vanished, leaving the dying Savage lying in the shell of his now-oversized armor.

His eyes turned to Maul.

"Brother, I am an unworthy apprentice," Savage said. "I am not like you. I never was."

He took a last breath and lay still.

Maul looked up, saber in his grasp, and stared into Darth Sidious's blazing eyes.

"Remember the first and only reality of the Sith," Sidious said. "There can only be two, and you are no longer my apprentice. You have been replaced."

Sidious raised his saber and flew at Maul, who parried desperately, his mechanical legs whirring as he sought to counter his former Master's blows. Sidious's sabers were a blur, a whirling cage of deadly plasma. Maul danced away from one blow, then reversed his movement to avoid another, and then there were too many to count, and then there were even more than that.

Maul's saber spun out of his hand, bouncing away across the floor. Then Sidious seized his former apprentice with the Force, hurling him against the wall. Maul's vision swam. He tried to get up, but realized he was already in the air, held aloft by the Force. Sidious slammed him into the floor. Then Maul was off the ground again, legs kicking for purchase in empty air. He could taste blood in his mouth. His head hit the wall with a sickening crunch.

A rhyme crept into his head, a nagging sing-song bit of poetry.

Far above, far above,
We don't know where we'll fall.
Far above, far above,
What once was great is rendered small.

Maul could no longer remember where he had heard it, or what it meant. He was broken, helpless, useless.

"No," Maul heard himself gasp. "Have mercy. Please . . ."

"There is no mercy," Sidious said.

Bolts of energy ripped out from the Sith Lord's fingers, tendrils of brilliant blue and purple that danced across Maul's tattooed skin and ripped through his muscles, his organs. His mechanical legs convulsed, shorting out.

"You belong to me," Sidious said. "Your existence is now perfectly meaningless."

He stretched out his fingers and the energy tore through Maul again. Sidious watched the lightning build in intensity, his eyes unblinking, his teeth gritted in a triumphant, terrible smile.

One of the most feared villains of all time!

This incredible story features never-before-told secrets about Darth Maul.

STAR WARS
THE WRATH OF
DARTH MAUL
SCHOLASTIC

STAR WARS
THE RISE AND FALL OF
DARTH VADER
SCHOLASTIC

STAR WARS
A NEW HOPE: THE LIFE OF
LUKE SKYWALKER
SCHOLASTIC

STAR WARS
THE LIFE AND LEGEND OF
OBI-WAN KENOBI
SCHOLASTIC

Look for these *Star Wars* biographies—now available as eBooks!

SCHOLASTIC

scholastic.com/starwarsgalaxy

SWCW0912

A chance to find her sister

The cloth bag blended into the landscape as if it had been lying there for a long time. I wondered how many times I'd walked past and not seen it.

I brushed off the dirt, pulled open the zipper, and looked inside. The bag held bundles of twenty-dollar bills!

"Whoa," I said.

I sat on the ground and counted the money: eight hundred and twenty dollars!

My hands shook as I stuffed the cash back inside the bag.

I zipped the bag, then stuck it inside my T-shirt, hoping the bulge wasn't obvious. I tucked the shirt into my jeans, to be sure the bag didn't slide out.

What should I do?

I knew two things for sure:

1. I had to try to find the bag's owner.

2. I wasn't going to tell Rita or my caseworker or anyone else what I'd found.

If the bag's owner showed up and could prove it was his money, I'd give it back. But if no one identified the bag, the cash was mine. It would be my secret, my ticket to find Starr.

Despite the warm June morning, goose bumps rose on my arms as I thought of my twin sister. No matter where she was living now, this was enough money to get me there, and give the two of us a fresh start, together.

All I had to do was find her.

OTHER BOOKS BY PEG KEHRET

Runaway Twin

PEG KEHRET

PUFFIN BOOKS
An Imprint of Penguin Group (USA) Inc.

PUFFIN BOOKS
Published by the Penguin Group
Penguin Young Readers Group, 345 Hudson Street, New York, New York 10014, U.S.A.
Penguin Group (Canada), 90 Eglinton Avenue East, Suite 700, Toronto, Ontario, Canada M4P 2Y3
(a division of Pearson Penguin Canada Inc.)
Penguin Books Ltd, 80 Strand, London WC2R 0RL, England
Penguin Ireland, 25 St Stephen's Green, Dublin 2, Ireland (a division of Penguin Books Ltd)
Penguin Group (Australia), 250 Camberwell Road, Camberwell, Victoria 3124, Australia
(a division of Pearson Australia Group Pty Ltd)
Penguin Books India Pvt Ltd, 11 Community Centre,
Panchsheel Park, New Delhi - 110 017, India
Penguin Group (NZ), 67 Apollo Drive, Rosedale, North Shore 0632, New Zealand
(a division of Pearson New Zealand Ltd)
Penguin Books (South Africa) (Pty) Ltd, 24 Sturdee Avenue,
Rosebank, Johannesburg 2196, South Africa

Registered Offices: Penguin Books Ltd, 80 Strand, London WC2R 0RL, England

First published in the United States of America by Dutton Children's Books,
a division of Penguin Young Readers Group, 2009
Published by Puffin Books, a division of Penguin Young Readers Group, 2011

13 15 17 19 20 18 16 14 12

THE LIBRARY OF CONGRESS HAS CATALOGED THE DUTTON CHILDREN'S BOOKS EDITION AS FOLLOWS:
Kehret, Peg.
Runaway twin / by Peg Kehret.—1st ed.
p.   cm.
Summary: Thirteen-year-old Sunny, accompanied by a stray dog, takes advantage
of a windfall to travel from her Nebraska foster home to Enumclaw, Washington,
to find the twin sister from whom she was separated at age three.
ISBN: 978-0-525-42177-1 (hc)
[1. Foster home care—Fiction. 2. Voyages and travels—Fiction. 3. Dogs—Fiction.
4. Runaways—Fiction. 5. Twins—Fiction. 6. Sisters—Fiction.]
I. Title
PZ7.K2518Run 2009
[Fic]—dc22   2008048974

Puffin Books ISBN 978-0-14-241849-9

Printed in the United States of America
Designed by Abby Kuperstock
Set in Berling Roman

Runaway Twin

For Jenny Moller and Jerry Lindsey,
who enrich my life in countless ways

ACKNOWLEDGMENTS

The character of Snickers is based on a real dog who was the cherished companion of Julie Carlton. Julie won the chance to memorialize Snickers in a book when she was the high bidder at The Dog Bowl, an auction benefiting Pasado's Safe Haven. Thank you, Julie, for your generous bid, which helped Pasado's care for their many rescued animals.

If it were not for Casey Karp, I would be a bald woman. Casey solves all my computer problems, thereby saving me from tearing my hair out.

My first proofreader for this book was Brett Konen, who gave me numerous helpful suggestions. She's an astute editor and a terrific granddaughter!

My wonderful pet-sitter, Karrie Kamcheff, enables me to travel without worrying about my furry friends.

Thanks, as always, to Rosanne Lauer and the rest of the talented group at Dutton Children's Books.

Runaway Twin

1

Most people who have a life-changing experience survive a terrible injury or disease. My life was transformed by a craving for Twinkies.

When I woke up on the first day of summer vacation, I yearned for something sweet, so I decided to celebrate the end of school by eating Twinkies for breakfast. I knew better than to suggest this to my foster mom, Rita, who is a total health-food freak. Rita thinks the perfect breakfast is raw carrots dipped in unsweetened yogurt. For an extra treat, she sprinkles a little flaxseed on the yogurt. Yum-yum.

I dressed, and pulled my hair into a ponytail. I heard

Rita's shower running, so I left a note on the counter. "Rita: I'm going for a walk. Sunny."

Since Rita is always urging me to exercise, I knew that going for a walk would be okay with her. She didn't need to know I was walking to the store to buy Twinkies.

Wouldn't you think the Nebraska Department of Human Social Services (HSS, known as Hiss) would try to match a kid's background with the lifestyle of the foster family she's placed with? In my opinion it is cruel and unusual punishment to put a thirteen-year-old girl who was raised on junk food into a home that serves tofu and cauliflower.

It's hard enough to adjust to a new school and a different neighborhood, often a new town, every few months. It would be comforting to at least get some Snickers bars once in a while, or a big plate of nachos. Instead, I live with Rita, who thinks if she feeds me enough healthy food I will learn to like it. So far this strategy hasn't worked.

Rita remains optimistic, though. She also hopes I'll write about my summer activities because the school gives extra credit to any student who turns in an essay, story, or poem on the first day of school in September. This year's topic is "What I Did This Summer." How boring! Eating Twinkies for breakfast will probably be the highlight of my summer, and it would be hard to make an essay out of that.

Two blocks from Rita's house, I left the sidewalk, cut diagonally across an empty lot, and took the trail. It isn't an official trail yet, although it will be someday when the county parks department gets enough money to maintain it. For now, it's a well-worn path that runs parallel to Silver Creek.

I have to watch where I walk because the trail is full of potholes created by the dirt bikes and quads that roar along it while thick curtains of dust drift down behind them. The morning sun warmed my shoulders as I relished the summer that stretched ahead with no homework and no tests. Rita had suggested summer school as a way to improve my grade point average, but she backed down when I threatened to run away again.

I had run away from my last two foster homes, and Rita was determined not to let it happen on her watch. She prided herself on winning over even the most uncooperative foster kids. That's why she'd agreed to take me.

I'm not a bad girl. I don't do drugs or shoplift or anything like that, but I don't do much schoolwork, either.

Why bother when I'll be in a different school by the end of the term anyway? Why participate in sports or try to make friends when I always leave so soon?

As for running away, I don't really want to leave Rita. I ran away before because Hiss put me in unbearable foster homes. In one, the man of the house believed he was Boss of the World. He had to have complete control of everyone, even his wife. He kept track of how long it took his kids to walk home from school, and punished them if they dawdled or stood on the corner talking with friends. He monitored how much toilet paper we used.

I left after he wouldn't let me have dinner because I had held the refrigerator door open too long while I looked for the mustard. It turned out I couldn't find it because the mustard had been used up the last time they had hot dogs, but that didn't matter. I still had to go to bed hungry. How was I supposed to know they needed a new bottle of mustard?

I sneaked out in the night and started walking. I didn't know where I was going, and I didn't care. Any place would be better than staying another day, with the Boss of the World. Hiss found me the next day but when I told the caseworker why I ran away, she said I didn't have to go back. I think the toilet paper part got to her.

Unfortunately, I went from the Boss of the World to living with She Who Hates Anything Pretty. She-Who didn't let me wear makeup, even if I had a zit to cover up. She-Who wouldn't let me curl my hair, which is straight as a shelf.

"If God had wanted you to have curly hair," she said, "you would have been born with it."

"Then why did God allow the invention of the curling iron?" I asked. I've noticed that people who claim to know what God wants always manage to have His opinion be the same as theirs.

She insisted I wear clothes that were a size too large and clunky, old-lady shoes. Small wonder I didn't make any new friends at school. I looked like an eighty-year-old weirdo.

After I ran away from She-Who, I was placed with Rita. It is my seventh foster home. Some were okay. The Boss of the World and She Who Hates Anything Pretty were the worst.

The one constant in my life, until now, had been that none of the people I lived with cared what I ate. Junk food was cheap and easy, so if I wanted to fill up on Doritos instead of salad, it was okay with them.

Until Rita.

Actually, if it weren't for her fetish about healthy food, I'd like Rita. At least she gives me some space and lets me make my own choices about clothes, books, and music. She's smart and makes me laugh—but she believes the axis of evil is sugar.

As I sidestepped around an especially deep pothole, thinking that maybe I would eat Twinkies for breakfast every day all summer, I almost missed the faded, water-stained bag that lay about three feet off the path. Its mossy green color matched the weeds growing beside the trail. I had already passed the bag when a tiny flash of light reflected from its zipper tab, and I realized I'd seen something that had not grown there.

I often picked up litter when I walked the trail after school. Usually I carried it to the trash or recycling containers outside Manny's Market.

It irritates me that people will use the trail along the creek, supposedly to enjoy Nature's beauty, and then, by littering, will pollute the very thing they have come to admire.

Over my weeks of trail walking, I've trained my eyes to search out man-made materials, those jarring bits of color that don't belong near the path. Expecting the usual candy wrapper or soda can, I stepped back to pick up the item that had caught my eye.

It wasn't litter.

The cloth bag blended into the landscape as if it had been lying there for a long time. I wondered how many times I'd walked past and not seen it.

I brushed off the dirt, pulled open the zipper, and looked inside. The bag held bundles of twenty-dollar bills!

"Whoa," I said. I looked around, half expecting someone wearing a ski mask to leap out from behind a tree, point a gun at me, and say, "Drop it right there."

No one leaped.

Sometimes I meet other people on the trail, often walking their dogs, but this morning I was alone. A slight breeze rustled the leaves; a bird called to its mate. I sat on the ground and counted the money: eight hundred and twenty dollars!

My hands shook as I stuffed the cash back inside the bag.

I zipped the bag, then stuck it inside my T-shirt, hoping the bulge wasn't obvious. I tucked the shirt into my jeans, to be sure the bag didn't slide out.

All thoughts of a Twinkie vanished as I ran back to Rita's house.

What should I do?

I knew two things for sure:

1. I had to try to find the bag's owner.

2. I wasn't going to tell Rita or my Hiss caseworker or anyone else what I'd found.

If the bag's owner showed up and could prove it was his money, I'd give it back. But if no one identified the bag, the cash was mine. It would be my secret, my ticket to find Starr.

Despite the warm June morning, goose bumps rose on my arms as I thought of my twin sister. No matter where she was living now, this was enough money to get me there, and give the two of us a fresh start, together.

All I had to do was find her.

2

Back **in my** room, I pulled the beat-up brown suitcase out from under my bed. It contained everything I wanted to remember about my life, which wasn't much. The most important item was a photograph of Grandma holding her little dog. I stood on one side of Grandma, and Starr stood on the other. We were three years old, wearing matching white shorts and pink T-shirts. Wispy ponytails on the sides of our heads were held in place by bright pink ribbons. Both of us grinned at the camera.

My dad had vanished before Starr and I were born, and if Mama knew where he was, she never told. Our last name, Skyland, was the same as Grandma's, and we all lived with her. A few days after the picture was taken, Grandma and Mama died in an auto accident. I don't know what happened to the dog. Maybe he had been in the car, too.

Starr and I didn't go to the funeral. Instead we played in the church's nursery room, supervised by a bored teenager whom we did not know. We were building towers with blocks and knocking them over when the service ended.

Starr and I were taken away in separate cars; I never saw my sister again.

Nobody mentioned Starr to me after that. She had been my constant companion, my playmate, the only person who could understand everything I said because we often spoke what Mama called "twin talk," a shortcut language that only the two of us knew. Then Starr disappeared, just like Mama and Grandma had disappeared a few days earlier.

I remember looking at the night sky through the car window as I was driven to my new home with my mother's great-aunt Cora. I wished Starr were sitting beside me, and I wondered where she was. I felt as if half of me was missing.

Even then, Twinkies were my favorite treat. I always nibbled the top off first, then scooped out the cream filling with my tongue. Grandma had often made me giggle by singing "Twinkle, Twinkle, Little Star" to me, changing the lyrics to "Twinkie, Twinkie, little star."

As I gazed at the sky that night and thought of my sister, I silently sang my own version:

"Twinkie, Twinkie, little Starr. How I wonder where you are." Of course I was too young to know that my twin's name was spelled with a double *r*. All I knew was that the song made sense to me.

Since then I had repeated the ditty every time I saw the first star in the evening sky. It was my mantra; it showed that I remembered my sister even though I didn't know where she was.

Great-aunt Cora was ten years older than her sister, my grandma, and had an ailing husband. A three-year-old proved to be more than she could cope with, so she talked her son, Jerod, into taking me. Jerod lived alone and had no desire to share his life with a little kid. Most nights I cried myself to sleep, missing Mama, missing Grandma, missing Starr.

Eventually, I ended up as a ward of the state. Jerod had taken me to Nebraska with him, and then left me behind, locked in an empty third-story apartment, when he moved again. By then I was four—only four but already too familiar with loneliness and loss.

When I woke up alone that morning, and saw that all Jerod's clothes were gone, my first thought had been, *Where will I live now?* I tried to open the door but the knob wouldn't turn. I thought I was locked in.

Mama had taught me to call 911 in an emergency. "Don't call unless someone's very sick, or there's a fire, or a burglar," she had said. I sat on the floor with my back to the locked door. I wasn't sick; there was no fire or burglar. I waited.

Did anyone know I was in the apartment? I waited for what seemed a long time, but no one came to get me. Even though I wasn't sick, I decided to call 911, but when I picked up the phone, there was no dial tone. The line had been disconnected.

I was hungry, and the only way to get food was to let someone know I was there. I found a blue towel crumpled on the bathroom floor. I opened the apartment window on the street side, and waved the towel out the window until a woman pushing a baby stroller looked up and noticed me. "I'm hungry!" I called.

"Are you alone?" she asked.

"Yes. I'm locked in."

"I'll get help," she said, and took a cell phone out of her pocket.

Ten minutes later, two police officers told me how to turn the small lever in the center of the doorknob to unlock the door. When it opened, one officer squatted down so he could talk directly to me. "What's your name, sweetheart?" he asked.

"Sunny Skyland."

"Where is your mother?"

"She died."

Those were the only questions I was able to answer. I didn't know Jerod's last name, or where he had gone. I didn't know who my father was. I had no address and no phone number.

Nine years later, sitting in my room at Rita's house, I still felt hollow inside when I remembered how the police officers took me with them and told me not to worry, that I'd be going to a foster home soon. One of them bought me an ice-cream cone, but her kindness didn't make me feel less alone.

My old suitcase contained the clothes I'd been wearing that day. I'm not sure why I kept them. They hold no happy memories, but somehow they prove that I have a past, that I came from somewhere. Someone had bought that flowered yellow sundress for me; someone had buckled those white sandals onto my feet. Someone had cared, at least a little bit.

The suitcase also contained a magazine article that I had read and clipped several years earlier about twin boys who were separated as babies and reunited as adults. I had read it so many times, I could have recited it from memory.

A friend of one twin saw a man in a restaurant who looked so much like his friend that he approached the man's table and asked if he had a brother.

The man said, "No."

"I'm sorry to have bothered you. It's uncanny, how much you resemble my friend. I would have sworn you were his brother."

As he turned to leave, the other man asked, "Was your friend adopted?"

It turned out that he was.

This conversation led to a meeting of the look-alikes where the two men discovered they had been born on the same day and had been adopted from the same agency. Further research proved that they were identical twins.

I didn't know if Starr and I were identical or fraternal twins, but ever since I had read that article, I had daydreamed about someone coming up to me and asking if I had a sister. This stranger would swear that I

looked exactly like someone she knew, and that someone, of course, would turn out to be Starr.

It made a good daydream, but I've learned that if
you want dreams to come true, you have to take action.
Sitting around and hoping someone might look at me
and notice a resemblance to Starr was not likely to produce my twin. If I was ever going to find her, I needed to
do it myself.

I put the bag of cash at the bottom of the suitcase,
laid my belongings on top, and added a pile of school
papers that I'd brought home the day before. I was pretty
sure Rita wouldn't snoop in my things, but the suitcase
didn't have a lock and if it got opened, I wanted the bag
of money to be well hidden.

I shoved the suitcase back under my bed and went
downstairs, humming "Twinkie, Twinkie, little Starr."
Usually the tune made me sad and lonely. That day it
made my heart soar.

I was going to find Starr. Somehow, some way, I
would find my sister and when I did, I would finally have
a family again.

3

That afternoon I went to the office of the local paper and paid cash for a classified ad. "Found money. To claim, identify amount, what it's in, and where you lost it."

I didn't want anyone to call Rita's house, so I used my e-mail address. Rita gave me an account on her computer, with my own e-mail address, even though I didn't have anyone to write to. I knew I'd be the only one who would read any responses to the ad.

I placed an identical ad on Craigslist, and then started watching my e-mail. I got one response right away that said, "I lost my rent money and I am going to be evicted tomorrow. I don't know where I lost it. You are my only hope. Please help me. Angie."

I noticed the writer did not say how much was lost, nor did she mention the zippered bag, so I figured this message was not from the rightful owner. Probably Angie hadn't lost any money at all but thought she could trick me into parting with what I had found. Well, Sunny Skyland is not easily tricked.

The newspaper ad ran the next afternoon. I checked the paper to be sure it was right.

My second response came a day later. It said, "The money is mine. I had it in my pocket and I'm not sure exactly how much there was, but now it's gone. I could have dropped it anywhere. I can meet you tonight to get it back, just tell me what time and where, and I'll be there."

I'll bet you will, I thought. How stupid do people think I am? If anyone had lost eight hundred and twenty dollars that was in a zippered bag, the bag is the first thing they'd tell me about.

I let both ads run for a week. A few more responses arrived, all equally unbelievable. As the days went by and there was no legitimate claim, my excitement grew. I started a list of things I wanted to tell Starr after I found her.

One e-mail said, "That money was left to me by my fathur who died of hart falure yesturday. It is all I have in the wurld. Pleez do not rob me of my futur by keeping it."

I shook my head. The ad had been running for five days before that person's father died—if he had died.

At the end of the week, I replied to all the people I'd heard from. I wrote, "Sorry. The money was claimed by someone who knew exactly how much it was, and what container it was in." I didn't say that the someone was me.

Meanwhile, I had searched for Starr online. It wasn't the first time I'd done that, and the result was the same as it had always been. I found towns named Skyland and people whose last name was Starr and even a group of amateur astronomers, but there was no record of a Starr Skyland in Google or Yahoo or anywhere else. She was not on Facebook or MySpace or any of the other social networks. It was as if my sister had fallen off the Earth. I tried spelling her name with only one *r*, but that didn't make any difference.

It occurred to me that whoever Starr was living with now might have had her use their last name instead of her own. For that matter, they might have given her a new first name, too. Maybe she wasn't bouncing around in foster homes like I was. Maybe she had been adopted.

I decided my best chance of finding her would be to return to where we had lived at the time of the accident. I would talk to people in our old neighborhood. Some of them might have been there when we were, and would remember us. They might know who had taken Starr, and where she is now.

I didn't know the name of the street where we had lived, but I knew the town because it was written, along with *Starr and Sunny, Loretta and Frisky*, on the back of that old snapshot. *Enumclaw, Washington.* I could also make out a house number, 1041, over the door.

According to the Census Bureau, Enumclaw has a population of eleven thousand two hundred people. That wasn't too big. Even without a specific street, I should be able to find someone who had known my mother or my grandma. I could go to every street in town and find number 1041. I could stop at the high school, and ask to see old yearbooks in case my mother had been a student there.

Starr might still live in Enumclaw. Wouldn't that be something? While I was driving away with Great-aunt Cora, Starr could have been moving in with our next-door neighbors. Perhaps she still lived there, in number 1039 or 1043. It was possible.

I studied a map of the United States. I was approximately thirteen hundred miles from Enumclaw, Washington. The closest airport to there was Seattle, but I had already decided not to fly. Instead, I planned to take the bus. It would take me longer to get there, but it would be harder for Rita and Hiss to find me if I bought a series of bus tickets from place to place than if I got on a plane.

I knew from watching the news that flying requires photo ID, which I didn't have because the photos for student ID cards at my current school had been taken while I was still living with She-Who and attending a different school. Also, a kid flying alone and paying cash for a plane ticket might attract attention. Better to travel a short distance by bus, maybe stay over a night or two, and then go a little way farther.

I decided to leave Rita a note. Although she'd probably still report that I was missing, if she knew I had not been abducted but had left on purpose, the cops wouldn't issue an Amber Alert, and the media wouldn't broadcast my picture. A foster kid who runs away, especially one who has run away twice before, would not be newsworthy.

I didn't want to waste the time of the police and others who would look for me if they thought I was lost or the victim of a crime. I wouldn't tell Rita where I was going, only that I was okay and would be in touch. Rita had been nice to me, so I added, "I'm not leaving because of anything you did."

If the whole state wasn't looking for me, I had a good chance of getting away. Just to be sure, I decided to change my appearance.

I made careful plans, thinking through each step. I would leave on Friday morning because Rita taught yoga classes on Fridays and was always gone from eight in the morning until two-thirty. It was the longest period of time that I could count on being alone.

I checked the local Greyhound bus schedule. A bus left at nine-thirty. If I started the minute Rita went out the door, I could cut and dye my hair and make it to the bus depot in time. I'd be off the bus before Rita got home and found my note.

Taking twenty dollars from the bag, I headed for the mall to purchase hair dye. I had no idea there would be so many choices. I read labels and instructions for thirty minutes before deciding on the one that sounded the fastest to use. I didn't care how I looked; I only wanted to look different.

Once I was safely out of town, I planned to let my hair grow to shoulder length again, and revert to its natural light sandy color. In the meantime, it was going to be Deep Burgundy Brown.

On Thursday night, I packed my backpack. I had decided to leave my suitcase and everything in it, except the money and the picture. A girl carrying an old suitcase would be identifiable; girls wearing backpacks are on every corner. I wanted to be as inconspicuous as possible.

Three sets of underwear. Toothbrush and toothpaste. Shampoo. An extra pair of jeans and two T-shirts. Socks. Pajamas.

I put in my favorite red Nebraska sweatshirt, and then took it back out. It was too easily identified because I wore it a lot. Instead, I packed a UCLA sweatshirt that I'd bought for a quarter at a garage sale but had never worn. I didn't think Rita had seen it.

The bulky sweatshirt took up a lot of space, but I was afraid I might be cold without it, even though I also planned to wear my Windbreaker. I hoped to find an inexpensive motel every night, but I needed to be prepared to sleep outdoors, if necessary. Even in summer the nights can get cool.

I looked longingly at my hair dryer and curling iron but left them on the bathroom counter, along with my nail polish and my creme rinse. I would worry about beauty after I found Starr. For now, I needed to travel light, taking only the essentials.

Food. I should have some food with me for times when I couldn't buy any, but the backpack was nearly full. I took two PowerBars and an apple from Rita's cupboard.

I sat on the bed and tried to think of what else I would need. I put in a small notebook and a pen, in case I needed to write down an address or phone number or directions, and the flashlight that Rita had given me. It doesn't require batteries; you just wind it up. Rita had one in every room, in case of a power outage.

I looked around my room. Of all the foster homes I'd had, this room was the best. Before I came, Rita had tried to make it a room that a teenager would like and not a babyish room all pink and with ruffles. The bedspread was two tones of purple, with three big puffy pillows on top. A matching purple Lava lamp perched on the bedside chest. A radio and CD player sat on a small white desk. If Starr could be here, too, I wouldn't mind staying in this room.

But Starr wasn't here and there was no guarantee that Rita would let me stay, even if I didn't run away. There are never any guarantees.

I awoke early on Friday and went downstairs to eat breakfast with Rita.

"Not sleeping in today?" Rita said. "Do you have plans?"

"It's too nice out to sleep," I said. "I thought I'd go for a walk." I didn't add, *To the bus station.*

"Would you like to learn to play tennis?" Rita asked. "One of the women in my yoga class gives tennis lessons and she offered to trade me. She'll come to my class for free, and you and I can take free tennis lessons from her. What do you think?"

"I don't know anything about tennis," I said. "I don't even know how to keep score."

"Neither do I, but it might be fun to learn."

"Okay," I said. I felt like a rat agreeing to tennis lessons when I knew I was not going to be here, but I didn't know what else to do. If I said no, Rita would ask a bunch of questions about why not. The truth is, tennis lessons sounded great, and if I had planned to stick around I would have wanted them.

"No cutesy little white skirts, though," Rita said.

"Shorts and T-shirts," I said, and then quickly changed the subject. "What's so nutritious about oatmeal?" I asked, knowing that if I could get Rita started on healthy eating, she'd forget about tennis lessons.

"All whole grains are good for you," Rita said. "Oat-meal provides all of the B vitamins, plus calcium, iron, and vitamin A. It's high in fiber and low in fat." While Rita extolled the benefits of oatmeal, I tuned out.

Ten minutes later, she waved good-bye and left for her yoga class. I fought an urge to hug her before she left. I couldn't do anything that might tip her off that today was different from any other day.

The minute the car pulled out of the garage, I dashed upstairs, put my note on her bed, and grabbed the scissors and hair dye.

I snipped about three inches off my hair, which put it just below my ears. It looked pretty good on the sides, but the back was uneven. I didn't have time to try to fix it. It took over half an hour to dye my hair. I put the empty box and the hair clippings in a plastic bag, to throw in a public trash can. If I left them here, Rita would know what I'd done and would change my description when she reported me missing.

My hair was still damp as I slipped on my backpack. I took one last look around my purple bedroom and left. Maybe Starr and I would come back sometime to visit Rita. I would tell her that of all the foster homes I'd had, this one was the best. Except for the food.

4

The bus station was not actually a station. It was a small counter in the back of a drugstore. I'd been there a few days earlier to get a schedule, so I knew exactly where to go to buy my ticket. On my way there, I stuffed the plastic bag in the trash container in front of the post office.

I told the woman behind the counter where I wanted to go.

"How old are you?" she asked.

I knew from the Greyhound Web site that kids under fifteen couldn't travel alone, so I said, "Fifteen."

"One way or round trip?"

"One way." I thought she might wonder why a kid

my age would be going somewhere alone and not coming back, so I added, "I'm meeting my dad there. We're going to go camping and then he'll drive me home."

The woman printed out my ticket.

There was a display of candy, potato chips, and other impulse-purchase items next to the counter. I picked up a package of Twinkies. "I'll take these, too," I said.

"The bus should be here in about ten minutes," the woman said. "Have fun camping."

"Thanks. My dad and I do this every summer." The ease with which false statements rolled out of my mouth astonished me. I didn't have much experience in telling lies, but I seemed to have a natural talent for it.

Those lies didn't hurt anyone, I told myself. I'm only making it harder for somebody to find me.

I sat on the bench in front of the store and ate my Twinkies while I waited for the bus. Each time a car went past, I looked down at my lap so that the driver and any passengers would see the top of my head rather than my face. It was unlikely that anyone I knew would happen along, but I wasn't taking any chances on being recognized.

The bus rolled in right on time and disgorged two young men wearing Chicago Cubs T-shirts. I climbed aboard, handed the driver my ticket, and started down the aisle.

I had hoped for a seat by myself, but that wasn't a choice. There were double seats on each side of the aisle and at least one seat in each section was occupied. I wanted to sit toward the front. Did I want to sit next to a white-haired woman who was reading a paperback book, a teenage boy listening to his iPod, or a tired-looking young woman holding an infant? I chose Granny.

I took off my backpack and held it in my lap. Since I was not carrying a separate purse, I had decided to hang on to the pack at all times, rather than put it in an overhead luggage space or in the storage area under the bus. I couldn't chance losing my eight hundred and twenty dollars, which, after the hair dye, bus ticket, and Twinkies, was down to seven hundred sixty-nine dollars and change.

As soon as I sat down, the woman beside me closed her book and smiled at me. I could tell she wanted a nice long chat. Even though I was quickly becoming a world-class liar, I did not relish making conversation with her for several hours, so I smiled, pointed at my throat, and said hoarsely, "Laryngitis. Can't talk."

"Oh, you poor dear," she said. She opened her purse, dug around, and came up with a cough drop. "Maybe this will help," she said.

I mouthed *thank you*, unwrapped the cough drop, and put it in my mouth. Then I leaned my head back against the seat, closed my eyes, and pretended to fall asleep. After a few minutes, I opened my eyes a slit, just enough to see that my seatmate was reading her book again.

Although I was too wired to actually sleep, it was pleasant to ride along with my eyes closed. I imagined how it would be when I found Starr. I pictured her initial surprise, and then her joy. I saw us throwing our arms around each other and exclaiming at how much we still looked alike, even with my new hair color.

She would tell me how much she had missed me, and how she had hoped to find me someday.

We would probably stay up all night the first night, telling our life stories. Maybe we'd discover that we like to do all of the same things.

In the article about the twins who had been separated at birth, then reunited as adults, it had turned out they liked the same food, played the same sports, and had similar jobs. They had even married people with the same first name! I wondered if Starr loved Twinkies.

When the bus stopped at the next town, my seatmate got out. After that I had the space to myself, so I didn't have to pretend to sleep anymore. I watched out the window, each mile taking me closer to Starr.

I arrived at my destination at two o'clock, wishing I could go farther. It seemed too early in the day to quit traveling. The bus stopped at a small diner, which served as the depot, and the driver announced that there would be a half hour lunch break.

I sat on a bench outside the diner, eating an ice-cream bar and looking at my map. It was thirty miles to the next stop and eight miles to the one after that. I had figured if I bought a ticket to one destination, stayed there overnight, and then bought a new ticket to continue, it would make it harder for anyone to track me. But did it matter if the second ticket was purchased tomorrow or right away? Probably not. Maybe I should buy another ticket now, get back on the same bus, and keep going.

As I was trying to decide what to do, an orange school bus pulled into the parking area and a group of girls my age swarmed out and went into the diner. A harried-looking chaperone trailed after them, followed by the driver. The side of the bus said SCHOOL DISTRICT 432.

I looked at the empty school bus. I looked at the diner. All of the bus riders were inside.

I boarded the school bus, walked to the last row of seats, and slid in next to the window. I checked the floor, to be sure nobody had left a sweater or anything that would make them want this particular seat. There was nothing, so I slumped into the seat and closed my eyes. I was good at pretending to be asleep.

About fifteen minutes later, the girls began returning, two or three at a time. An older woman called out, "Get on board, girls. We're leaving in five minutes."

I heard talking and shuffling as everyone boarded the bus. I didn't dare open my eyes. I hoped there were enough seats that mine wasn't needed, which turned out to be the case.

"Sit down, girls," the woman said. "Clear the aisles so we can leave."

The engine started. If anyone had noticed me, they apparently decided not to wake me up.

The bus made a *beep beep* sound as it backed up, then it headed out of the parking area.

It wasn't until we were rolling down the road that it occurred to me that this bus might be going in the wrong direction. I had no idea where these girls were from or where they were headed. What if I ended up right back where I had started from this morning?

5

It's a good thing I didn't really want to sleep, because someone started singing, "Ninety-nine bottles of beer on the wall," and each verse got louder. By the time they got down to one bottle of beer, the noise level was equal to that of a rock concert.

Next the girls began yelling school cheers. "We won! Sis boom bun! Sunrise School is number one!"

After much screaming, clapping, and whistling, they shouted, "No joke! No jest! Sunrise School is the best!"

I had never been on a team, had never even played a sport. As I listened to the girls cheering for themselves, I wondered what it would feel like to be a part of such a group. Clearly they had won some sort of tournament.

Did they have medals, or a trophy? Would they be written up in the local newspaper tomorrow?

I wondered if Starr was an athlete. I had always thought if I could learn a sport, I'd like to do gymnastics or volleyball.

After another hour or so of raucous singing and cheering, the girls quieted down, and by the time the bus pulled into the parking lot of Sunrise School, at least half of them were asleep.

"Wake up, girls!" called the chaperone. "Time to get off the bus. Be sure you take all your personal items with you, and don't leave the parking lot until your parents have arrived to take you home. I'll be checking each of you off my list before you leave."

Uh-oh. This could be trouble.

I sat up, watching as the chaperone exited the bus and stood at the bottom of the steps with a clipboard. The first girl to disembark was met by an adult woman. "Hi, Mom," the girl said. "Good-bye, Miss Lilton." The chaperone made a checkmark on the paper that was on her clipboard.

The next girl pointed to a car and said, "There's my dad." Miss Lilton checked the name off her list.

One by one the girls got off and were greeted by adults. I noticed that one girl was still in her seat, sleeping soundly. When she and I were the only ones left, I hurried to the front of the bus, stepped off, and pointed across the parking lot. I said, "There's my mom, Miss Lilton." Then, before she could ask my name and look at her list, I added, "You'd better check the seats in the rear of the bus. Somebody's still asleep back there."

Looking flustered, Miss Lilton boarded the bus and headed toward the slumbering girl, while I walked as quickly as I could across the parking lot and around the side of the school. I ducked into a doorway to wait. When the bus pulled away, I peeked around the corner and saw Miss Lilton get in a car and drive off.

Nobody would be able to track me here. There was not one person in the whole world who knew where I was. That knowledge excited me and made me nervous at the same time. What if I got sick? What if I fell and broke my arm, as I had when I lived with Jerod?

Stop it, I told myself. *You're where you want to be, doing what you want to do. Don't spoil it by worrying.* Besides, I knew Rita's phone numbers. If I ever broke a bone or got in other serious trouble, I knew I could call her and she'd come.

I walked away from the school and kept going until I came to a main street. Looking both ways, I saw a strip mall to my left. There were fast-food restaurants, a gas station, and, only half a block farther, the Dew Drop Inn.

I ate a chicken sandwich and drank a chocolate milk shake, then went into the lobby of the Dew Drop Inn. "Has Mrs. Webster checked in yet?" I asked. "I'm her daughter."

The clerk said nobody named Webster had arrived.

"I'll go ahead and register then," I said. "She should be here shortly."

"Do you have a credit card?" the clerk asked. "A double room is sixty-nine dollars. Or you can get a single room with a cot for forty-nine."

"The single's fine," I said. "I don't mind the cot." I gave him cash, which seemed to surprise him, and he handed me the key to room nine.

As soon as I got to my room I opened my backpack and checked the map, happy to see that the school bus I'd stowed away on had gone nearly two hundred miles in the direction I needed to go. I was a whole lot closer to Starr than I'd been a few hours earlier, and it hadn't cost me anything for a ticket.

I couldn't afford many nights at fifty bucks a pop, though. It wasn't even a good motel. Not that I was used to five-star accommodations, but the carpet was worn, the bathroom tile was chipped, and the ancient air conditioner protruding from the window sounded like a NASCAR race. Well, the room would be fine for my purposes. All I needed was a bathroom, a bed, and some privacy; it had all three of those.

Tomorrow night I'd try to find a YWCA where I could rent a less-expensive room.

The next morning I asked the motel clerk to direct me to the Greyhound bus terminal. He raised his eyebrows. "I thought your mom was meeting you here."

"She called. She got hung up in a business meeting and said for me to catch the bus and she'll pick me up at the other end."

I must have been convincing, because the clerk told me how to find the bus stop. On my way there, I passed a fast-food restaurant; I bought an order of french fries for my breakfast. I started to order a Pepsi, but then, hearing Rita's voice in my mind, I changed it to an orange juice.

I carried my meal to one of the outdoor tables. Movement in the bushes that lined the parking area caught my attention as I ate. Looking closer, I saw a dog lying with his head on his paws, watching me. As I ate a french fry, the dog's eyes followed the movement of my hand to my mouth. He licked his chops.

I tossed a fry toward him. It landed in the dirt about three feet in front of him. I expected him to lunge forward and grab it, but instead he rose slowly, and looked cautiously around before approaching the food. He sniffed the fry, then raised his head and looked at me, as if asking permission.

"Go ahead," I said. "That one's for you."

The dog ate the french fry. Then he sat down and stared at me. I knew he wanted more.

Something about the dog appealed to me. He wasn't a cute little puppy. In fact, his muzzle showed some gray and he moved as if his joints were stiff. He appeared to be an unlikely combination of basset hound and black Lab, with long drooping ears and big sad-looking brown eyes. The fur on his face was black, with a tan spot over each eye. His legs seemed too short for his body, but he had a certain presence, a dignity, that belied the fact he was hanging around a fast-food restaurant, hoping for a handout.

His ribs stuck out like the pickets in a fence and it had been a long time, if ever, since he'd had a bath.

"Good dog," I said, and he wagged his tail.

I went inside and ordered a plain hamburger, just the meat and the bun. I carried it outside and broke it into pieces to cool. With the pieces piled on a napkin, I approached the dog. His eyes stayed on the hamburger as I came closer.

"Here you are," I said, and I put the food on the ground in front of him. Again, he did not lunge and gobble it all down. He stood, looked at me, and wagged his tail.

"You're welcome," I said.

He ate slowly, as if savoring the treat.

When he had finished, I extended my hand, fingers curled in a fist, so he could sniff me. His tongue came out and slurped my hand. I petted him then and he sat down beside me, leaning on me so hard that if I had moved suddenly, he would have fallen over.

Now what? I thought. How could I walk away and board a bus and leave him here with no way to get his next meal? But I couldn't take him with me, either. I was pretty sure dogs would not be allowed on the bus.

Unless it was a service dog. I might be able to convince the ticket agent that this was a service dog, except that every service dog I'd ever seen wore a special coat with a service-dog logo. This dog didn't even have a collar.

I sat for a while, petting my new best friend. After a few minutes I went back inside.

"There's a dog in your parking lot," I told the girl who had sold me the hamburger. I pointed through the window.

"He's there every day," she said.

"Do you know who he belongs to?"

"I don't think he belongs to anyone. He hangs around and eats food that people leave behind."

"Where does he sleep?" I asked.

She shrugged. "I don't know. In the bushes, I guess."

"He's a nice dog," I said. "Friendly. Has anyone tried to find his owner?"

"You mean, like, put an ad in the paper or make flyers for a Found Dog?"

"Right."

"Nah. He's been out there for a long time."

"How long?"

"Well, I've worked here for, like, three months and he's been here that whole time."

I stared at her. For three months she had watched that dog beg for food and she had never tried to help him!

"Could I have a cup of water for him?" I asked.

"We charge twenty-five cents for water."

"That's okay."

She filled the cup, and I gave her a quarter.

The dog slurped eagerly, sticking his tongue down inside the cup. I poured the last of the water into my hand, and he licked it. *He needs a bowl,* I thought. *He needs a collar and a leash.*

He needs me.

I knew it would take me twice as long to find Starr if I had a goofy-looking old dog tagging along with me.

"I'm sorry, dog," I said. "If I lived nearby, I'd take you home in a heartbeat. But I don't live near here. I don't live anywhere."

The dog wagged his tail, acting as pleased as if I'd said, "Come on, pal. You're going with me."

I don't live anywhere. What an awful thought! It made me sound like one of those homeless people who shuffle along pushing a stolen shopping cart that contains everything they own.

I wasn't really homeless, not like those street people. I could always go back to Rita's and, even though she'd be mad at me for running away, I knew she'd take me back. Rita would probably take the dog, too.

I patted the dog, daydreaming about showing up at Rita's with this big old mutt.

"Who's your friend?" Rita would ask, and I would say he had followed me home, uninvited, and she'd know I was pretending and wouldn't care.

No! I pushed the image out of my mind. First I had to find Starr. Then the two of us would come back here and, if the dog was still hanging around, we'd adopt him and take him home—to my real home, with Starr.

I stood and walked away from the dog. I didn't look back until I reached the corner.

The dog was right behind me.

"You can't come," I said. "Stay!"

He hung his head.

His tail drooped.

My heart broke.

I knew exactly how he felt. I remembered all the times I had felt unwanted, times when I desperately wished to be welcomed and cherished. How could I do to him the very thing that had hurt me the most?

I couldn't. He was a stray, like me. We strays need to stick together.

6

We were standing in front of a supermarket.
"I'll be right back," I said. "Sit." To my surprise,
the dog sat down. "Stay," I said. The dog watched me go
inside. I found the aisle that had pet supplies, and I
bought a collar, a leash, a water bowl, and a box of dog
biscuits. I also got a small box of plastic sandwich bags
so that I could clean up after the dog. One of my pet
peeves on the trail by Rita's house was people who left
their dogs' poop behind for other people to step in.

I fastened the collar around his neck and snapped
the leash on. I opened the box of biscuits and gave him
one.

"You need a name," I said.

The dog crunched his biscuit.

"Maybe it should have something to do with the sky," I told him. "I'm Sunny and my sister is Starr and our last name is Skyland."

I thought of sky words: moon, cloud, blue. The dog's tan and black color suggested Earth words, not sky words. I saw that he had been neutered.

"Somebody loved you once," I said, "the same as me."

The dog's tail thumped the ground, making me smile.

"Now someone loves you again."

I crammed the box of biscuits into my backpack and put the pack on. I picked up the leash and walked down the sidewalk. The dog trotted at my side as if I had spent the last month teaching him to heel.

Maybe I could name him after one of the planets. Mars was the god of war; this dog seemed too peaceful to be called Mars. Venus was a goddess; I couldn't saddle a boy dog with a girl's name. Mercury didn't seem right, either. A dog named Mercury should be silver colored, and a fast runner. This dog plodded. Neptune? Uranus? Saturn? None seemed quite right.

Next I thought of Pluto. This old boy didn't look anything like the Disney cartoon dog Pluto, but I had always liked those old cartoons. What I didn't like was that Pluto is no longer considered a planet. Back in third grade when I had memorized the list of planets, Pluto was one of them. Pluto had been discovered in 1930 and had been a planet ever since until, all of a sudden, I heard that it wasn't a planet any longer.

How can the scientists arbitrarily get rid of a planet? How can an important part of the solar system be demoted? It seems to me that once a planet is called a planet there should be no mind-changing allowed. The same with dogs, and kids. Once you were part of somebody's family, you should get to stay forever.

I didn't want to name my dog after a planet that had lost its status. This dog was too good for that. Maybe I should name him after a constellation. Orion? Ursa?

The word *comet* popped into my head. I liked that because comets have tails. But comets orbit the sun, streaking across the heavens. This dog wasn't going to streak anywhere.

I decided to forget sky words and try to think of a name that fit the dog's looks and personality. His black fur was accented with the colors of caramel and dark chocolate. He had a sweet personality.

Snickers, I thought. I could name him after my favorite candy bar. It even starts with an *S*, the same as Sunny and Starr.

I said it aloud, trying out the sound. "Snickers."

He wagged his tail.

"Good dog, Snickers," I said. "After we find Starr, I'll get you one of those little tags to hang on your collar. I'll have it engraved SNICKERS, with my phone number on it, in case you ever wander off."

It did not appear likely that Snickers would wander off. Since he stayed as close to me as he could get, a more apt name might have been Velcro.

I'd never had a dog. She-Who had a cat, a big white Persian named Snowball, but he wasn't very friendly. He kept to himself, probably because he didn't like She-Who, even though she fed him. I didn't blame him. She fed me, too, and I didn't like her, either.

I didn't remember Grandma's dog, the one that was in the picture with us, but I'd always thought how great it would be to get a dog someday. I hadn't planned to do it when I was on the road alone, but you can't always anticipate what's going to happen.

In my experience, unplanned events were usually bad and often began with a foster parent saying, "Sunny, there's something I need to tell you," which meant I was going to be uprooted again. This time, finding Snickers, was good. He had been my dog for less than an hour and I already knew we'd be together for as long as he lived. No matter what else happened, we'd always have each other. I wondered if this is how it feels when you truly belong to a family.

The bus ticket counter was in a health food store. I tied the leash around the leg of a park bench in front of the store, said, "Stay!" and went inside.

I walked past the bins of oat bran and wheat germ. Organically grown produce lined one wall. Instead of Twinkies, there were sugar-free carob cookies. Yuck. Rita would have loved this place.

I picked up a bus schedule and saw that the next bus going west would arrive in an hour. "Do you know if dogs are allowed on the bus?" I asked the woman who was unpacking boxes of egg substitute.

"Seeing Eye dogs are," she said. "I don't know about regular dogs."

I had already decided I couldn't take a chance on trying to pass Snickers off as a service dog. There was too much risk that it would lead to being questioned by the authorities.

"This is a plain old dog," I said. "A pet. He's really well behaved."

"You'll have to talk to the bus driver," she said.

I had noticed a small park down the side street, so while I waited for the bus I took Snickers there for a walk. He loved sniffing the grass and the trees.

When Snickers squatted to do his business, I saw a young woman with a toddler frown at us. I removed one of the small plastic bags from my pack, slid my hand inside, and picked up Snickers's waste. I quickly turned the bag inside out and dropped it in a trash bin. The woman smiled approvingly, and I was glad I'd had the foresight to buy bags.

When the hour was almost up, we walked back to wait for the bus. Ten minutes later, it wheezed to a stop. I waited while the driver, a bearded middle-aged man, helped two people retrieve their luggage. Then I approached him.

"Excuse me," I said. "I'm planning to take the bus and I'm wondering if it's okay to bring my dog. He's friendly and well behaved."

"No dogs allowed."

"I could pay extra for him."

I saw the man hesitate and realized that any extra would probably go straight into his pocket rather than the bus company's coffers.

"He'll probably sleep the whole trip," I said.

"How big is he?" the driver asked, which seemed like a stupid question, since Snickers was standing right beside me.

I pointed, and the man seemed to notice Snickers for the first time.

"No way," he said. "I thought you meant a little lapdog. Too many folks are scared of dogs. I could lose my job if I let you take him on board."

I made my lower lip tremble and tried to force a few tears from my eyes. "He's the only family I have," I said. "My dad left years ago and my mother died and I need to get to my sister's house. I can't leave my dog behind. I just can't!"

"Save your acting for the movies," the man said. "I'm not risking my job over a mutt." He walked away from me and entered the coffee shop on the corner. When he returned carrying a paper cup, he refused to look at me.

As I stood at the curb watching the bus pull away, I got a face full of exhaust fumes, but they weren't the only reason I felt sick. What was I going to do now?

I walked to the coffee shop and sat at one of the outdoor tables. I spread my map out, found where I was, and calculated how much farther I had to go. More than nine hundred miles. Could I walk that far? Could

Snickers? If we made twenty-five miles a day, it would still take over a month.

I had enough money for a month's worth of food, but where would we sleep? I had no sleeping bag or tent and didn't want to carry them anyway, so campgrounds were out. I was pretty sure that places that rent rooms, such as the YWCA, would not allow a dog and even if they did, my money would run out before we got to Enumclaw. What about weather? Sometimes in summer there are thunderstorms and even tornadoes.

I thought briefly about hitchhiking but quickly decided against it. Too risky. I wanted to find Starr, and I wanted to keep Snickers, but I did not want to climb into a vehicle with somebody who I knew nothing about.

Maybe I could board Snickers at a kennel and then come back for him. He would be safe and fed while I continued my journey on the bus. As soon as I found Starr and had made plans for my permanent home, I would retrieve Snickers and take him to live with me. I wondered how much it cost per day to board a dog.

I tied Snickers's leash to the table leg, went into the coffee shop, and asked if I could look at a phone directory. I turned to the Yellow Pages and looked under kennels.

When I saw an ad for dog boarding, I wrote the number in my notebook, untied Snickers, and found a public pay phone.

"How much do you charge to board a dog?" I asked, when Kanine Kennels answered.

"How much does your dog weigh?"

"I don't know."

"The charge varies, depending on if the dog is Small, Medium, Large, or Extra-large."

"I think he's mostly bassett hound with some black Lab."

"That would be considered a large dog. It's thirty-five dollars a day."

I gulped. "Where would you keep him?"

"We have six- by ten-foot covered kennels with concrete floors. Each dog gets a blanket to sleep on unless you bring his own bed."

"Would you take him out for walks?"

"Twice a day."

"Thanks," I said. "I have to think about it."

Mentally, I marked off a six- by ten-foot space. It wasn't very big, especially when I tried to imagine Snickers inside it.

It wasn't cheap, either. It would probably be at least two weeks before I could bail him out. That would be four hundred ninety dollars! It might take longer than two weeks to locate Starr, and then come back to get Snickers. Meanwhile his stiff old body would be resting on hard concrete. Even with a blanket, that didn't sound comfortable.

Snickers nudged my knee as I stepped out of the phone booth. I scratched him behind his ears while his tail whacked the ground. I looked into his brown eyes and knew he'd be miserable in a kennel. He'd think I had abandoned him, the same as everyone else. Even if I could afford to board him, there had to be a better solution.

I looked at my map again. If I took an older two-lane road, rather than the highway, it was twelve miles to the next small town. Snickers and I could walk twelve miles. It would give me time to think of a plan, and I'd end the day closer to Starr than when it began. Not as close as I had hoped, but twelve miles was better than nothing.

Before we left, I filled Snickers's bowl with water in the coffee shop's restroom and carried it out to him. After he drank, I used what was left to water a shrub.

It felt good to walk briskly along with Snickers at my side. Maybe Rita was right about exercise. She always said it was good for the mind, as well as the body, and I did feel optimistic as I headed down the road. I still didn't want to try to walk all the way to Enumclaw because it would take too long, but maybe I should walk whenever there were short distances between towns, just to stay in shape. It would be like training for a sport, except I would be accomplishing an even greater goal—finding Starr.

7

Unfortunately, **Snickers was** not up to a twelve-mile walk. After an hour of walking, Snickers began lagging behind instead of walking beside me. He didn't limp, exactly, but he walked more and more slowly, as if his legs hurt. I realized an old dog who had been sleeping outside with no medical care probably had arthritis. Maybe his joints ached, and if he had been accustomed to spending his days in the bushes next to the restaurant's parking lot, where he got little exercise, he was badly out of condition. The pads on his feet were probably sore by now, too.

I needed to find my twin sister, but Snickers needed a nap.

Flat fields stretched as far as I could see. Farm country. I didn't know what crop these fields were. Potatoes? Soybeans?

I sat on the shoulder of the road, at the edge of a plowed field. Snickers sank down beside me, heaved a sigh, and closed his eyes. The air smelled dusty, as if it had not rained for a long time. I dug my hands into the dry dirt between two rows and let it sift through my fingers.

The rural setting felt peaceful and spacious—and lonely. I wondered what Rita was doing, and hoped she wasn't too worried about me. I wished I had a way to let her know I was okay without also giving away my location.

If I saw a café with Wi-Fi in one of the towns ahead, maybe I'd ask someone with a laptop if I could send an e-mail. I didn't think that could be traced to the town it came from, only to the person who had the e-mail account. If the police asked the service provider where the person who had the account lived, did AOL, or whoever the account was with, have to reveal it? I wasn't sure. Better to be safe and not send an e-mail at all.

While Snickers slept, I examined the bottoms of his feet. His toenails needed to be trimmed, but he had thick, tough pads that looked as if he could walk many miles on them without a problem. His muscles must have been what ached. I didn't know what to do to help that, except to let him rest.

I let Snickers sleep for an hour, then roused him and headed on down the road, walking until he trailed behind me on the leash again, rather than trotting by my side. We continued the day's journey on a one-hour-on, one-hour-off schedule.

Just before sunset, we arrived at a town that consisted of a water tower, a one-pump gas station, a feed store, a combination drugstore/hardware store, and a grocery store. No motels. At first I didn't think there was a restaurant, either, but then I saw a faded, hand-painted sign that said JUNE'S HOME-COOKED MEALS. June's restaurant turned out to be one large room at the front of June's house.

A bell jingled when I went in. A short, plump woman entered, wiping her hands on a purple towel. Her blond hair formed a frizzy halo around her head.

"Howdy," she said. "I'm June."

"I'd like to get a meal," I said.

"Have a seat."

She gestured at three round wooden tables that

seated four people each. The centerpieces consisted of a bottle of ketchup, a paper napkin holder, and a salt and pepper set.

I chose a table and sat down. I was the only customer.

"You have your choice of a grilled cheese sandwich or a bowl of chili."

"Grilled cheese would be good."

"Anything to drink?"

Since there was no menu, I asked, "What is there?"

"Hold on a sec, let me check," she said, and disappeared into the back room. When she returned, she said, "I have milk, apple juice, and water."

"Apple juice, please. And could I also get water for my dog? I have his bowl."

As I took Snickers's bowl out of my backpack, June walked to the window and looked out.

"Good gracious," she said. "Don't leave your dog out there like some poor relation. Bring him in. He can rest under the table."

"That would be great," I said. "Thanks."

I brought Snickers inside.

June rubbed his ears and said, "Well, aren't you a handsome boy? Just look at you! What's your name?"

"His name is Snickers."

"Snickers?" she said, as if it were a foreign word that she'd never heard before.

"Right," I said. "Snickers, as in candy bar."

"Oh, *that* kind of Snickers. I was thinking of a mean type of laugh."

She petted Snickers again, then headed back to the kitchen. Soon she returned with a plate of table scraps. "I thought Snickers might enjoy some leftover stew," she said.

Snickers stood as she placed the plate before him. He wagged his tail.

"It's for you, Snickers," I said. "Go ahead."

"Would you look at that?" said June. "He's trained not to gobble down his meal until you tell him it's okay? I never saw the likes!"

"I didn't train him," I admitted. "He just always waits until I say he can eat."

"Now that is the most polite dog I've ever seen," June said. "He's welcome here anytime." She poured water from a pitcher into Snickers's bowl. "You new in town?"

"Passing through," I said. "Is there a place to rent a room?"

"Are you alone?"

"No. I'm with Snickers."

June laughed so hard that she had to wipe her eyes on the bottom of her shirt.

I didn't think it was that funny, but then there probably isn't a lot of comedy in this town.

"Myrtle Fishby used to take in boarders, years ago. She might rent you a room. Depends on whether her Social Security check covered the utilities this month. I'll call her."

I could hear June's side of the conversation. "Myrtle? Do you want a tenant tonight? It's a young girl and her dog. I don't know; a funny-looking dog, with big ears. He's very polite. Yes, I did say a girl; I meant the dog is polite. The girl is nice, too. Just a minute, I'll ask her." She held the receiver against her chest and asked, "Are you staying only one night?"

"Yes."

"One night, Myrtle."

June spoke to me again. "It would be ten dollars."

"I'll take it."

"Okay, Myrtle. I'll send her over after she eats."

It was the best grilled cheese sandwich I'd ever had—golden brown with a buttery taste, and the cheese all melted and gooey and oozing out the edges. It was real cheddar cheese, too, not the "cheese food" they use for nachos at fast-food restaurants.

The apple juice was served icy cold in its can and tasted great with the hot sandwich. I wished I could have all my meals at June's.

"That was delicious," I said as I swallowed the last bite. "How much do I owe you?"

"Two dollars."

Only two dollars? For a home-cooked sandwich, a can of juice, and stew for my dog? I couldn't believe my good fortune. I laid three dollar bills next to my plate, and asked how to find Myrtle's place.

June pointed. "One block down, on the corner. The yellow house with the pots of petunias on the porch." As I left, June said, "I'm cooking breakfast tomorrow. Pancakes and eggs. If you're interested, come on down any time between seven and nine. You too, Snickers."

"We'll be here," I said.

Myrtle had turned on the porch light, so I had no trouble finding her house, even though it was dark by then. She led me to a small room furnished with one twin bed, a wooden chest of drawers, and a table lamp. A braided rug on the floor would work for Snickers. I handed her the ten dollars.

"You don't have to pay until you leave," she said.

"That's okay. This way you know you have it."

The sheets on the bed smelled of sunshine. Rita always

hung the sheets outside to dry, so the smell of fresh air made me think of her. Until I had lived with Rita, my sheets and pillowcases had always come out of a clothes dryer, except at Jerod's apartment, where they never got laundered at all. At first I had thought Rita was foolish to lug the wet sheets into the backyard and hang them on the clothesline, even if it did conserve energy, but once I got used to that fresh, clean smell, I found I enjoyed it.

I slept soundly, awakening once when a train rumbled through town and blasted its whistle. As I fell back asleep, I heard Snickers snoring softly on the rug beside my bed. I felt safe here and wondered what it would be like to grow up in a small rural town, to live one's whole life in a place where a dog gets invited into the restaurant and served a free meal of table scraps. That would be against all the Health Department regulations in every place I'd ever lived. It was probably against the rules here, too, but the difference was that here nobody cared.

The next morning as I ate scrambled eggs and blueberry pancakes at June's, she brought her cup of coffee to my table and sat down across from me. "Where are you headed?" she asked.

"Enumclaw, Washington," I said.

"You have kin there?"

"My sister. I'm going to live with her."

"How are you fixing to get there?"

"The bus, if the driver will let me take Snickers along. The last driver wouldn't allow him on the bus, so we walked awhile."

"Tell you what," June said. "I need to visit my aunt today and I'd just as soon go now, before it gets too hot. You and Snickers could ride along, if you want. It's about fifteen miles west of here. The Trailways bus stops there."

"That would be great," I said. "Thank you."

I helped her wash the dishes. When she put a CLOSED sign in the window, I said, "Aren't you worried that you'll lose customers if you close in the middle of the day?"

"If I'm not here and they're hungry, they'll wait until I get back. Where else are they going to go for a meal?"

We piled into June's Jeep and off we went, with Snickers's nose aimed into the wind and his ears flapping out behind him.

The town where June's aunt lived turned out to be a sad-looking cluster of houses, some unkempt mobile homes, and a large grain silo. A one-pump gas station appeared to be the only commercial establishment in town. The peeling paint and dirty windows made me wonder if it was open for business or abandoned.

"I'm afraid it isn't much of a town," June said as she pulled up in front of the dilapidated gas station. "The bus will be along soon, though."

"Thanks for the ride," I said.

"You be careful, honey," she said. "Stop for a meal if you ever get back this way."

Snickers and I climbed out. I watched June's car cross the road and turn left, disappearing behind a windbreak of trees.

8

There wasn't a real bus stop—no shelter of any kind, no bench to sit on, not even a sign. I opened the door to the gas station and went inside, where I was surrounded by loud music, the kind the radio stations call "golden oldies." I didn't recognize the song—something with a saxophone solo. An old man in coveralls sat on a high stool behind the small counter with his eyes closed, tapping his fingers to the song.

"Excuse me," I said.

The radio band continued with the sax replaced by a string section. The man swayed to the beat, a half-smile on his lips.

I spoke louder. "Excuse me!"

The man opened his eyes, frowning. He turned the knob on a large brown radio, and the music faded. "What can I do you for?" the man asked.

"I want to catch the bus, and I was told it stops here. Do I get a ticket from you?"

"From the driver. Just stand on the side of the road, and when the bus comes, wave your arms to signal the driver to stop. He'll pull over, and you can pay your fare then."

"How soon does it come?"

He consulted a large, round wall clock. "About fifteen minutes. Don't miss it; it only comes by once a day."

I thanked the man, and went back outside. Before the door closed behind me, I heard the music swell again.

The gas station provided a rectangle of shade that felt several degrees cooler than the air beside the road. I was tempted to wait there, but I feared I wouldn't see the bus in time if I didn't stand close to the road.

When Snickers started to follow me, I pointed to the shade and told him, "Stay!" There was no reason to make him swelter out in the hot sun while I watched for the bus. He lay down beside the building, and I wondered again about his past. Who had trained him? He kept his eyes on me as I walked to the edge of the road, but he didn't try to follow me.

As the mid-morning sun beat down, waves of heat echoed up from the asphalt. Sweat trickled down my neck, but I didn't bother to wipe it off. Thoughts of my room at Rita's house sneaked in the back door of my mind. Her house wasn't air-conditioned, but Rita closed all the windows and pulled the curtains shut early each morning to keep out the sun, so the house stayed cool. In the evening, she opened the curtains and the windows to let the breeze blow through. She called it Nature's air-conditioning, and it worked.

Voices approaching brought me out of my memory. I turned to see three boys emerging from behind the gas station. All wore jeans and T-shirts. The two in front, who looked about sixteen, swaggered and punched each other as they walked, full of their own importance. One was tall and lanky, with biceps that shouted "I lift weights!" His sidekick had an unlit cigarette dangling from his mouth.

The third boy was younger, maybe ten or eleven, and he lagged behind the other two.

The boys stopped when they saw me.

"Well, now, looky here," said the tallest one. He pointed at me. "Somebody new has come to town."

"Maybe we should introduce ourselves," said the second one. "I'm Hunker. This here is Zooman." He pointed to the tall boy.

"Hi," I said, then looked at the younger boy.

"I'm Randy," he said.

"We're the welcome committee," said Zooman.

Something about the older boys made me uneasy. Zooman's eyes were blank, and he seemed to look right through me. I wondered if he used drugs. Randy shuffled his feet and kept glancing nervously at Zooman and Hunker, as if he needed their permission to breathe.

I forced a small smile but did not say my name.

"What's in the backpack?" Zooman asked.

"Extra clothes. I'm going to visit my sister."

"Taking the bus?" asked Hunker.

"That's right."

"If she's taking the bus, she must have bus fare," said Zooman, "and maybe some cash for while she's at her sister's house." He stepped closer, with Hunker beside him. Randy stayed behind, making a circle in the dirt with the toe of his sneaker.

I clutched the backpack's straps and watched the boys warily.

"You owe me ten dollars," Zooman said.

"For what?"

"I'm the one who gives permission to catch the bus here. Ten dollars is the permission fee."

"No way," I said.

"You're refusing to pay the permission fee?" Zooman said, sounding as if he had never heard of such an outrage.

"Then we'll have to take it ourselves," Hunker said.

I stared at the boys but said nothing.

"Hand over the backpack," said Zooman.

I shook my head no.

"Didn't you hear him?" asked Hunker. "The man told you to give him your backpack."

My thoughts raced. Should I scream? Would the man in the gas station help me? Would he even hear me over his radio? Should I try to fight? Maybe if I kicked Zooman in the groin, he'd back off and the other two would follow. Or maybe that would only make them angry and they'd really hurt me.

I glanced up the road. No bus. No cars. No people.

Zooman held out his hand.

"Now," he said.

"This is a public road," I said. "Anyone can catch the bus here."

"Not without paying me first," he said.

Zooman and I stared at each other for a second. Then he lunged at me and grabbed hold of the backpack. He yanked so hard that one side slipped off my shoulder. I held on to the other strap and yelled, "Help!"

Hunker ran around behind me and tried to slide the other strap down my arm. I kicked at Zooman and missed.

A flash of brown and black fur shot out from beside the building, the loud barks startling all of us. Hunker dropped my arm. Zooman let go of the backpack.

Snickers rushed to me, then stood beside me, facing the boys, with his teeth bared. A menacing growl rumbled from his throat.

"He's trained to protect me," I said. "Take one step toward me, and he'll go for your throat."

The three boys backed away.

"Hey, we were only kidding," Zooman said. "We wouldn't really have taken your money."

"Yeah, right," I said.

"Nice doggy," said Hunker.

Snickers growled louder. He sounded vicious.

"Lucky for you he only attacks when I tell him to," I said. "Otherwise the three of you would be hamburger." I slid my arm through the strap and settled my backpack where it belonged.

The boys inched farther away, sliding their shoes on the dirt as if they wore skis.

I patted Snickers's head. "Good boy," I said. *We're even now*, I thought. I saved Snickers from a life of begging for scraps, and now he had saved me from being robbed and possibly beaten.

When they were about fifteen feet from me, the three boys turned at the same time, like a school of fish, and ran down the road. As I watched them, I saw the bus approaching in the distance. The boys dashed toward it, shouting and waving their arms.

Oh no, I thought. *Don't tell me they're going to take the same bus I am. If they get on, maybe I should try to find June and stay at Myrtle's house another night.*

The driver stopped beside the boys and opened the door, but they did not board the bus. I couldn't hear what the boys said, but the door quickly closed again and the bus drove forward. I saw the boys watching me and wondered what they had told the driver.

I waved my arms over my head. The bus slowed but didn't come to a complete stop.

As it rolled up beside me, the driver shouted through an open window, "The next time you kids flag me down when you aren't going anywhere, I'm calling the cops!" Then he stepped on the gas and pulled away.

"Wait!" I shouted. I ran a few feet after it, but the bus kept going.

While I watched the rear of the bus grow smaller in the distance, I heard the three boys laughing hysterically as they loped off in the opposite direction.

I stood there with the sun beating down on me and wondered why some people are so mean. Those boys knew that if they hailed the bus but didn't get on, the driver would be unlikely to stop for me. I could see why the driver assumed I was with them; what I didn't understand was why the boys wanted to make me miss my ride. Was it because Snickers had foiled their attempt to rob me? Did causing trouble for me make them feel superior? Or was it simply that they were bored and unhappy and not smart enough to figure out better ways to use their time?

I sighed. There was no way I would wait here twenty-four hours for another bus to arrive. I didn't want to spend twenty-four more *seconds* in the same town with those delinquents. I really didn't want to go back to Myrtle's, either, even if I could find June. They lived in the wrong direction. I wanted to continue my journey. I wanted to find Starr.

"Looks as if we're going to do some walking again today," I told Snickers. I went back in the gas station.

This time the man saw me enter, and he turned the radio down. "Miss the bus?" he asked.

"The driver didn't stop. He thought I was playing a trick and didn't really want to get on."

"Were the Jenley boys out there again?"

"Three boys waved at the bus before it got to me, but when it pulled over, they didn't get on."

"Yep. That would be Will Jenley's two boys and their cousin who's visiting from Alabama. They flag that bus down two, three times a week and then run off when the driver stops. I keep telling them, one of these days the driver's going to get fed up with their shenanigans and sic the law on them. Teach 'em a lesson." He shook his head. "Not the brightest bulbs in the box, those Jenley boys."

The one shelf in the glass counter held a few candy bars and other snack items for sale. There weren't any Twinkies, so I bought a Milky Way and a package of salted cashews. Then Snickers and I set off down the road together.

I glanced frequently over my shoulder, in case the three stooges decided to follow me, but I didn't see them again. Like most bullies, they disappeared as soon as there was a chance that they might get hurt themselves.

As I walked, I thought about what could have happened if Snickers hadn't come to my aid. I didn't think Zooman planned to hurt me, but he would have stolen all my money. He might have let me keep the backpack with my clothes in it, since he probably had no use for girl's clothes, but without any cash I'd have been in terrible trouble. I realized it wasn't smart to carry all of my money in one place.

As soon as I got away from town, and was certain nobody could see what I was doing, I stopped. I sat on the side of the road and opened my pack. First I poured some water in Snickers's bowl. The Milky Way was starting to melt, so I ate it. Then I folded some of the twenty-dollar bills into tight rectangles and put them in my shoes. When I slipped the shoes back on, I could feel the mounds of money under each foot's arch.

I wished I had a dog collar with a little container on it like rescue dogs wear in the mountains. If I had one of those, Snickers could carry some cash, too. I unsnapped the leash and put it in my backpack. Since Snickers stayed next to me, leashed or not, it didn't seem necessary to use it when no one else was near.

While Snickers finished slurping his water, I stuck some money in my jeans pockets. If anyone stole my backpack now, I'd still have enough funds to keep traveling. I'd still be able to find Starr.

With the cash distributed, we set off again. I never thought I'd be the kind of person who talks to her dog, but as we walked along, I found myself telling Snickers about my early memories of Starr.

"We used to lie on a blanket in the yard and watch for shooting stars," I said. "That's when Grandma first sang 'Twinkie, Twinkie, Little Star' to me, and I had a giggle fit and couldn't quit laughing."

As we plodded along the shoulder of the road, I tried to empty my mind of everything except memories. When people get hypnotized they sometimes remember events from long ago that they hadn't even known they could recall. I hoped that if I concentrated on scenes from my early years, new images might flood into my brain and give me some fresh clues about exactly where we had lived. It didn't happen, though. I only replayed the few events that I'd remembered all my life.

I soon ran out of my meager supply of family memories, so I told Snickers about Rita. "She got me a library card right away so I could read whatever I want," I said. "She let me use her computer, and trusted me not to look at sleazy stuff. When we shopped for clothes, she let me pick out my own and told me I looked pretty. If I had stayed there, I was going to have tennis lessons."

Snickers was a good listener.

"If I ever write my autobiography," I told him, "I'll skip all the years between when Mama died and when I went to live with Rita. I'll only tell the good parts of my life. First I'll write about Mama and Grandma and Starr; then I'll write about Rita. Next I'll tell how I found you, and finally I'll report the happy ending where I'm reunited with Starr. After that, I'll be so busy having fun and doing everything with my twin sister and you that I won't have time to write more chapters in an autobiography."

Snickers stopped walking. He looked around and whined.

"You can't be tired already," I said.

Snickers looked up at the sky and gave a short, high bark.

I followed his gaze and realized that the sky had grown darker while I was absorbed in my thoughts. A bank of clouds filled the sky ahead, darker clouds than I had ever seen. They had an odd greenish tinge, the color of an old sea turtle.

I realized the temperature had dropped, too. Even though I'd been walking at a steady pace, I no longer felt warm.

"Is it going to rain?" I said. "Is that what you're telling me?"

Snickers whined again.

9

A wind rustled across the road, and drops of rain spattered on my head and shoulders. Snickers poked my leg with his nose, as if urging me to hurry.

I know animals sometimes sense bad weather approaching before humans are aware of it. Maybe a severe storm was headed this way. I scanned the countryside around me for some place to take shelter. I saw rows of cornfields and, about fifty yards ahead, a big tree on the side of the road. Not too far beyond the tree, a ramshackle shed leaned sideways, as if trying its best to fall over. Probably it had once housed a tractor or plows or other farm equipment. Now it looked abandoned.

Even though its walls looked less than sturdy, the shed did have a roof, and right then Snickers and I needed a roof over our heads.

As I hurried toward the shed, the rain turned to hail. I ran, holding my arms over my head, as Snickers trotted beside me. A flash of lightning lit up the dark sky. Thunder followed the lightning. I wondered if Snickers had heard far-off thunder that my ears couldn't hear, and that's why he had barked.

Hail the size of gum balls pelted us, stinging my arms and the top of my head, as if the pieces had been shot from guns. Snickers yelped. By the time I reached the big tree, the ground was covered with round white ice balls, making it impossible to run. I tried to remember if you're supposed to stay under a tree during lightning, or get away from trees. I wasn't sure, but when I stood close to the tree trunk, most of the hail got deflected by the tree's branches before it could hit me or Snickers, so I stayed there. It seemed better to remain under the leafy canopy than to let huge hailstones pound us and risk turning an ankle or falling while we ran to the shed.

I knelt on the ground beside the tree trunk, with Snickers beside me. I took off the backpack. I put Snickers's muzzle on my legs, bent over him to protect his head, and held the backpack over my own head.

Some of the hailstones still hit us, but they were slowed by the leaves and did not strike with as much force as when we were out in the open.

The lightning and thunder continued. One huge lightning bolt zigzagged straight down, as if flung to earth by an angry god. Others bounced from cloud to cloud, seeking a place to penetrate. The wind increased. The earth vibrated. I could feel Snickers trembling.

"It's okay, boy," I said, trying to convince myself as well as my dog. "It's only a thunderstorm."

But was it? I had never experienced such a high wind before.

I had always counted seconds in a thunderstorm to estimate how close the lightning was: one, one thousand; two, one thousand. I'd been told that each second that elapsed indicated one mile; if I could count two seconds between the lightning and the thunder, it meant the lightning was two miles away. The thunder now followed the lightning with no space between them. Flash, *boom!* Flash, *boom!* The storm was no longer somewhere in the distance. It was here, beside us, all around us. I buried my face in Snickers's fur and pressed myself against him.

The wind whipped through the tree above my head, stripping leaves from the branches. My ears popped the way they do if I ride downhill really fast on my bike.

The hail stopped as abruptly as it had started, perhaps blown away by the strong wind.

Crack! A large branch snapped off the tree and fell onto the road.

Even with my backpack on my head and my palms pressed against my ears, the howling wind seemed to come from a boom box whose volume was on high.

Snap! Another branch broke off, this one dropping to the ground beside me.

Snickers began to pant, his sides heaving and his tongue hanging out of his mouth. His drool soaked my pant leg.

The noise increased to a roar. I raised my head to look toward the bank of greenish clouds that I had seen earlier, and gasped.

A tornado!

Beyond the shed, a funnel cloud whirled its way from sky to earth. I couldn't tell how far away it was. Not far. The tornado came toward me across the cornfield, its long, narrow funnel dangling down, twisting like a snake held by its tail.

I had seen enough nature programs on television to know I could not outrun a tornado. Besides, the wind was now so strong that I knew I would not even be able to stand up, much less run. I leaned hard against the tree trunk, slipping one hand through Snickers's collar to keep him close and grasping one strap of my backpack with the other.

Maybe the tree would act as a shield, protecting us from the storm's fury. If it didn't—if the tree was uprooted—I didn't think Snickers and I could survive.

The noise grew louder. It sounded as if a train track had been installed between two corn rows, and the train was rushing toward me at full speed.

The twister came closer.

Another branch snapped off, but this time instead of falling to the ground it flew across the road like a huge bird. I didn't watch to see where it finally landed because I heard a different noise, like fingernails scraping a chalkboard but magnified a thousand times. As I looked toward the noise, I saw the roof come off the old shed. A long, flat piece of rusty corrugated tin lifted up like a magic carpet and skimmed across the rows of corn, flattening them. It banged to the ground once, then rose again and continued its destructive journey.

Without the roof, the shed walls collapsed. If I had taken shelter there, the walls would have come down on Snickers and me. The center of the funnel swerved away from us after it hit the shed, but the edges swirled with such intensity that I felt as if Snickers and I were Dorothy and Toto in *The Wizard of Oz*.

One hand curled around Snickers's collar so tightly that my fingers cramped, but I was afraid to let go. With my other hand, I opened my backpack. I planned to snap the leash on Snickers and tie the other end around my waist. Whatever happened to us in this tornado, I wanted to stay together.

Like a giant scoop, the wind lifted up big chunks of the shed walls and sent them sailing into the air.

Then the wind ripped my backpack right out of my hand. The strap simply pulled from my grasp and the backpack rose as if it had sprouted wings.

"No!" I screamed. I grabbed at it, but it was far beyond my reach. All I could do was watch my backpack disappear into the distance, along with pieces of the shed, tree branches, and other debris.

Snickers panicked when I screamed. He jerked so hard that I could not hold on to his collar. He ran from me, racing blindly into the storm as if he believed he could run away from this nightmare.

He did not get far.

The whirling wind chased him, and as I watched in horror, a big branch dropped from the dark sky above Snickers and struck him in the head. He went down.

Feeling sick to my stomach, I tried to crawl to him, keeping myself flat on the ground while I pulled my body forward with my forearms. If he had been killed, I would never forgive myself. Even though I had no control over the weather and could not have prevented a tornado, I had brought him to this desolate place. I had made him endure a horrible storm, with nowhere to take shelter. As frightening as it was to me, I could only imagine how scary it must be to a dog, who did not understand what was happening. Snickers knew *sit* and *stay* and *good dog*, but he did not know what *tornado* meant.

The wind blew dirt in my eyes even at ground level, and bits of mud stung my cheeks. I kept my lips clamped shut, trying to keep the grit out of my mouth. I kept expecting some unknown object to drop on me, as it had on Snickers.

How could my trip to find Starr—the trip I had dreamed about for so many years—have ended like this, with my dog unconscious or worse, and me crawling in the mud while a tornado swirled around me?

Before I reached Snickers, the noise let up, and the wind became less intense. I raised my head and could not see the tornado. It had moved on or had worn itself out. Either way, it was gone.

The wind eased more. Several seconds elapsed between the lightning and the thunder that followed.

Snickers still lay motionless. I got up, ran to him, and knelt beside him. I put my hands on his side, relieved to feel the slight rise and fall as he breathed. "Good dog," I said. "Good boy."

Now what? He needed to be seen by a veterinarian. How would I get him there? He was too heavy for me to carry. Not a single car had gone past since the bus, so I couldn't wait to flag down a passing motorist.

Much as I hated to leave him, I decided the best chance of helping him would be for me to walk back the way I had come. I'd return to the town and ask the man in the gas station to help me. Even better, I might be able to find June. Maybe she had waited out the tornado in her aunt's basement or maybe the tornado had bypassed the town.

If I couldn't find her, I'd ask the gas-station man to help me find a phone number for June's Home-cooked Meals, and I'd call her. June would come to get Snickers, and help me lift him into her car. She would drive him to a vet.

I worried that Snickers would come to while I was gone. If he woke up and didn't see me, he might go wandering through the countryside, looking for me. If he did that, I might never find him again.

I wished I still had my backpack so I could write a note and tuck it into Snickers's collar. That way if anyone happened to see him, they would know he wasn't a stray, that he belonged to me and that I would come for him.

But my backpack was nowhere in sight and I couldn't take time to search for it. I needed to get help for Snickers as quickly as I could.

I stroked his side. "I need to leave," I whispered. "I'm going to find help for you, but I'll return as soon as I can."

I kissed his forehead lightly. He didn't move. "Stay where you are until I come for you," I said. "Stay."

Blinking back tears, I walked away. When I looked at Snickers, he lay still, like a big brown and black rock in the field.

10

I picked up two boards that the storm had deposited in the field, and arranged them in an X at the side of the road so that I'd be sure to remember where Snickers was.

The scenery on my return trip was far different from what I had walked through only a couple of hours earlier. The cornstalks that had stretched tall in straight rows now lay broken, their tops angled in all directions. Some had been completely uprooted. Others looked as if someone had driven a large vehicle at random through the field, crushing everything in its path.

The green-black sky had brightened, but clusters of

melting hailstones offered further proof of the horrible storm that had passed through.

I walked faster without Snickers, jogging part of the time. I felt an urgency that I had never experienced before, a fierce desire to save my dog. Except for Starr, Snickers was the only family I had. I had quickly learned to love him, and now, when he was in danger, my fear that he might not make it made me love him even more. I had to find a vet for him as fast as I could.

This is farm country, I told myself. People probably have horses and cows, plus barn cats and family dogs. Surely there will be a veterinarian in the area. Snickers will get the treatment he needs. He will get well. He has to!

One bright spot: I still had part of my money. If I had left it all in the backpack it would be gone now, but by dividing it up when I did I still had half, enough to pay the vet. Maybe even enough to get me to Starr.

As I hurried forward, my eyes scanned the horizon, looking for the town. I was almost upon it before I realized that what I saw ahead was not what I had seen two hours ago. Instead of the gas station and the clumps of old houses, piles of debris littered the ground. The gas pump itself rested on its back, on the wrong side of the road, with the hose and nozzle missing.

A crumpled car lay upside down, squashed like an aluminum can that had been stomped on. Uneasily, I peered in the car's shattered window. The vehicle was not occupied. Either the driver and any passengers had managed to climb out and walk away or the car had been empty when it was lifted up somewhere else and deposited here.

The building where the old man had listened to his radio was only a heap of broken boards. Its tin roof was rolled back like the pop-top on a can of tuna, and pieces of pink insulation looked like mounds of cotton candy. Was the man buried under the rubble? Might he still be alive?

With my heart pounding, I approached what was left of the building. "Hello?" I called. "Are you there? Can you hear me?"

Nobody answered. I looked around. Where was everyone? Some of the houses on the other side of the road must have been occupied when the tornado hit. Were there survivors? Staying clear of a downed power line, I walked toward the houses, past a flowered sofa, an old refrigerator, and a baby's high chair that had three legs snapped off.

As I approached the closest house, I heard a hissing sound. I quickly looked around for a snake. Were there rattlers or other poisonous snakes in this part of the state?

I didn't see a snake, but the hissing continued. Then I smelled an odd odor and realized I heard propane leaking from a broken line. I'd noticed a white propane tank near every house, and wondered why they weren't painted green so they'd blend in with the landscape. Fearing an explosion, I skirted that house and approached what looked like a huge pile of kindling that had pieces of furniture mixed in with the wood.

A piece of paper fluttered down and landed in the dirt beside me. I picked it up. It was a child's drawing: a family of smiling stick figures with a bright sun overhead. SUZY was printed in wobbly block letters on the bottom of the drawing.

Where was Suzy now? What had happened to the people who lived in these houses? Where was June, and her aunt? I folded the drawing and put it in my pocket. The still air made it feel like a ghost town, and I shivered in spite of the heat.

"Hello?" I called. "Is anyone here?" As I zigzagged through the splintered wood and rain-soaked contents of the former houses, I heard a sound.

I stopped, listening. It came again, a faint cry. "Help."

I went toward the voice. "I hear you," I called. "I'm coming! Keep talking so I can find you."

"Here," said the voice. "I'm under here."

The voice came from beneath a heap of rubble, all that remained of one of the houses. I began to dig, throwing pieces of wallboard and roof shingles off to the side, trying to reach the voice.

"Don't worry," I said. "I'll get you out."

"Hurry," replied the voice. It sounded like a child.

When I tried to pry a piece of siding loose, I got a splinter under one of my fingernails. I tried to pull the splinter out with my teeth, but it broke off. Ignoring the soreness, I kept working toward the voice.

After I pulled away a large chunk of ceiling tile, I was startled to see the soft brown eyes of a cow looking at me. I had uncovered a large oil painting that, except for being dirty, did not appear to be damaged. I lifted the painting, shook the dirt off, and set it aside. If the owners of this home returned, they would be surprised to find their cow painting in such good condition when the rest of the house was demolished.

Beneath where the painting had been, I glimpsed hair. Human hair. I was looking at the back of someone's head. No wonder the voice seemed so muffled. The person was lying facedown in the dirt. I removed more debris until the whole head was uncovered.

"I see you!" I said. "Can you turn your head? You'll be able to breath better if you can turn."

The head turned slowly and I saw the profile of Randy, the youngest of the three boys who had tried to rob me. He looked at me for a second, then closed his eyes.

"I'll keep digging," I said, "until you can crawl out of there."

He moaned.

I tugged at the rubble that covered Randy's shoulders and back. When his arms were free, I said, "Can you raise up on your elbows and pull yourself loose?"

He struggled briefly, then started to cry. "My legs hurt," he said. "My legs hurt really bad."

"I'll dig them free," I said.

But I didn't.

I couldn't. When I yanked a piece of ceiling off Randy's legs, it revealed a cast-iron sink lying on top of him. The sink covered his legs from mid-thigh to mid-calf. His ankles protruded out the bottom at an unnatural angle. His legs were surely broken.

If I lifted the sink off him, I could fashion splints from pieces of board and make him more comfortable while he waited for medical help.

I tugged with all my strength, but I was not able to remove the heavy sink.

"There's a sink on top of your legs," I said, "and it's

too heavy for me to move it. I'm going for help. I'll send someone back to get you out of here."

"Don't leave me," Randy whimpered. "I don't want to stay here alone."

"Where are Zooman and Hunker?" I asked.

"I don't know. We came home to their house to get some lunch and we heard hail on the roof. I was in the bathroom when I heard Zooman yell, 'It's a twister! Run to the shelter!'"

Good, I thought. *Maybe there are other survivors who are still in a storm shelter.*

"By the time I got out of the bathroom, Zooman and Hunker were gone. When I called to them, they didn't answer." Randy spoke haltingly, as if it hurt to talk. "I stepped outside, but I didn't see them, and then the wind blew so hard I fell down, and then something landed on top of me and I blacked out." Sobs temporarily replaced words as he struggled for control. "When I woke up, I couldn't move or see and my legs hurt. I lay here, and then I heard you calling, and I answered."

I patted Randy's shoulder. How could the older boys have run to the shelter and left him behind?

"I'll get help for you," I said. "You need to lie as still as you can while I'm gone. I promise I'll find someone and send them here to get you out."

"Cross your heart?" he asked.

"Cross my heart."

Tears trickled down his muddy cheeks. "We were mean to you," he said.

I wondered if he was afraid I wouldn't really help him because of what had happened earlier. "Zooman and Hunker were mean," I said. "I don't think you wanted to take my money, but you were scared of them."

"I'm scared now, too."

"I'll hurry," I said. "I'll send help as fast as I can."

I left Randy pinned under the sink. I wasn't going to find a veterinarian here, or a doctor for Randy, or aid of any kind. I returned to the road and hurried back toward Snickers. I had spent a long time trying to free Randy, and my dog still needed help.

My arms ached from lifting and digging to get to Randy, and my fingernail throbbed where the splinter was lodged under it. I wished I could take a warm shower and then crawl into my comfy bed at Rita's house and have a nap.

As I headed back to Snickers, I thought back to televised news accounts of natural disasters. The Red Cross usually sent workers. So did the government, although I remembered that the government aid was often slow to arrive. After Hurricane Katrina, animal-rescue groups had gone to New Orleans to aid with injured or lost pets. Maybe that would happen here and an animal-rescue group would help Snickers. Not today, though. It takes a day or two for rescue groups to arrive. I wasn't sure Snickers could wait that long.

I should have spent some of my money on a cell phone. When I planned this journey, I didn't think I would want to call anyone. Who would I call? Now I wished I had considered the possibility of an emergency. I could have used a phone to call for help.

I'm coming, Snickers, I thought. *Stay where you are. I'm coming!*

I ran, even though my knees felt as if they would buckle at any moment. My breath came in short gasps, and a persistent pain jabbed my side, but I kept running. I ran toward Snickers, and away from the devastation I had seen. I wanted to run until I was miles away from this place. I wanted to run and run, until Snickers and I were safe.

Eventually I saw the boards that I had used to make my X beside the road. When I reached them, I turned to the right, to where I had left Snickers.

I saw only the empty field.

Snickers was gone.

11

My eyes scanned the field, searching for a black and tan dog. Instead I saw battered rows of corn and debris from the tornado.

Snickers must have awakened and gone to look for me.

Fear rose in my throat. Sometimes when an animal is sick or injured, it will crawl away and hide somewhere, and wait to die. What if Snickers had done that?

"Snickers!" I shouted. "Here, Snickers! Come, boy!"

Wouldn't he have smelled me and followed my scent? But if he had gone after me toward town, we would have found each other. Did the rain-soaked ground dilute my odor, making it harder for him to track me?

Perhaps he had gone back to the tree where we had waited out the tornado. That's where I had been when he panicked and ran. That's where he had last seen me.

I ran toward the tree.

Paw prints circled the base of the tree, and my hopes soared, even though I knew they could have been made before the tornado hit.

"Snickers!" I yelled again. "Here I am! Snickers!"

I heard him before I saw him—a soft whimper coming from a patch of corn that was still standing.

"Snickers!" I called, and then he emerged, walking slowly toward me as if it hurt him to move.

I ran to him, and threw my arms around him. Relief flooded through me as he licked my cheek.

I had told Randy I'd find help for him, but it was clear that Snickers was in no condition to travel and I couldn't leave him alone again.

Knowing I was as likely to find help by waiting here for it to arrive as I was by walking any farther with an injured dog, I decided to stay with Snickers until we were rescued, and then I'd direct the rescuers to Randy. Maybe he'd be found first. Search teams would look in the remains of a town before they'd hunt in a cornfield. I should have told him where I would be so that he could send help my direction if he got found before I did.

I sat on the ground, and Snickers lay beside me. The wound on his head had formed a scab, and there was a lump the size of an egg. I didn't touch it. I wished I still had my backpack so that I could give Snickers a drink of water and a dog biscuit. All I could offer him were words of comfort.

"Someone will find us," I told him. "There are probably people searching already, looking for survivors of the tornado. They'll find us before long. They'll help us."

I knew that I spoke the truth, and my heart filled with gratitude for these strangers who would come to our aid. There may be mean people like Zooman and Hunker in the world, but there are also good people who leave their comfortable homes and rush to help in times of trouble.

I stroked Snickers's fur. He put his head on my leg, closed his eyes, and sighed.

We sat like that for about an hour before I heard the helicopter. I stood and looked up, shielding my eyes from the sun. The helicopter approached from the west, flying low. It appeared to be following the road that Snickers and I had walked on. I could see two people inside it.

I waved my arms over my head, trying to signal the pilot and his passenger. The helicopter passed to my left, then circled back over me. I waved again, and watched as it hovered over the road and then slowly landed. Snickers began to pant again, afraid of the noise, and I held tight to his collar. The chopper blades sent swirls of dust into the air. A man jumped down and ran toward me.

"Are you okay?" he called.

"I'm not hurt," I yelled, "but my dog needs a veterinarian. He got hit on the head with a branch during the tornado."

The man stopped beside me. "An emergency shelter is being set up in an old school about ten miles west of here. I can give you a lift there," he said.

"What about Snickers?"

"The dog?"

I nodded.

"You'll have to leave him here. You can probably come back for him in a day or two."

"I can't leave him," I said. "He would try to follow me. He'd get lost."

"I can't take him in the chopper," he said. "I need to keep the space open for any injured people I find. We're not equipped to rescue animals."

"Then I'll stay here," I said.

"Don't be foolish," the man said. "I know you love your dog, but you need to get to the shelter where there's food and people to help you. What if another twister comes through?"

I had not considered that possibility, but I realized it could happen. Tornadoes sometimes come in bunches. Even so, I shook my head. "Snickers is my best friend," I said. "I can't leave him behind."

The man shrugged his shoulders, as if he thought I was making a huge mistake. "Suit yourself."

"Could you tell the people at the shelter where we are?" I asked. "Maybe someone could drive here to get us. Maybe even a veterinarian would come."

"I'll tell them you're here," he said, "but don't get your hopes up. In an emergency like this, most people are busy trying to find family and friends or helping those who were injured or left homeless. Destruction from this storm is widespread. A few miles west of here we saw three boxcars that had been lifted off the railroad tracks. You're lucky to be alive."

"There's a boy, Randy, who needs help right away," I said. "He's about two miles that way." I pointed. "A house came down on top of him. I tried to dig him out, but his legs are pinned by a sink that was too heavy for me. The town is destroyed; he's the only person I found. I think his legs are broken."

The man started back toward the helicopter.

"Wait!" I yelled, and he looked back. "I think there's a broken propane line near Randy."

"Thanks. We'll check that out." Just before he got to the place where he had to duck down and run through the wind caused by the chopper blades, he called back, "Are you sure you want to stay here?"

I waved, to signal he should go without me.

I stood beside Snickers and felt tears drip down my cheeks.

As the helicopter rose, I saw something fall from it and land in the dirt. I walked toward it, and found a bottle of water. My would-be rescuer had thrown down the one thing Snickers and I needed the most.

"Thank you!" I shouted as I held the bottle over my head. I knew he couldn't hear me, but I yelled it anyway. "Thanks for the water!"

The helicopter flew off, headed toward Randy.

I opened the bottle of water and took a drink. Then I cupped one hand and poured some water into it for Snickers. He lapped it quickly, wagging his tail. I thought about pouring some water on his wound, to clean it and try to keep it from getting infected, but I decided I should save the water for drinking. I didn't know how long it would be before we got rescued.

For a while I scanned the sky, watching for the helicopter to go back the way it had come. I was sure that two adults would be able to lift the sink off Randy's legs.

An hour passed, and then two hours. By now, I thought, they should have carried him to the helicopter and flown him to a hospital, or at least to a waiting ambulance. Maybe the closest hospital was not this way. Maybe they had flown Randy in the opposite direction.

While I watched for the helicopter, I also kept alert for the possible sound of a vehicle coming my way. I fantasized that a minivan drove up and a woman who looked like Rita jumped out and said, "I'm a veterinarian. I've come to take you and your dog to my clinic." It didn't happen, though.

The sun turned a fiery golden red as it sank below the horizon, casting an orange glow on the scattering of clouds. The temperature dropped, and I was glad for the warmth of Snickers beside me.

My stomach grumbled. I wished I had eaten the cashews instead of saving them in my backpack. I tried not to think about food, but the more I tried not to think of food, the more images of food danced in my mind. Mac and cheese. A chocolate milk shake. Pizza. Even one of Rita's healthy vegetable soup and salad dinners sounded good. I wondered if Snickers was visualizing a box of dog biscuits or a bowl of kibble or more of June's stew. I took another drink of water and gave some more to Snickers, hoping to fill our empty stomachs with liquid.

Darkness descended. I lay on my side, with my knees bent. Snickers curled next to me. He fell asleep immediately and began snoring softly.

I wondered if I should wake him up now and then during the night, because of his head injury. Once when a girl I knew had fallen off her scooter and hit her head on the pavement, her parents had been instructed to wake her up every two hours all night long, to be sure she was sleeping and not unconscious.

While Snickers slept, I lay there with my mind racing. I was sure I'd get to the shelter the next day. If nobody came to rescue us, Snickers and I could walk there. But what should I do when I got to the shelter? People would ask where I lived. They would want to know who my parents or guardians are. I couldn't give my real name.

I decided to say my name was Kaitlyn Smith. If asked, I'd say I had missed the bus and was walking when the tornado hit. That part was true. Although I was becoming an accomplished liar, I knew if I told too many untruths it would be hard to remember what I'd said and I would be more likely to be found out.

When I shifted position, Snickers opened his eyes and looked at me as if he wanted to be sure I was still there. Then he went back to sleep. Good. I wouldn't need to wake him on purpose.

I stroked his back and found that petting him relaxed me. Soon my eyes closed, too.

Several times during the night, I woke up because I was stiff. Even cuddled next to Snickers, I couldn't get comfortable and I longed for my bed at Rita's house, with the purple bedspread and the soft patchwork quilt. Thinking back, I realized how many things I had liked about living with Rita—physical things like the quilt and the computer access, but also intangibles, such as Rita's willingness to let me choose my own clothes and her sense of humor as she encouraged me to do homework. Rita had a curiosity about the world that made ordinary events more interesting. She carried binoculars in her car, in case she spotted an unusual bird. She always asked store clerks and waiters about their jobs. "You can learn a lot by listening to the people you meet every day," Rita said.

Two days before I left, I had found her knitting like crazy, and I asked her what she was making. "A bagel," she said.

I stared at her. "What?" I asked, thinking I had misunderstood.

"This morning I was toasting a bagel," she said, "and I thought it was the perfect shape to be a bracelet, so I decided to knit a bagel bracelet."

I thought she was crazy until I saw the finished

product. The next day, she held up her arm and said, "I finished my bagel bracelet. How do you like it?"

It was a round knitted tube, about an inch in diameter, made of a soft light tan yarn. Rita had sewn a variety of funky old buttons around the outside rim. It was unlike any bracelet I'd ever seen, and I loved it.

"Cool," I said. "Can you make one for me?"

"Sure. Go through the old buttons in my button jar and pick out which ones you want for decoration."

I wished now that I hadn't left before Rita had knit my bagel bracelet. It would have been perfect to remember her by. I wondered if she had knit a bracelet for me anyway, in case I came back. If Starr and I go to visit Rita, I'll ask her to knit matching bagel bracelets for us.

Thinking about Rita made me sad, and it occurred to me that I was a little bit homesick. How could I be homesick for a place that wasn't really my home? I told myself I only felt that way because I was hungry and tired and uncomfortable.

Tomorrow I would push Rita out of my thoughts and get on with my quest to find Starr. I felt sure that she had longed for me all these years, just as I had yearned for her. Once we were reunited, I would truly be home.

12

The **sound of** a vehicle approaching woke me. The sun had not yet risen, but the sky was growing light. I saw a pair of headlights coming toward me.

Snickers stood and shook, making his ears flap. I stood, too, and walked toward the road, waving at the lights.

A large black pickup truck, the kind with a backseat, pulled up next to me. The driver, a man in a baseball cap, leaned out the window. "Need a lift?" he asked. "There's temporary housing and food available about ten miles up the road."

"Is it okay to bring my dog?"

The man laughed. "They may not let him inside the building, but I don't mind giving him a ride. Hop in."

I hesitated briefly, wondering if I should ask him for identification. Under normal circumstances, I wouldn't dream of getting in a truck with a man I didn't know. Then I saw that he wore a white smock over his shirt; the smock said AMERICAN RED CROSS VOLUNTEER in big red letters.

He opened the passenger door. Snickers scrambled in first and sat between me and the man as if he had ridden there a hundred times.

"My name's Jake," the man said.

"I'm Kaitlyn," I replied, silently congratulating myself for having chosen the pseudonym ahead of time so that I could answer without hesitation. "My dog's name is Snickers."

"Where do you live?" he asked. "Should I drive you home instead of to the shelter?"

"I'm not from around here. I'm on my way to my sister's house, but I missed the bus yesterday. Snickers and I were walking a while and got caught in the tornado."

"You were outside?" he asked. "With no protection?"

"We sat under a tree to try to get out of the hail, and it ended up shielding us from the wind."

He looked at me as if I were the eighth wonder of the world. "You are one lucky girl," he said, "and your dog, too. Half the trees in the county were uprooted. The wind hit one hundred and fifteen miles an hour in some places. The next town east of here is gone, every building wiped out."

"I know," I said. "I saw it. I tried to dig out a boy who was buried in the rubble, but I couldn't get everything off him. I told a man in a helicopter where the boy was."

"That was you?" Jake said. "You're the one who saved the boy from Alabama?"

"You know about Randy?"

"They airlifted him to the hospital and he couldn't stop talking about a girl who he had been mean to, but she tried to help him anyway. The TV station is having a field day with the story. According to the reporters, you saved the kid's life."

I hoped that was true.

"They're trying to locate you, for an interview."

I immediately regretted saying anything about Randy. I certainly did not want a reporter interviewing me and broadcasting my picture.

"Please don't tell anyone else it was me," I said. "I don't want a big fuss."

Jake smiled his approval. "Well, that's refreshing," he said. "Most people mug shamelessly at a camera, trying to get on TV."

"I'm shy," I said. Then, hoping to change the subject, I asked, "Were there other survivors there besides Randy? I didn't see any people, but I didn't see any bodies, either."

"Some folks weren't home, and everyone else made it to the town's underground storm cellar. The siren that was supposed to sound the warning malfunctioned, but people saw the hail and wind and realized what was happening in time to get to the shelter. When you live in tornado country, you learn to watch the skies and be cautious. We're always supposed to stay in the shelter until the all clear siren sounds, but this time it never went off. They waited almost three hours before they finally tried to open the door, and then it was blocked shut by rubble."

"So nobody was killed?" I asked, thinking about June and the old man at the gas station.

"Nope. The only serious injury was the boy with the broken legs and the crushed pelvis, and he'll survive."

A crushed pelvis, too. Poor Randy. At least he was alive and had not had to wait alone too long after I left him. I wondered if he had told Zooman and Hunker's parents how the older boys had deserted him.

"Tornadoes are unpredictable," Jake said. "They hop about at random, creating chaos in some places and completely missing other spots. The town of Alliance, where I live, didn't even get the rain or hail."

"Is there a veterinarian near here?" I asked. "Snickers got hit on the head and was knocked out."

"He seems okay now."

"I'd like to have him examined, just to be sure."

"Maybe somebody at the school will give you a ride to a vet. I'd take you myself, but we were assigned territories to look for survivors and I need to stay in my area."

Jake's truck pulled up to an old brick school building. A banner draped over the door of what appeared to be the gymnasium said AMERICAN RED CROSS TEMPORARY SHELTER.

A big silver van, the kind where a window opens on the side for serving food, was parked in the yard. A car next to it had its trunk open and two women were unloading boxes of food and supplies.

"Are you hungry?" Jake asked.

"I'm starving. All I've had since breakfast yesterday morning is a candy bar and some water."

"Wait here," Jake said, and he jumped down from the truck and walked to the women who were unloading the boxes. A moment later he climbed back in the truck and handed me a sandwich wrapped in plastic wrap. "I hope you like ham and cheese," he said.

"Right now I'd be willing to eat cauliflower," I told him.

I unwrapped the sandwich, picked out the ham, and gave it to Snickers, who gulped it down without even chewing. I bit into the sandwich. "Yum," I said. "Thank you." I gave Snickers a couple of bites of bread and cheese, and ate the rest myself. No meal had ever tasted better.

As soon as I finished eating, Jake said, "I need to leave you here. I'm supposed to be out driving around, looking for survivors who need assistance."

"Thanks for your help," I told him. I got out of the truck, and Snickers jumped out, too. He followed me to the door of the school, and up the three concrete steps.

"Stay," I told him, before I opened the door.

Snickers obediently sat down on the top step and watched me go inside.

Rows of cots formed lines in the center of the building. People slept on some of the cots. A few people sat on others, talking quietly. Chairs lined the periphery of the room. A woman sat on one of the chairs, playing peekaboo with a toddler. Two little boys chased each other between the rows of cots until their mothers made them stop.

A table stood just inside the door, with two women behind it. The table held a notebook computer, lined tablets, pens, and a first-aid kit.

One of the women smiled and said, "Hello. Do you need a temporary place to stay?"

"Yes."

"Let's get you registered on our Safe and Well Web site. Sign in here, please." She pointed to a list of names, addresses, and phone numbers.

Stalling for time while I tried to figure out a reason to refuse, I said, "The what?"

"The Red Cross maintains a Safe and Well Web site. After a disaster, people can search for family members, as long as they know the phone number or a complete address. Once you're registered, your parents will be able to find out that you survived."

I almost said, "That isn't necessary because I don't have any parents," but I caught myself. A statement like that would only call attention to me and probably bring Hiss to the scene. Instead, I gave my name as Kaitlyn Smith and made up a fake address and phone number. "I'll enter your information on the Red Cross website," she said. She handed me a folded blanket and a pillow.

"Pick out any empty cot you want and it will be your bed as long as you're here."

"I have my dog with me," I said. "Is it okay to bring him in?"

"No, it isn't."

"He'll stay on the floor by my cot. He won't bother anyone."

"I'm sorry. Animals are not allowed inside. Some people are allergic to them. He can be outside with you, as long as he's leashed."

"The leash was in my backpack, and it blew away in the tornado."

"You can't keep an unleashed dog on the premises," she told me. "There's too much risk that it would bite someone, or get in a fight with another animal."

"Do you have something I could use for a leash? A piece of rope, maybe?"

She looked down at the table, as if expecting a coil of rope to miraculously appear in front of us. Then she shook her head.

"Sorry."

"Thanks, anyway," I said, handing back the pillow and blanket. I turned to open the door.

"Where are you going?" she asked.

"I don't know, but I can't stay here without Snickers."

"If you can find a way to leash your dog, you can try keeping him here. As long as he's under control and nobody complains, I don't see what it would hurt." She smiled at me. "I have a dog myself," she added.

"Thanks. I'll look for something I can use as a leash."

I didn't want to leave the shelter. Snickers and I both needed a source of food, and some sleep. I'd slept little the night before and I felt a weariness deep in my bones. I knew Snickers needed rest, too, and I still hoped to find a veterinarian to examine the lump on his head. It made sense to stay here, at least for a day or so.

I asked the people who were distributing food if they had something I could use as a leash. "I can't stay at the shelter unless I find a way to tie my dog," I explained.

They looked around but found nothing suitable.

Then one of the women said, "You can have my belt, if you want it. That might work." She unbuckled her belt and slid it free from the loops of her jeans. It was a woven belt, so the tongue of the buckle would pierce through at any spot. I looped it around Snickers's neck and fastened it. The belt length that was left was a lot shorter than his real leash had been, but it worked to keep him beside me.

"Thank you," I told the woman. "I'll return it if I can find something else to use."

"Meanwhile, I hope my pants stay up," she said, and we both laughed.

I led Snickers back to the shelter building and this time I took him inside. I asked the woman at the table if she had tweezers, and she helped me get the splinter out from under my fingernail.

Then I picked up a blanket and pillow, claimed a cot, and lay down. Snickers did not want to lie on the floor beside me; he hopped up on the cot. Although it was crowded that way, I decided to let him stay. Once I fell asleep, my grasp on the belt would loosen and I wouldn't know if Snickers wandered off. If he was lying next to me, I would know if he moved. With me under the blanket and Snickers on top of it, I closed my eyes. Even with the low murmur of strangers talking, I fell asleep right away.

When I woke up, the room was crowded. Every cot was occupied, and so were the chairs. Some people sat on the floor. I took Snickers outside and walked him for a while, then returned and got in the food line, which now snaked around the corner of the building. When I got to the window, I was given a tuna sandwich, an apple, and a bottle of water. "Could I please have an extra sandwich?" I asked. The man inside handed it to me.

Most people took their food inside and sat on their

cots to eat, but I walked to the edge of the yard and sat in the grass. I didn't want to take a chance that some fussbudget would complain about me giving a sandwich to a dog. Tuna is not my favorite, but I ate it. Snickers gobbled his sandwich, including the lettuce. All of his months of scrounging for scraps had apparently made him an unfussy eater.

Back inside, I noticed that the walls were now covered with papers, photos, and other items that were attached with masking tape. People were walking around the room looking at them, as if they were in an art gallery.

Leading Snickers with the belt/leash, I circled the room, too. There was a graduation photo of a pretty young woman in a red cap and gown, with a gold tasseled cord draped around her neck. There were pictures of a black cat. A loop of bright blue beads hung from a pushpin that had been jammed into the wall. A page from a calendar, with notations on the dates, hung between a lace doily and a packet of pumpkin seeds. Most of the papers and photos were torn and dirty, and I realized these were things people had found and brought here, hoping the people they belonged to would reclaim them.

I remembered the drawing I had found. I took it out of my pocket, smoothed it open, pricked it with a pushpin, and stuck it on the wall. Maybe Suzy's parents were here; maybe they would be happy to find her drawing.

Two women walked around the room ahead of me. "I wouldn't mind losing my house so much," one of them said, "if I could still have the pictures of my grandparents, and of my kids when they were little."

A few minutes later the same woman said, "Oh! Here's Grandma and Grandpa!" She was standing in front of a long table that was piled with items that had been picked up. I saw her hug a small framed photo to her chest.

The table also contained a tattered blue baby blanket, a leather-bound Bible, and a teddy bear. Curious, I went closer.

When I reached the table, I stopped and stared in disbelief. A pink diaper bag sat at the edge of the table and there, partly hidden behind it, was my backpack! While I had slept, someone had brought my backpack to the shelter and left it on the table. With trembling hands, I opened it.

I took out my UCLA sweatshirt, my underwear, the bag of cashews, Snickers's bowl and biscuits, and, yes, my money. All of it. I clasped the backpack, holding it tightly as a wave of gratitude swept over me. Whoever had found my backpack could have removed the money before they brought it here. No one would ever have known. But they didn't take my money. They brought the backpack here and left it with the contents intact, hoping the owner would find it. And I did.

I took Snickers's leash out of my backpack and snapped it on his collar. Then I removed the belt and took it back to the woman in the food van.

"Thanks for the loan," I told her.

She smiled. "Anytime."

The backpack gave me fresh hope and determination. Nothing could stop me now. I had survived a tornado!

13

The next morning, as Snickers and I ate scrambled eggs and toast, with orange juice for me and dog biscuits for him, I saw Zooman and Hunker waiting in line for food. I wondered what they would do if they saw me. Probably they'd complain that Snickers was a vicious dog who had tried to attack them.

I turned my back to them and positioned myself between them and Snickers so they wouldn't notice him. He's definitely a one-of-a-kind dog; if they saw him, they'd recognize him.

A white van with green lettering on the side pulled in to the parking area, and a man with a large video camera got out. I heard him introduce himself as the reporter for a TV station. "We're doing a feature story on heroes of the tornado," he said.

Remembering what Jake had told me about the media wanting to find the girl who had helped Randy, I decided it was time to move on. Keeping my face turned away from Zooman and Hunker, I led Snickers inside and went back to our cot.

Many of the people who had slept at the shelter had already gone. Some had been picked up by friends or relatives; others had left on foot or had hitched a ride with a volunteer. Everyone was eager to return to their homes to survey the damage.

Although the food was tasty, and the cot comfortable enough, I knew I needed to leave before any questions were asked about where I lived, and before Zooman and Hunker caused trouble.

I folded my blanket and put my pillow on top of it. We had all been instructed to sign out when we left permanently so that anyone searching for us would know we weren't coming back to the shelter. I didn't need to do that. No one would come here looking for Kaitlyn Smith, or for Sunny Skyland.

I waited until the woman at the entry table was engaged in a conversation with someone else, then I added my blanket and pillow to a stack that was already started, and walked out the door. Zooman and Hunker were at the food station, receiving their breakfasts. I quickly went around to the back of the building, passed a chugging generator, and headed into town.

Snickers seemed to have recovered from his blow to the head. The lump was barely noticeable. Although he still walked as if his joints needed oiling, he apparently felt okay. I decided it wouldn't be necessary to find a veterinarian, after all. What I needed to find was transportation to Washington State.

An hour later I saw restaurants, motels, and other businesses ahead. As I neared the edge of town, lights suddenly came on in all the buildings.

While I waited at a traffic light, a taxi idled in the street beside me, giving me a new idea.

I waved for the cab to pull over. The driver, a man about Rita's age, looked as if he should do more walking and less driving. His cheeks were chubby and his ample stomach barely fit behind the steering wheel. His face had laugh lines, and he smiled as he said, "Where to, Miss?"

"How much would you charge to drive me to Washington?" I asked.

The smile turned to a scowl. "Don't play games, kid," he said as he looked over his left shoulder, preparing to pull away.

"Wait!" I cried. "I'm serious!"

Looking skeptical, he stayed at the curb. "Where do you want to go?" he asked.

"Enumclaw, Washington."

"Washington State?"

"Yes." I fished my map out of my backpack and offered it to him, but he didn't take it.

"I can't do that," he said. "I only work an eight-hour day. My back kills me if I drive longer than that."

"How much would it be if you drove me west for four hours, and then returned alone?"

"I'd have to charge you for both directions. I can't drive an empty cab for four hours."

That seemed reasonable. "How much?" I asked.

"How are you going to pay me?"

"Cash."

"Where did you get the money?"

"I didn't steal it, if that's what you're wondering, and I didn't sell drugs or do anything else illegal. I found the money and I advertised for the owner and nobody claimed it. It's mine, fair and square."

He thought for a few seconds. "Four hundred dollars," he said.

For eight hours, that came to fifty dollars an hour. I doubted he averaged fifty dollars an hour. If he did, lots more people would want to be cab drivers.

"How much do you make in a normal eight-hour day?" I asked. The taxi said CHARLEY'S CAB on the side, so I was pretty sure he owned the vehicle and didn't have to share what he got with a boss.

"Four hundred dollars," he said.

I didn't believe him. "I don't have that much," I said, figuring if he could lie, so could I. "I'll give you one hundred-fifty dollars."

"Two-fifty, paid in advance."

"Two hundred, half now and half in four hours."

I could tell he was tempted, so I added, "And I'll buy lunch."

He laughed. "You drive a hard bargain," he said. "Hop in."

As Snickers and I climbed into the backseat of Charley's cab, I looked at my watch. It was eleven o'clock. I wondered where we'd be in four hours.

"You're lucky I just started today," he said. "Otherwise I couldn't do this."

"Are you Charley?" I asked.

"At your service. And you are . . . ?"

"Brenda." I have no idea where that name came from since I've never known anyone named Brenda. It just jumped out of my mouth. So far on this trip, I'd been Sunny, Kaitlyn, and now Brenda. At least Snickers stayed the same.

Charley did not drive off. He seemed to be waiting for something. Finally I realized what it was. I opened my backpack, took out five of the twenty-dollar bills, and handed them to Charley. "Here's your down payment," I said.

One at a time he held each bill up to the light, checking to be sure it was not counterfeit.

"Thanks," he said, and pulled out into traffic.

I had never spent that much money at one time before. I hoped we'd go many, many miles in the four hours.

"Nice dog," Charley said. "What is he?"

"A mutt."

"Mutts are the best kind," Charley said.

"His name is Snickers." I almost added that we were taking a cab because the bus driver wouldn't let him on the bus, but I caught myself. I needed to be careful about how much information I divulged. I didn't know whether or not Rita had honored my request not to report me missing. Cops all over the country might be searching for me.

It dawned on me that even if Rita had reported me missing, nobody would be looking for a girl with a dog. Snickers was now part of my disguise.

"Good dog," I said as I patted his head. "Good Snickers."

Snickers put his head on my knee, heaved a sigh, and closed his eyes. I leaned my head on the back of the seat and closed my eyes, too. *I'm coming, Starr,* I thought. *I'm getting closer by the minute.*

A short time later I felt the cab stop. Looking out, I saw a sign that said WELCOME TO WYOMING. "You need to walk across the state line," Charley said. "You're a minor. I'm not certain, but I think I could get in trouble for driving you into a different state, even if you've asked me to do it."

I got out and walked past the sign while Charley pulled the cab ahead, into Wyoming. Then I climbed back in, we drove on, and I soon fell asleep.

I jerked awake when the cab stopped. We were parked at a highway rest area.

"Sorry to wake you," Charley said, "but this is the last rest area for a while."

I looked at my watch. Twelve-thirty. I had slept for more than an hour! "That's okay," I said. "I need to stretch."

While Charley was in the restroom, I snapped the leash on Snickers and led him to the dog-walk area. Then Charley held the leash while I took my turn in the restroom.

"I used to have a dog," Charley said as we pulled back onto the road. "A mutt named Freddie. He was a good dog."

"What happened to him?"

"He lives with my ex-wife. She got him when we divorced. We didn't have any kids, so we had a custody battle over the dog. She won."

"Do you ever see him?"

"No. She took him along when she moved back to Iowa, where she was from. I miss him a lot. More than I miss my ex-wife."

"Why don't you get another dog?" I asked.

"I will, someday. Right now I'm still missing Freddie."

I understood. A Hiss caseworker had once asked me why I was sad, and I told her I missed my friend Jessie. I'd left Jessie behind when I moved to a new foster home and I missed playing with her.

Using her cheerful kindergarten-teacher voice, Ms. Hiss had said, "You can make a new friend. Then you won't miss Jessie."

I had glared at her. A new friend would be nice, and I might make one, but that person wouldn't stop me from missing Jessie. The new friend would not know the secret code that Jessie and I had made up. She wouldn't call me Sunnysideup, or let me sleep with her stuffed elephant when I stayed at her house overnight. I felt like saying, "People are not interchangeable. If you lose one friend, you can't just substitute somebody else. It doesn't work that way."

I didn't say anything, though. If Ms. Hiss had to be told how friendship works, she wouldn't have understood what I was talking about.

The taxi approached a small town, and Charley asked if I was hungry. "There's a deli ahead," he said. "Might be a good time for some sandwiches."

We left Snickers in the cab while we went in, but we got our food to go so we could eat with him. Even with the windows rolled partway down, it was too warm to leave him in the vehicle. As promised, I paid for lunch.

I ordered a plain ham and cheese, no mayo, no oil and vinegar, for Snickers.

"Do you always feed your dog people food?" Charley asked.

"Only when we're traveling. It's easier than trying to carry dog food along."

Charley moved the cab to a shady spot, and we opened the doors while we ate.

I had just finished my sandwich when Charley asked, "Are you running away?"

"No," I said.

"I don't believe you," he said. "I'm not going to turn you in, if that's what you're thinking."

"Then why do you care?"

Charley shrugged. "I like you. You seem like a good kid, and you're nice to Snickers. People who are kind to animals can usually be trusted. I don't want to see you making a mistake."

"I'm going to see my sister," I said, then instantly regretted saying it.

"She lives in Enumclaw?"

"Look, Charley, I like you, too. It's real nice of you to take Snickers as a passenger and to drive so far knowing you'll just have to turn around and drive back by yourself. It's nice of you to worry about me, too, but I really don't want to get into a discussion about where I'm going. Okay?"

"Okay." He turned on the radio then and we listened to country western music and commercials while we drove on.

As it got close to three o'clock, when the four hours would be up, I watched out the window for a town. All I saw were acres and acres of empty fields, stretching as far as I could see. We were in the middle of ranch country, with no town in sight. It looked as if Snickers and I were going to walk a while today whether we wanted to or not. I was glad I'd bought a fresh bottle of water at the deli.

By 2:55, I began to get uneasy. It was isolated out here. What if some sleazebag came along and tried to get me to go with him? Would Snickers protect me again, or would he wag his tail as I was forced into Sleazebag's car? What if there was another tornado? Stop it, I told myself. Instead of imagining the worst possible scenario, try to think positive. Maybe Snickers and I could find a nice barn to sleep in overnight.

When the dashboard clock said 3:00, Charley pulled the cab onto the shoulder of the road and looked back at me. "Four hours are up," he said.

"Right."

Fences crowded the road on both sides. I didn't see a barn, or a farmer on a tractor, or even a silo or water tower in the distance.

I wanted to beg Charley to drive farther, but a deal's a deal and he had kept his end of the bargain. I snapped the leash on Snickers.

"Wait," Charley said. "I can't dump you off here, in the middle of nowhere. I'll drive you to the next town."

"What about your sore back?" I asked.

"I'll survive. I want to be sure you do, too."

"Thanks, Charley."

It was another fifteen minutes before we saw buildings. Calling it a town would be a stretch. There was a grain elevator by the railroad tracks, a ramshackle gas station, and a cluster of houses.

"Where do you want me to drop you?"

I didn't have much hope that a different bus driver would let me take Snickers along, but I didn't know what else to try. "The bus probably stops at the gas station," I said.

Charley pulled up to the gas pump and filled the tank. While he did that, I went inside. The gas station attendant, who wore bib overalls and no shirt, seemed surprised when I opened the door. I don't think he got a lot of customers.

"Does a bus stop here?" I asked. "Going west?"

He removed the toothpick from his mouth and said, "Yep."

"When does it come?"

He looked up at a big clock on the wall. "Usually goes through a little after six," he said.

"Goes through? It does stop here, doesn't it?"

"Yep. So long as you flag it down. Stand out there by the gas pump and when you see the bus coming, you wave your hands over your head so the driver knows to stop. Otherwise he don't bother."

I knew the routine, and hoped there were not any smart-aleck boys in this town.

I was sure I knew the answer to my next question, but I asked it anyway. "Do I buy a ticket first, or pay the driver?"

"You pay the driver."

I thanked him and went back outside. What was I going to do for almost three hours?

"The bus stops here," I told Charley.

He went inside to pay for his gas.

I walked Snickers to a sparse patch of grass and wondered what I would do if this bus driver refused to allow a dog on board.

14

When Charley returned, Snickers wagged
his tail as if Charley had been gone all day. Charley leaned down and scratched Snickers behind both
ears. As I watched, I had an idea.

"I have a favor to ask of you," I said. "A huge favor."

"Now, I hope you aren't going to tell me you don't
have the other hundred bucks, because I would not be a
happy man if you tried to cheat me."

"I have the money," I said. I quickly took five more
twenty-dollar bills out of my backpack and handed them
to Charley. This time he put them in his wallet without
holding them up to the light first.

"So, what's the favor?"

"Would you keep Snickers for a few days? Once I get to my sister's house, I'll be able to come back and get him. That should only be a week or so, and I can pay you for his food."

"You want me to board your dog."

"I'd get there a lot faster if I was traveling alone, and I know you'd be good to Snickers."

"You could put him in a kennel."

I looked around the sorry excuse for a town. "What kennel?" I said. "Even if there was a boarding kennel, Snickers would be miserable. He'd think I had abandoned him. He needs a warm bed and somebody to pet him and play with him and take him for walks." I could feel the tears trying to leak out of my eyes, and I blinked to keep them from falling. "I'm afraid the bus driver won't let me take Snickers on board," I said. "The last driver wouldn't take him. We had to walk, and we were caught in a terrible tornado. Snickers already knows you, and likes you. He wouldn't be scared if he stayed with you." My bottom lip trembled, and I bit it, to make it stop.

"Where are your parents?" Charley asked.

"I never knew my dad. My mom was killed in an accident ten years ago, and so was my grandma."

"Who do you live with now?"

"I'd rather not say."

"Look, Brenda, if that's your name. If you are going to trust me with Snickers, who loves you and who is your loyal companion, then you should be able to trust me enough to tell me the truth."

I hesitated.

"I think you could use some help right now," Charley said, "and I don't mind giving it to you, but I can't do it unless I know exactly what's going on. You need to level with me."

"If I do, will you keep it to yourself? Not tell anyone?"

"I can't promise that without knowing what you're going to tell me."

I looked at the concern in Charley's eyes and thought what my options were.

I decided to take a chance.

"My name is Sunny Skyland," I said. "I was separated from my twin sister when our mom died, and I haven't seen or heard about her since. I've been in a string of foster homes; I don't know where Starr is, but I hope to find her soon."

"Why are you going to Enumclaw, if you don't know where she is?"

I showed him the photo, and what was written on

the back. I explained my plan to find the house and talk to the people who live there now, and maybe the neighbors.

"Where did you get the cash?" Charley asked.

"I found a bag of money, just like I said, and I tried to find the owner, but nobody claimed it, so I'm using the money to look for Starr."

"Does your foster family know about this, or did you run away?"

"I ran away. But I left a note so my foster mom would know I hadn't been abducted."

"Were the foster people mean to you?"

"Not this time. My current foster mom is actually the best one I've ever had. Rita lives by herself and she's smart and nice."

"Why didn't you ask her to help you find your sister?"

I stared at Charley. It had never occurred to me to ask Rita to help me. I was used to living with people who didn't care about me. I was used to keeping my dreams secret. I realized Rita would have helped me, if I'd asked her to.

"I thought it was something I had to do by myself."

"You could call her now."

I shook my head. "Rita would make me come home. Even if she was willing to help me find Starr, she'd want me to come home first. I've gone through a lot to make it this far. I want to go the rest of the way, and see if I can find Starr by myself."

We stood quietly for a moment while Charley thought about what I'd told him. "So, will you take care of Snickers for me?" I asked.

"On one condition."

"What's that?"

"You let me call this Rita and tell her you're okay."

"She'll trace the call. She'll send Hiss after me."

"Who?"

"The social workers who run the foster-care system. If Rita told them I'm gone, which she probably did, she'd have to let them know that she's heard from me. They'd be here instantly to drag me back and probably put me in a different foster home, or maybe even in juvenile detention."

"You like this Rita?"

"Yes. I like her a lot."

"Do you know how much she's probably worrying about you? She has no idea if you're okay or if you're lying in a ditch somewhere with a knife in your back."

I knew Charley was right. Rita was undoubtedly frantic with fear over my safety.

"I'll use a public phone to call my brother in Florida," Charley said. "Then I'll ask him to call Rita from a public phone down there. He'll do it, no questions asked. He won't say anything except that you're okay and you'll be in touch with her soon."

I felt guilty about making Rita worry after she'd been so good to me, and Charley's plan sounded foolproof. Rita would know I was okay, Hiss wouldn't find me, I'd get on the bus for sure, and Snickers would be safe.

"Deal," I said.

We shook hands. Charley wrote his name, address, and phone number on the back of the gas receipt and handed it to me. "Here's my card," he said, grinning. "Call me when you're ready to pick up your pal."

I put the paper in my backpack. Then I wrote Rita's name and number on a sheet of my notebook paper and gave it to him. I set the box of dog biscuits, the water dish, and the plastic bags on the floor of the cab. "Thanks, Charley," I said.

"Do you have enough money left?" he asked. "If you don't, I can lend you some, and you can pay me back later."

"I'm okay," I told him, "but thanks for offering."

I hugged Snickers. "Be a good dog," I told him. "Charley's going to feed you and take care of you until I can come back for you." Again, I blinked back tears. For years I had prided myself on being a tough kid who never cried. Now I was on the verge of bawling practically every other minute. Snickers gave my cheek a big slurp, and I lost it, letting my tears fall onto his fur. I felt Charley's hand, patting my shoulder.

"He'll be fine," Charley said. "I'll take good care of him."

I took a deep breath, and put Snickers in the cab.

"Good luck," Charley said. "If you get into trouble, call me."

I stood in the dirt beside the gas pump and watched the cab drive away. The last thing I glimpsed was Snickers's nose, pressed to the back window, watching me. I hoped I was doing the right thing. Although I missed Snickers already, I knew he'd be better off with Charley than he would be traveling with me.

Once again, I was by myself. *The story of my life*, I thought as I found a shady spot where I could wait for the bus.

15

Without Snickers by my side, the bus driver hardly looked at me. I waved, he stopped, I paid my fare—and the next afternoon I was in Auburn, Washington. A meal, a shower, a night in a motel, and then I boarded a Metro bus. This time when I got off, I was in Enumclaw. Was Starr here, too? For the first time since our mother's funeral, were my twin and I in the same town?

My first stop was a Welcome Center, where a friendly man asked if he could help me.

"I need a map of Enumclaw," I told him.

"We have two," he said. "Take one of each." He removed two maps from a holder and handed them to me.

"There's plenty of other information," he told me, nodding toward a rack of brochures for various attractions. "There's lots to do in this area."

I thanked him and hurried out the door. I went into a small café called The Hornet's Nest, ordered a soda, and studied the maps. I decided to start with what appeared to be the two main streets, Griffin and Cole. I'd walk down one and look for number 1041. If I found it, I'd compare the house with the one in my picture and either knock on the door or go a block over and see if there was a number 1041 there. How many 1041s could there be?

If I didn't find a 1041 on the main streets, I'd keep looking, one street at a time, until I found my house.

The adrenaline began pumping as I paid for my drink and went back outside. I was close now. I might find the right 1041 today. Maybe I would even find Starr today!

At the corner, I noticed a cardboard Garage Sale sign taped to a telephone pole. Half a block away, the front yard of one house contained card tables filled with household merchandise for sale. As my eyes swept the scene, I saw a bicycle at the edge of the sale. I hurried closer. A sticker on the handlebars said ten dollars. It was a plain blue bike with no extra gears, but I knew I could travel a whole lot faster on a bike than I could if I walked.

"Is that your best price?" I asked the woman who was running the sale.

"It's a good bike," she replied. "You can try it, if you want to."

I mounted the bike and rode it a short way down the street. When I returned, the woman said, "I'd take eight dollars for it."

"Sold." I paid her and pedaled away, watching the house numbers as I rode.

It took me only ten minutes to find a house numbered 1031. Thinking I was close, I rode slowly, but the next house was 1051. I rode to the next street, where the numbers jumped from 1031 to 1043. It seemed that every street had a 1031, but instead of progressing to 1041, they skipped up to higher numbers.

Many of the homes were ramblers. In the picture, my family stood in front of a two-story house, with steps leading to a front porch.

I continued to ride my bike around Enumclaw, going farther away from the downtown area.

It was mid-afternoon when I found a house numbered 1041. The numbers themselves were missing, but I could see the outline of where they had been, over the porch. As soon as I saw the house, I knew it was the right one. The redbrick chimney matched the photo. A large fir tree grew off to the side, in the area between the sidewalk and the house. The tree seemed familiar, like an acquaintance whose name I couldn't remember. The tree couldn't be seen in the picture, yet I was sure it had been there when the photo was taken.

The house needed paint, and the roof shingles were dotted with patches of green moss. Dandelions had gone to seed in the front lawn and the seeds had blown away, leaving behind empty stems.

As I looked at the house, I saw Starr and myself as we had been in the picture—two happy little girls posing with their grandma and her dog while their mom aimed the camera. We had played in this yard, and slept in this house. This very same house!

Even though it now needed some repair, I felt a deep fondness for the house where I had lived with Mama and Grandma and Starr. This had been my home.

Feeling as if I had traveled backward in time, I walked up the porch steps and knocked on the door. A woman opened it about an inch, leaving a chain in place.

"I'm looking for some people who used to live in this house," I said. "Their last name was Skyland."

"I don't know them."

"Have you lived here long?" I asked.

"That isn't any of your business."

"I'm sorry," I said. "I'm trying to find my sister. We used to live here. I have an old picture of us standing in this yard with our grandma."

The woman's eyes softened slightly. "We rent this house," she said. "I don't know who lived here before we did. You'd have to ask the owner."

"What's the owner's name?"

"I don't know that, either. We pay the rent to a property management company. Just a minute, I'll get their card." She handed a business card through the crack. I thanked her and walked down the steps, feeling discouraged. I wasn't likely to find someone at a big company who would help me. Privacy rules would probably prevent them from telling me the owner's name.

I went to the house next door and knocked, but nobody answered. Nobody answered at the house on the other side, either. I would have to come back in the evening, when people were more likely to be at home.

As I nudged the kickstand up with my foot, I saw movement at the window of the house across the street, and realized someone was watching me. I wheeled my bike over there and approached the door. Before I could ring the bell, the door opened. A white-haired woman in an orange and blue flowered muumuu said, "What are you selling?"

"I'm not selling anything." I held up my empty hands. "I'm looking for someone who used to live there," I said, pointing. "I wonder if you might know where she is."

"Who are you looking for?"

"Her last name was Skyland."

"She's gone. Loretta Skyland was killed in a car wreck years ago, and her daughter, too."

Chills ran up my arms. This woman had known my grandma and my mother. "Loretta was my grandma," I said. "My sister and I lived with her when we were little. So did my mom."

"You're one of the twins?" The woman's eyes widened. "You're one of Marie's girls?"

I swallowed the lump in my throat. "Yes. I'm Sunny."

The woman opened the door wider and waved me inside. "Come in," she said. "I'm Connie. I'll fix us some tea."

I followed her into the kitchen and watched while she filled an old kettle with water and put it on the stove. "Sunny," she said, as if trying to remember more about me. "Sunny. You're the one who went to live with Loretta's sister. What was her name?"

"Cora. My great-aunt, Cora."

"Cora! Yes, that's right. Cora. Is she still living?"

"I don't know. I didn't stay with her very long. She sent me to live with her son."

"Jerod? That no-good who caused her nothing but trouble from the day he was born? He took you?" She sounded genuinely shocked.

"He didn't keep me long, either."

"Well, that's no surprise. I can't imagine Jerod putting himself out for anyone, not even an orphaned cousin. Where did he send you?"

I didn't want to go through the whole long list of people I'd lived with, so I said, "I became a ward of the state. I've been in foster homes."

"Maybe you were better off that way. Jerod had a mean streak." Connie poured tea into two china teacups, placed them on matching saucers, and set them on the table.

I sat across from her. "Now I'm looking for my sister, Starr. I hoped someone here in the neighborhood would know where she went to live."

"You came to the right place," she said.

"You know where she is?"

"I don't know exactly where she is now, but I know who took her after the accident. It was the Andersons, Al and Becky Anderson. They used to live down the street, and they didn't have any children, and when Loretta's sister said she could take only one of you girls, Becky and Al offered to adopt the other one." Connie's head bobbed up and down as she spoke, as if confirming her own facts. "They were a nice young couple."

Knowing how many rules and regulations Hiss has about foster kids, I was amazed that Starr and I had apparently been placed in new homes without anyone ever notifying the authorities.

"You said the Andersons used to live in this neighborhood. Do you know where they went?"

"No. They moved not long after they took the girl," she said. "Becky said they needed a bigger yard, with room for a swing set."

"Did any of your current neighbors live here back then?" I asked. "Maybe someone else kept in touch with them."

"No. The street has changed a lot these past few years." She shook her head sadly. "Nobody stays put anymore. They move in, live here a year or two, and move on. Some of the houses are rentals, and they're all owned by the same company. I think the company's trying to buy the whole block so they can tear everything down and build condominiums." Connie sipped her tea. "It isn't like it used to be, when folks raised their family in one spot."

"Do you have a telephone directory that I could look at?" I asked. Anderson was a common last name, but maybe first names would be listed.

"You aren't going to make a long distance call, are you?" Connie asked. "My phone bill's too high as it is."

"I'm not going to call anyone," I said. "I only want to see if there's a listing for Al and Becky Anderson. Maybe they still live in Enumclaw, and I can find their address."

She handed me the directory, and I turned to the *A* section. Several Andersons were listed, but no Al and no Becky. However, there were two Andersons with the initial *A*. I copied down both addresses.

"If you want to call the Andersons, it's okay," Connie said. "As long as it's a local call."

I could tell she was curious as a cat to know if one of the names in the directory was the one I wanted.

"I think it will be better if I go in person," I said. "Thanks for the tea and for your help."

"You let me know if you find your twin," Connie said. "I always liked Loretta. She made the best banana bread."

I rode back to the main part of town to get something to eat. While I ate, I marked the addresses for the two A. Andersons on my map. One was only eight blocks away; the other was a couple of miles east of town.

I tried the closer house first. When I rang the bell, a chorus of barking dogs erupted. They yipped and yapped so loudly that I didn't hear the door click. A young man with purple spiked hair put his foot in the door to keep a pack of Chihuahuas from rushing out.

"Stay back!" he said. "No barking!" The dogs kept yapping.

The heavy silver chains around the man's neck clinked as he edged out the door. He kept it cracked open, and the dogs pressed their noses to the crack, sniffing and barking.

"I'm looking for Al and Becky Anderson," I said.

"Not here."

"Are you Mr. Anderson?"

"I am, but my name isn't Al. It's Aaron."

"Sorry to have bothered you," I said.

He used his foot to shove the dogs back so that he could go inside. The door closed, but the barking continued.

I rode to the other address, hoping I was not nearing a dead end in my search. If this was not the right Anderson, what would I do next? How would I find Starr?

As I pedaled along, the homes I passed became bigger. Most had three-car garages and large lots. The address, when I found it, was a big white house with green shutters. Window boxes bloomed with pink geraniums and the lush green lawn made me want to walk barefoot on it. It was the kind of house you see on the cover of a magazine. While I sat on my bike, looking at the house, a young boy rode by on a scooter.

"Hi," I said. "Do you live around here?"

He stopped. "I live on the corner."

"I'm looking for the Anderson family," I told him. "Do you know if this is where they live?"

"That's it," he said.

"Do they have any kids?"

"Nope. No kids."

I tried to swallow my disappointment. This wasn't the right Anderson, either.

"They have a teenager, though," the boy said. "She babysits me sometimes."

A teenager! My scalp tingled as I asked, "What's her name?"

"Starr."

I could barely breathe. This was Starr's home. I had found her! I felt like shouting to the skies, *I found her! I found my twin sister!* but I tried to stay calm. I didn't want this little kid to be the first to know who I was. I wanted Starr to be first.

The boy pushed off on his scooter, rode down the street, and turned into the driveway of the corner house.

Suddenly I was aware of how scruffy I looked. Maybe I should get cleaned up before I went to the door. I wanted Starr's first impression of me to be favorable. I sat on my bike and debated. One part of me wanted to rush to the door and another part of me didn't. I realized my hesitation had nothing to do with my appearance. I was frightened. I felt the way I had the one time I had been in a school play, just before I went on stage—nervous, afraid I'd make a mistake, scared the audience wouldn't like me.

I had dreamed of my reunion with Starr for so long. In my dreams, it was always the same. I told her my name, she gasped and flung her arms around me. We cried tears of joy and swore we would never again be separated. Never!

Starr won't care what I'm wearing, I told myself. *She'll be so glad to see me that nothing else will matter.* I got off my bike and started up the curved brick path that led to Starr's front door.

16

I approached the house slowly. A honeysuckle twined around a trellis near the door, and I paused to inhale the sweet scent. After imagining this moment for so many years, now that it was here I wanted to savor it. It was really happening at last; I was about to be reunited with Starr.

My heart beat faster as I rang the doorbell.

A girl my age opened it. My eyes swept over her, noting the similarities. She had the same oval face as I have, the same dimple in the left cheek. Her hair was the color mine had been until I dyed it. It was Starr!

I could barely speak over the lump in my throat. Finally I managed to whisper, "Hi, Starr. I'm Sunny."

She raised her eyebrows, looking quizzical. "Who?" she said.

"I'm Sunny," I repeated.

She still looked blank.

"Your twin sister."

"You have the wrong house," she replied. "I don't have a sister." She started to close the door.

"Wait!" I said. "You were born on April tenth, right? And your mom was killed in a car accident when you were three."

A voice from behind Starr said, "Who is it, honey?"

"You'd better come," she said. "It's some girl claiming she's my sister."

A blond woman wearing a blue sweatsuit appeared behind Starr. She gasped when she saw me. Even with my dark hair, I could tell she saw the resemblance.

"Are you Becky Anderson?" I asked.

"Yes."

"I'm Sunny Skyland," I said. "I'm Starr's twin sister."

"I told her she has the wrong address, that I don't have a sister," Starr said. "You tell her, Mom. Maybe she'll listen to you."

The woman said, "I'm Starr's mother. Her adoptive mother. Come in, Sunny. We need to talk."

Starr gaped as her mother held the door for me.

Mrs. Anderson sat in an overstuffed chair, and motioned for me to sit, too. I chose the sofa. Starr remained standing.

"As you can see," Mrs. Anderson said, "this is something of a shock to us."

"Mother!" Starr said. "Are you saying I do have a sister? I'm a twin?"

"Yes," Mrs. Anderson said. "When your mother was killed, you and Sunny were separated. We got you, and Sunny went to your grandmother's sister." She looked at me. "Isn't that right?"

"Yes," I said. "She didn't keep me, though."

"She didn't?" Mrs. Anderson seemed stunned by that news. "But she loved you! She loved both of you. She wept when she signed the document that allowed us to adopt Starr. She only did it because she knew she couldn't possibly cope with two young children."

"Why didn't you tell me?" Starr said. She looked furious. Instead of being thrilled to find me again, she was angry at her mother for having kept me a secret.

"Your dad and I did not intend to deceive you," Mrs. Anderson said. "At first we had planned to arrange visits so that you girls would remain close, but you never talked about your twin. You never wondered where Sunny was, or said you missed her. If you had asked about your sister we would have tried to contact her, but you never once mentioned Sunny. As the months went by, it seemed best for us not to bring up the subject, either. You were happy; you had adjusted well. You didn't seem to miss your family, or your old life. We were afraid if we talked about your past, about your mother and your grandma and your sister, it would only stir up your grief."

The words hurt terribly. During those times when I had cried myself to sleep every night, missing Starr, she had not even asked where I was.

Mrs. Anderson continued, "We never heard from your great-aunt Cora, so we assumed she had made the same decision about not keeping in touch. After your adoption was final, and your last name was the same as ours, we decided to let the past be forgotten."

Starr sank into a chair, looking shocked.

Mrs. Anderson turned to me. "If your great-aunt didn't keep you, Sunny, where have you been?" she asked. "Who raised you?"

"First I went to live with her son, but he abandoned me. Since then I've been in a series of foster homes."

Starr stared at me as if I'd said I'd been living on Mars.

"Oh, my," Mrs. Anderson said. "Oh, that's terrible! We wanted both of you. At the time, I said it didn't seem right to separate twins, but everyone felt you should stay with a blood relative, if possible, and Cora swore she wanted one of you but couldn't handle both of you." She stood suddenly and told Starr, "I need to call your father."

"By all means," Starr said. "Let's hear what Daddy's excuse is for not telling me the truth all these years."

Mrs. Anderson clamped her lips together, clearly stung by her daughter's words. Then, without replying, she went to the phone and dialed. "Al?" she said. "Can you come home? Starr's sister just showed up."

They talked briefly while I looked at Starr and she looked at the floor.

"He's on his way," Mrs. Anderson said, after she hung up. She returned to her chair. "You say you've been in foster care," she said to me. "Here in Enumclaw?"

"In Nebraska."

"Nebraska! You've been living in Nebraska?"

"Yes. Great-aunt Cora's son took me along when he moved there."

"Who brought you here?" She looked out the window, as if expecting to see a car waiting for me out front.

"I came alone. Mostly I took the bus. A cab driver helped me. I walked a lot."

"Your foster parents let you take off across the country all by yourself?"

I hesitated. Should I tell the truth? I didn't want to begin my new life with Starr by telling lies. "My foster mom didn't know I was going," I said. "She doesn't know about my sister."

"You ran away?" Starr said.

"I had to find you," I said. "All these years, I've thought about you every day. When I finally had enough money to travel, I knew I had to look for you."

"But how did you know where to look?" Mrs. Anderson asked. "Starr has our last name now, and we moved years ago."

I handed her the picture. "It says Enumclaw, Washington, on the back," I said, "and you can see a house number. I decided the best way to find Starr would be to come to Enumclaw and see if I could find the house that's in the picture, so that's what I did. I hoped some of the neighbors might remember Mama and Grandma and us. One neighbor did remember; she told me your name."

"I'll bet it was Mrs. Polson," Mrs. Anderson said. "Connie Polson lives across the street from where you girls used to live. She is a big snoop, always watching everyone in the neighborhood. She's lived in the same house for decades."

"That's right," I said. "Connie Polson told me you took Starr, and I found your address in the telephone directory."

"So some old woman knows I have a twin sister?" Starr stood and began pacing around the room. "She knew all this time, but I didn't! She's probably told half the town. Everyone knows my background except me!"

Before Mrs. Anderson could answer, a man in a business suit rushed in. He stopped when he saw me. "Hello, Sunny," he said. "I'm Al Anderson, Starr's dad."

I stood, and we shook hands. Then he wrapped his arms around me and gave me a hug.

"Except for the hair color," Mrs. Anderson said, "she's a mirror image of Starr."

"She is not!" Starr declared. "How can you say that? She doesn't look anything at all like me. We probably aren't even related. Where's the proof?"

"She has a picture of the two of you, with your grandmother," Mrs. Anderson pointed out.

"That doesn't prove anything. Anyone could find an old photograph and pretend it was their own. She's probably an imposter who wants to con you out of your money."

"Calm down, Starr," Mr. Anderson said.

I couldn't believe how angry Starr was. I understood why she felt deceived at not knowing about me, but she must realize the secret had been kept with the best of intentions. If anyone had a right to be angry, it was me. Here were the Andersons, who seemed like nice people, telling me that they had wanted to adopt me. Instead of living with She-Who and the Boss of the World, I could have been here, with Starr. All these years, I could have been loved.

What bothered me the most, though, was that Starr apparently did not remember me. How could she forget the experiences that I cherished?

"If you're my sister," Starr said, "prove it."

"Our grandma was Loretta Skyland," I said, "and our mother's name was Marie Skyland."

"You could learn that from public records, or from an old obituary notice," Starr said. "Tell us something that isn't available in print or online."

"We used to play house," I told her. "We had white

wicker doll buggies and we pretended that our dolls were twins, the same as we were."

"I remember those buggies!" Mrs. Anderson said. "Loretta used to let you push them around the neighborhood, while she sat on the porch and watched."

Starr's expression changed. I suspected she *did* remember pushing our dolls in the wicker buggies.

"Do you remember our song?" I asked. I sang, "Twinkie, Twinkie, little star."

"It's twinkle, twinkle," Starr said, "not Twinkie, Twinkie."

"Not in our version." I stared at her. "You don't remember eating Twinkies and watching the stars come out?"

"No."

"We were in lawn chairs in the backyard. I was in Grandma's lap and you were in Mama's. We had blankets tucked around us and I remember feeling snug and safe." Again, I thought I saw a flicker of remembrance in Starr's eyes.

"I ate my Twinkie," I said, "while Mama sang, *Twinkie, Twinkie, little star.*"

"I don't like Twinkies," Starr said. "They're too sweet."

"You don't remember any of it?" I asked.

"No, and I'm not convinced you do, either. Maybe you're making all this up."

I felt as if a dark shade had been pulled across the sky, blocking out the sun. Starr didn't remember me. She didn't remember the Twinkies, or the song, or playing together. She didn't remember having a sister. What's more, she didn't *want* to remember.

"How can you forget your twin sister?" I whispered.

"I was only three," Starr said.

"So was I."

17

I looked down, twisting my hands in my lap. This reunion was nothing like the one I had envisioned. "Maybe I ought to leave," I said.

"No!" said Mrs. Anderson. "Please don't go yet. We want to know all about you, and what's happened to you over the years."

"It doesn't sound as if you've had much stability," Mr. Anderson said. "Not the life you would have had if they had let us take you both. I wonder why Cora didn't call us if she couldn't keep you herself. She knew we wanted you."

"She probably still wanted Sunny to stay in her family,"

Mrs. Anderson said. "And she hadn't heard from us. Maybe we were wrong not to keep in touch."

"That's water over the dam," Mr. Anderson said. "The important thing now is to find out what red tape we need to cut in order for Sunny to stay here for a while."

"What?" Starr exploded. "You're inviting her to live with us? We don't even know her!"

"I can't think of a better way to get acquainted," Mr. Anderson said. "Sunny, could you stay with us for the summer? And then, come fall, we can all decide if you should stay permanently."

"I've already decided," Starr said.

No one asked what her decision was. We knew.

Mrs. Anderson said, "We should start by calling the foster mother. We must do that anyway, to let her know that Sunny is with us and that she's safe."

For the first time, calling Rita sounded like a good idea to me. I wanted to talk to her; I wanted to get her opinion about what I should do. "I'll call her," I said.

"I am going upstairs," Starr announced, and she stomped out of the room. Her mother followed her.

I dialed Rita's number. When she answered, I said, "Hi, Rita. It's Sunny."

"Sunny! Are you all right?"

"I'm fine. I'm sorry I worried you, but . . ."

"Worried me? Do you have any idea how scared I've been?" I heard Rita pause and could tell she was trying to get herself centered, as she called it. "Where are you?"

"I'm in Enumclaw, Washington."

"Washington! I thought you were in Florida. I got a call from someone telling me you were okay, and I had the call traced to Florida. What are you doing in Washington?"

"I found my twin sister."

There was a stunned silence. Then Rita said, "You never told me you have a sister."

"We were separated when we were three. I didn't know where she was until today."

"Have you seen her?"

"Yes. I'm at her house now."

"How's it going?" Leave it to Rita to cut right to the important part. It was as if she could tell from my voice that I was unhappy.

"Not exactly like I thought. Starr got adopted right after we were split up. Her parents want me to stay here with them for the summer."

"I see. Is that what you want to do?"

"I—I don't know. When I left, I thought I wanted to

be with Starr more than anything in the world, but now that I'm here, I'm not sure. We haven't had much time together yet. She—she doesn't remember me."

"Oh, Sunny, I'm so sorry."

"Yeah. Me, too."

"How did you get there? Where did you get enough money for such a trip?"

I told Rita about the bag of money I'd found and my efforts to locate the owner.

"Let me speak to one of Starr's parents," she said.

I held the receiver toward Mr. Anderson. "She wants to talk to you," I said.

The two adults spoke for a few minutes. I heard Mr. Anderson give Rita his phone number. Then he gave the phone back to me.

"I told him you could stay for a week," Rita said. "That's *if* you want to stay that long. Do you?"

Did I? I wasn't at all sure, but I'd gone through so much to get here, it seemed as if I should stay the week, no matter how unwelcoming Starr was. Once she got used to me, she'd probably warm up. "Yes," I said.

"Then I'll get you a plane ticket to come home next Thursday. Even if it turns out that you want to return and stay there longer, you'd still need to come back here first and go through the channels with the foster-care system."

"Okay," I said.

"Is this what you really want to do?" Rita asked. "You don't sound sure."

"If I leave now, I'll always think I should have stayed and tried to make it work."

"Call me if you want to come home sooner. Call any time, day or night," Rita said. "It's all right to call collect. I'll accept the charges."

"Thanks."

"You want to know how worried I've been?" Rita asked. "I ate a whole package of Oreo cookies! I bought them to have on hand in case you came home, and then it was typical stress eating; they were gone before I knew I had opened the package."

"I'm flattered," I said. I had never seen a cookie enter Rita's mouth. She had never bought cookies for me before.

"I'm trying to make you feel guilty, not flattered."

"Rita, there's one more thing," I said. "I have a dog now."

"A dog!"

"He's staying with a friend of mine and I need to make arrangements to pick him up."

"Where did you get a dog?"

"It's kind of a complicated story," I said. "I found Snickers in a restaurant parking lot, and he was homeless, the same as me, so—"

"You are not homeless," Rita interrupted. "You have a home here with me. You will always have a home here."

"I adopted Snickers," I said, "but the bus driver wouldn't let me take him on the bus so we had to walk and we got caught in a tornado and—"

Rita interrupted again. "A tornado! Were you outdoors in that awful tornado? I saw pictures of it on the news."

"Yes. I wasn't hurt, but Snickers got hit on the head and was unconscious. We stayed overnight at a Red Cross shelter and then I met Charley, who's a cab driver, and he drove me more than four hours, and then I asked him to keep Snickers until I could come for him. I need to go get Snickers as soon as I can."

"You are a girl of many surprises," Rita said. "Let me speak to Mr. Anderson again, please. Maybe he can get Snickers and take him to Enumclaw and then I'll make arrangements for Snickers to fly home on your flight."

I gave the phone to Mr. Anderson. He listened a minute and then said, "The dog can't stay here. Starr is afraid of dogs."

"Snickers is as gentle as a kitten!" I said. "He wouldn't hurt anyone and I'll take care of him. He won't be any trouble."

"If I go get the dog," Mr. Anderson told me, "we'll board him at a kennel until you leave. Where is this dog?"

I got out Charley's address and told him the name of the town. It turned out that Charley lived almost as close to Rita as he did to the Andersons, so in the end, Rita said she would go get Snickers herself. "It will give me something to do while I wait for you to come home," she said, "and the dog will be waiting when you get here."

After we finished talking to Rita, I called Charley.

"Hey!" he said. "Glad to hear from you. Did you find your sister?"

"Yes. I'm at her house now."

I told him the plan and asked if it was okay for Snickers to stay with him for a few more days, until Rita could pick him up.

"He can stay as long as he wants," Charley said. "I was kind of hoping you wouldn't come back for him so I could keep him."

"No chance," I said. "Thanks, Charley."

When I'd completed my call, Mr. Anderson said, "You're probably tired. Maybe you'd like to rest a bit before dinner."

As soon as he said it, I realized I was exhausted. Besides riding my bike for hours, this had been an emotional few days, especially this afternoon. My thoughts were still whirling like the tail of the tornado, and I longed to lie down and replay everything that had happened, to try to sort it out.

Mrs. Anderson came in. "We're going to give Sunny the den for now," she said.

"What about Starr's room? She has twin beds," Mr. Anderson said. "No pun intended."

"I think Sunny needs some privacy," Mrs. Anderson said. What she probably meant was, Starr will throw a fit if we make her share her room, even with her twin sister.

"The den will be great," I said.

"Do you have luggage?" Mr. Anderson asked.

"Just my backpack. I left my bike out in front."

"Let's put it in the garage, where it's safe," he said. I followed him to the garage and watched while he pushed a button that made one of the garage doors open. I got my bike and wheeled it in beside a new Prius.

"You're going to need more clothes," Mrs. Anderson said as she led me to the den. "Tomorrow we'll go shopping. Starr loves to shop. Do you?"

"Yes," I said, although the only time anyone had ever taken me shopping was when Rita bought me new clothes when I first went to live with her. We'd had a great time that day. She let me try on anything I wanted, and then I'd step out of the dressing room to show her how I looked and we'd decide if we liked the item or not.

It wasn't only the new clothes that made this a happy memory; it was the feeling I'd had that someone cared about me and wanted me to look good. I realized Rita had given me more than jeans and tops that day; she had given me love.

Her words came back to me: *You'll always have a home here.* I realized how foolish I'd been to assume that once I found Starr, I'd instantly have a permanent home. I'd had a simplistic dream for a complicated situation.

Mrs. Anderson opened a hide-a-bed that was already made up with sheets and a blanket. "For now, you can sleep here," she said. "There's a bathroom across the hall. Let me know if you need anything."

"Thanks," I said.

"I'm glad you're here, Sunny," she said. "Starr will be glad, too, once she gets used to the idea. She's really a wonderful girl."

"I should have called first, instead of just showing up."

"It doesn't matter. You rest now, and we'll talk later."

I went across to the bathroom and took a long shower and shampooed my hair. According to the information that had come in the box of dye, it would take twenty-eight shampoos before my hair returned to its natural color. However, I had not left the dye on the full amount of time, so it was already beginning to fade, and I wanted to hurry that process along. I knew the resemblance to Starr would be greater if our hair was the same color.

I lay on the bed, trying to put myself in Starr's place. How would I feel if a stranger appeared with no warning and claimed to be my twin sister? I'd probably feel apprehensive, too, if I had no memory of a sister, but I didn't think I'd be as negative as Starr was. I would be curious. Whether I liked the idea or not, I'd want to know who my sister was and what her life had been like since we were separated.

Dinner that night was strained. Mr. and Mrs. Anderson tried to ignite the conversation, but I felt ill at ease.

Starr gave only one-syllable answers to questions and appeared not to listen when I talked.

"Starr is a poet," Mr. Anderson told me. "She's been writing poetry for years. Do you write poetry, Sunny?"

"No," I said. "I love to read it, though. I used to read only novels, but Rita likes poetry and she got me started on that." I turned to Starr. "I'd like to read some of your poems."

When Starr didn't respond, Mr. Anderson said, "You'll be impressed. Starr has a lot of talent."

I took a bite of my baked potato.

"Tell us about Rita," Mrs. Anderson said.

"She's single," I said. "She works at home most of the time, editing a business journal. One day a week she teaches yoga classes."

"How long have you been with her?"

"Five months." It seemed longer than that. In some ways, I felt as if I'd known Rita for many years.

"So you don't have a long-term relationship," Mr. Anderson said. "She probably wouldn't fight to keep you."

I put down my fork and looked at him, surprised. Was he saying they wanted me to live with them permanently? Starr looked horrified, and I knew she was wondering the same thing.

"Rita lets me make my own decisions," I said.

18

While we ate brownies for dessert, Mrs. Anderson said, "What shall we do tomorrow? Do you girls want to pack a picnic and go up to see the wildflowers? They should be in full bloom at this time of year."

"I'm going swimming with Abby tomorrow," Starr said.

"Do you have a swimsuit with you, Sunny?" Mrs. Anderson asked.

"No."

"We'll buy you one, first thing tomorrow. We can see the wildflowers another day."

"Mother," Starr said, "Abby invited me to go swimming at her club. I can't just bring along an extra person."

"Of course you can. If you call Abby and tell her that your twin sister is here, I'm sure she'll be eager to meet Sunny."

"No," I said. "It's okay. Starr, you go ahead with your plans. I'll be fine. Really."

"Then the two of us will go shopping," Mrs. Anderson declared.

And that's what we did. While Starr was off swimming with her friend, Mrs. Anderson took me to a dozen stores. It was almost like shopping with Rita. Almost. The differences were that Mrs. Anderson never looked at the price tags, and she didn't make me feel special, the way Rita had. I got the feeling Mrs. Anderson wanted me to be well dressed so as not to reflect poorly on Starr.

I felt ashamed for having such thoughts when Mrs. Anderson was being so nice to me. I pushed them aside and promised myself I'd make every effort to be friendly to Starr, no matter how much of a brat she was.

By the end of the afternoon, I had two new pairs of jeans, a pair of shorts, three tops, a sweater, some socks and underwear, new sandals, and a pink duffel bag that was the right size to fit in the overhead luggage space on my flight home. She also took me to a bookstore and let me choose a couple of new novels.

"Thank you," I told Mrs. Anderson. "I love everything you got for me."

"I hope this is only the first of many shopping trips," she replied. "Next time, Starr can come with us. Even though you and Starr are fraternal twins rather than identical twins, you have the same sweet personality." I didn't know what to say to that, so I said nothing.

When we got home from shopping, there was a voice-mail message from Starr saying she'd been invited to stay at Abby's for dinner and would be home around eight. Mrs. Anderson looked angry when she listened to the message, but she didn't call Starr and tell her she had to come home.

Mr. Anderson arrived home from work shortly after we returned from shopping. "I thought I'd take my girls out to dinner, to celebrate being together," he said.

"Starr is eating at Abby's house," Mrs. Anderson said.

His eyes narrowed briefly before he said, "Do you like Mexican food, Sunny?"

"It's my favorite."

"Then that's what we'll do."

We had a delicious dinner at a Mexican restaurant and then they showed me the town's public art. There was a huge loggers memorial sculpture that showed a pair of oxen pulling a downed tree while a logger urged them on. "Logging was an important industry here for many years," Mr. Anderson explained.

They showed me two other sculptures. My favorite was a bronze colt that stood on a street corner in the downtown area. I had seen it when I went to the visitor's center, but I enjoyed seeing it again.

After the tour, we went home and had ice cream. We had just finished when Starr arrived. "There's still plenty of ice cream," Mrs. Anderson said.

"No, thanks. I had dessert at Abby's house."

"Sunny and I had a good shopping trip," Mrs. Anderson said. "Would you like to see what we bought?"

"I'm really tired," Starr said. "I'm going to bed early."

Mr. Anderson opened his mouth as if he wanted to object but then said nothing. I got the feeling Starr's parents had decided not to push her to be nice to me but instead were hoping she'd come around by herself.

After Starr went upstairs, I excused myself and went into the den. I heard the TV go on, and Mr. and Mrs. Anderson talking together in the living room. I went quietly up the stairs and tapped on Starr's bedroom door.

"Who is it?"

"It's Sunny. Can I talk to you for a minute?"

"About what?"

"Nothing special."

"Oh, I suppose so. Come on in."

I went in. Starr was sitting on the bed, propped up with pillows. I sat on a small upholstered chair.

"I know you're unhappy that I'm here," I said, "and I'm sorry about that. I thought you would have the same memories that I have. I never dreamed that you wouldn't remember me."

"You could at least have written first, or called. It's a shock to find out I have a twin sister and nobody bothered to tell me about her."

"I know. I assumed you knew about me."

"Well, I didn't."

"You really don't remember me at all?"

"I vaguely remember playing with someone. I thought it was a friend."

"I'm not going to stay all summer, if that's what you're worried about," I said. "I'll be here only until Thursday. When I get back to Rita's, I plan to stay there."

"Mom is trying to bribe you," she said. "Buying all

those clothes for you is supposed to make you want to stay longer."

"I don't think that's true. Your mom was only being nice. She wanted me to have enough to wear during my visit."

"Think what you like," Starr said, "but I know her better than you do."

"I just—I just want to say that I'd really like to get to know you better. I mean, how often do you get a chance to meet a twin sister? It'll probably be years before we see each other again."

"If ever."

"If ever," I agreed. "So let's be friends for these few days."

Starr didn't respond.

"Are you afraid of me?" I asked.

"Afraid? Why would I be afraid?"

"I don't know. You act as if you fear something bad will happen if you get to know me."

"You're crazy. I'm just not thrilled to have my life disrupted by someone I don't know who moves in and wants to instantly become best buddies."

"Okay," I said as I stood. "I get the message."

I went back to the den and sat on the edge of the bed. Thursday seemed a long way off.

The old song ran through my mind, but this time I changed one word: "Twinkie, Twinkie, little Starr. How I wonder *who* you are." For ten years, I had wondered where my sister was. Now that I had found her, I realized I didn't know *who* she was. I had searched for a girl who existed only in my mind.

I picked up one of my new books, hoping it would be the kind of story where I'd forget about my regular life and become totally engrossed in the lives of the characters.

I had just finished Chapter One when Starr screamed. The first scream was followed immediately by another, even more shrill. I dropped my book and rushed to the den door.

Starr was at the top of the stairs, jumping up and down as if her shoes were on fire. Mr. and Mrs. Anderson came running from the living room and looked up at her.

"What's wrong?" Mrs. Anderson asked.

"What happened?" Mr. Anderson said.

Starr was waving a sheet of paper over her head. "I won!" she shouted. "I won! I won! I won!"

"Won what?" her dad asked.

Starr stopped jumping and bolted down the stairs. "I won the district poetry contest!" she yelled. "I'm going on to compete in the regionals!"

"Oh, Starr!" Mrs. Anderson said. "That's wonderful! I'm so proud of you!"

Starr handed the piece of paper to her dad. "They sent me an e-mail," she said. She grabbed the paper back and read it aloud: "Dear Ms. Anderson: I am pleased to inform you that your poem, 'Lilacs in Summer,' has won first place in the District Poetry Competition. It will automatically advance to the regional contest. That judging will take place in two weeks, and the winner there will go on to the State Poetry Competition.

"Congratulations on your winning entry. Attached is an affidavit for you to sign and return, stating that your poem is your own original work. This affidavit is required by the regional judges, so please return it as soon as possible."

Starr handed the paper to her dad again.

"I knew you would win," Mrs. Anderson said. "It's a lovely poem."

"Congratulations, Starr," I said.

"I told you she had talent," Mr. Anderson said. He was beaming with pride. "We need to call your grandparents."

"It's eleven o'clock in Chicago," Mrs. Anderson said. "They'll probably be in bed."

"For news like this, they won't mind being awakened."

I listened as he told his parents of his daughter's accomplishment. Then Starr got on the line and accepted congratulations. I kept waiting for them to mention me, but nobody did. Did the grandparents already know I was there or had my arrival not been newsworthy enough to merit a call?

When the call ended, Mr. Anderson said, "Do you have extra copies of your poem?"

"No, but I have it on my computer."

"Let's print a few. Grandpa asked me to mail one to him."

The three of them went up to Starr's room, talking about who else they needed to tell. "I'll notify the *Courier-Herald* tomorrow," Mrs. Anderson said. "They'll want to send a reporter out, and a photographer."

I returned to the den and picked up my novel. I thought about how many times in my life a good book had offered me a way out of a problem situation. From the time I had learned to read, whenever I was placed in a new foster home I got myself a library card as soon as I could. I tried to always have at least two unread books so that if I needed to escape my real life, I had other, fictional lives waiting for me. Books had taught me new ideas and had shown me ways of life that I would not have known about otherwise, and they offered a refuge when, like now, real life seemed too hard.

I was glad Starr's poem had won. I was happy to see Mr. and Mrs. Anderson's pride in their daughter. But I wasn't a part of their celebration, or their family. My dream of a permanent home with Starr had been a foolish fantasy.

I picked up my book and began to read.

19

When I went to the kitchen for breakfast the next morning, I saw that Starr's poem was taped to the front of the refrigerator. While I waited for my toast to pop up, I read it. Then I read it a second time. It was a good poem—an excellent poem—but Starr had not written it. I had read it before!

I tried to remember where I had seen it. A magazine? An English textbook? Surely Starr wouldn't be so stupid that she would copy a poem from one of her classroom books and enter it in a contest. She must have taken it from some out-of-print book or other source that she thought nobody would remember or find.

Rita had lots of poetry books and I sometimes browsed through them during the commercials when I was watching television. That's probably where I'd seen "Lilacs in Summer."

I debated what to do. If I said anything to Starr without proof, I was sure she would deny that she had copied the poem. If she was willing to sign an affidavit, swearing that it was her own original work, she wasn't likely to back down on my say-so, and the Andersons would take her side against me.

I found a sheet of paper and copied the poem, word for word. I had just finished when Mrs. Anderson came in. I folded the paper and put it in my pocket.

"I'm wondering if you and Starr would like to go into Seattle today," she said. "We could go to the Pike Place Market or walk along the waterfront."

Before I could answer, Starr came into the kitchen. "Count me out," she said. "Angie and Sarah and I are going to work on our routine for cheerleader tryouts."

"They could go with us," Mrs. Anderson said. "We'll take the van. There'll be plenty of time to practice cheerleading after Sunny leaves."

"I really need to go to the library today," I said. "I thought I'd ride my bike there." I felt sorry for Mrs. Anderson. She was trying so hard to plan fun outings that would create bonding between sisters, and everyone except her knew it wasn't going to happen.

"I can drive you to the library," Mrs. Anderson said.

"That's okay. I need the exercise and I'm not sure how long it will take me. I'm working on a project."

I could tell Mrs. Anderson was disappointed, and Starr was relieved. I wondered what she had told her friends about me. Maybe she had not told them anything. I knew she was counting the days until I left. Well, so was I.

The library didn't open until eleven, but I went early and walked around a while, wondering if I was doing the right thing. Maybe I should not try to find the published poem. Maybe I should just stay out of it and let Starr fool everyone. Of course, even if I didn't speak up, she might not get away with her deception. There was always a chance that someone else would recognize the poem. The judges in competitions of this kind must read lots of poetry. If I knew immediately that I'd seen it before, the odds were good that someone else would recognize it, too.

When the library opened, I went to the computer section, signed up for fifteen minutes online, and did a Google search for "Poem: Lilacs in Summer." Almost instantly, I got several responses and the second one I clicked was what I was looking for. It showed the whole poem and the author's name. "Lilacs in Summer" by Lois M. Kringdell. It had been published in 1896.

I got out the poem I'd copied and compared the two. Starr had not changed a single word. She had made no attempt to make the poem her own but had simply used it, word for word.

I printed out two copies.

Since I still had time left on the computer, I decided to check my e-mail to see if there had been any late responses to my ad. When I opened the in-box, there was a message from Rita, dated last Friday, the day I left.

> Dear Sunny,
>
> Please, please call me. I don't know what happened to make you leave, but whatever it was, we can fix it. I miss you like crazy and I'm scared that something bad will happen to you. I had hoped you would stay with me permanently, but if you want to live somewhere else, I'll help you do that as long as you are safe. Please come home! Love always, Rita

I logged off, then went to the magazine section, picked out some current issues, and found a soft chair. I was in no hurry to return to the Andersons' house. For one thing, I knew Starr and her friends would not want me there, and who wants to show up when they aren't welcome?

Also, I wasn't yet sure what to do about the poem. I could imagine how Starr's parents would react if I showed the published poem to them. They had welcomed me warmly and I didn't want to make them unhappy, no matter how much Starr deserved to get caught.

I tried to read one of the magazines but finally gave up. I sat in the library, staring at the shelves and wishing I had never found my sister. If I had not come, I could have kept my happy memories all of my life. I would always have thought that somewhere I had a wonderful twin who was exactly like me and who longed for me as much as I yearned for her.

Now I was stuck with reality. My twin sister not only did not remember me, she didn't want to know me at all. The fact was, I didn't like Starr. She was spoiled and self-centered and dishonest. When I left here to go home, I knew I'd never again make any effort to contact her.

Home. I smiled, thinking of Rita. While I had been traveling all those miles, I'd thought I was coming to find my family. It turned out I'd left my real family behind.

I put the magazines back. I asked the librarian if there was a public telephone that I could use and she told me where to find one.

I made a collect call to Rita, hoping she had not already left this morning to go pick up Snickers. I had her cell phone number, too, but she never answered when she was driving because she said it wasn't safe to talk and drive at the same time.

Please, I thought. *Please, please answer the phone!*

She did.

"I want to come home right away," I told her. "That way we could go together to get Snickers. It would be a lot easier for you to manage a dog in the car if I was there, too."

"I was planning to leave tomorrow," she said, "but Charley was flexible. He seems really fond of your dog." She paused, then added, "I don't think Snickers is the only reason you want to come back early. Things aren't going well?"

"My sister is a total jerk," I said. "We have nothing in common, and she doesn't want to get to know me."

"Her loss," said Rita.

"Mrs. Anderson keeps suggesting fun things for us to do together, but Starr always has an excuse. And you won't believe what I found out about her. She copied a poem and pretended she wrote it, and entered it in a contest and she won."

"Are you sure she copied it?"

"I'm at the library. I just found it online."

"Have you told the Andersons you want to leave?"

"No. I'm calling from a public phone."

"I'll see what I can do about an earlier flight," Rita said. "You'll need to go back to the Andersons' house so I can reach you to tell you the plans."

I started to cry. I couldn't help it. I was so relieved at the thought of not staying with Starr for another five days. "Thanks, Rita," I said. "I'm sorry I ran off without talking to you about Starr. It was a stupid move."

"Hey, we all make mistakes," she told me. "I'm just glad you're coming home. And your little dog, too."

I laughed. "He isn't so little," I said.

"I was afraid of that."

When I got back to the Andersons' house, Mr. and Mrs. Anderson were playing gin rummy.

"Starr and her friends went to a movie," Mr. Anderson said. "I can drive you to the theater, if you want. I'm sure you'd be able to find them. Sarah's mother is driving them home."

"No, thanks. I need to talk to you." I drank some water, took a deep breath, and said, "You've both been wonderful to me and I can't thank you enough for making me feel welcome here. But I realize now that I should have given you some warning. It was hard for Starr to have me just appear when she didn't even know I existed."

"It was a shock," Mrs. Anderson said.

"I called Rita from the library," I told them, "and asked her to see if she can get me on an earlier flight. I'd like to leave as soon as I can. That way I can go with her to pick up Snickers."

Even though they both said they wanted me to stay the full week, I could tell they thought it was a good idea for me to leave.

Ten minutes later, Rita called. Mr. Anderson answered. I heard him say, "Yes, I can take her to the airport. That will work out." Then he handed me the phone.

"Hey, Sunny," Rita said. "How'd you like to take the red-eye special tonight? It leaves Seattle at ten. You'd better say yes, because I already changed your ticket and it cost me a hundred-dollar transfer fee."

"Yes," I said.

After I hung up, the Andersons seemed at a loss for words.

"I need to pack," I said, and I headed for the den.

I folded my clothes and put them in the new duffel bag. It didn't take long. When I carried it out and set it by the front door, Mr. Anderson said, "I'm sorry this has not been a happier visit for you. I want you to know that if you ever need anything, anything at all, you can call us."

"Thank you," I said, although I knew I would not be calling.

"You could come back," Mrs. Anderson suggested, "after Starr's had time to adjust. We wanted to adopt you years ago, and we'd still like to explore that possibility."

"Starr's very lucky to have you for her parents," I said.

"We won't need to leave for the airport until seven tonight," Mr. Anderson said. "Would you like to go out for a Mexican dinner?"

"I want to talk to Starr alone," I said. "There's something I need to tell her."

"Maybe we'll send out for a pizza then," Mrs. Anderson said. "We'll eat at home, and then you girls can have plenty of time to chat."

"As soon as I've talked to Starr," I said, "I'd like to leave. I can get something to eat at the airport while I wait for my flight."

They looked surprised but didn't argue.

The remainder of the afternoon dragged. The Andersons quit playing cards and went outside to do yard work. I tried to read my book, but mostly I wandered around aimlessly.

Starr called at four to say she was at Sarah's house and had been invited to stay for dinner.

"No," her dad told her. "You need to come home. Sunny is leaving tonight and she wants to see you before she goes."

I could tell Starr argued with him, but for once she did not get her way. "I'll pick you up in ten minutes," Mr. Anderson said. He hung up, got in his car, and drove off.

When Starr arrived, she gave me a scathing look and said, "So, here I am. What do you want to talk about?"

"I need to see you alone," I said. "Let's go up to your room."

She led the way. She sat on her bed and glared at me.

I reached in my pocket and took out the copy of the poem, the one I'd printed at the library that included the author's name and the date the poem had been published. I handed it to her and watched as she read it.

Her face turned pale. "Where did you get this?" she whispered.

"As soon as I read 'Lilacs in Summer,' I knew you hadn't written it," I told her. "I'd seen it before. I wasn't sure where I'd read it, but I knew you weren't the author. I didn't want to use the computer here because I didn't know how long it would take me to find the poem and I didn't want to be interrupted, so I went to the library. I Googled the title and it popped up instantly."

Her hands were shaking so much, the paper rattled. She laid it on the bed.

"Are you going to show this to my parents?" she asked.

"No."

"Oh, I get it. This is blackmail. You keep quiet about the poem and, in return, I pretend it's okay with me for you to live here."

"I ought to be insulted," I said, "but instead I feel sorry for you."

"You feel sorry for me? That's a joke! You're the kid nobody wants."

"Not anymore. Rita wants me, and your parents want to consider adopting me."

"You're lying!"

"Ask them."

"They wouldn't adopt you unless I agreed to it, and I'll never do that."

"It doesn't matter," I said. "I wouldn't agree to it, either."

"What?"

"You heard me. I don't want your parents to adopt me. I like them a lot, but I want to live with Rita and Snickers."

"You're crazy. You'd choose a foster home and a flea-bag mutt over the chance to live here?" She waved one hand around. "What about the clothes and the big allowance?"

"Not important. Rita and I are going to take tennis lessons, and there's a trail where I can walk Snickers. I'm happy there."

Starr was quiet for a moment. Then she said, "You really aren't going to tell my parents about the poem?"

"No, but I think you should tell them."

She shook her head. "I can't. You don't know what it's like to have parents who think you're perfect. All my life they've expected me to be better than I am, to accomplish more than I'm capable of. No matter what I do, they always want more."

This is a problem? I thought. Nobody ever expected me to succeed at anything. Then I corrected myself: until Rita. Rita believes in me.

"They seem very proud of you," I said.

"They're proud of who they want me to be, not who I am." Tears dribbled down Starr's cheeks. "You were right when you guessed that I was afraid of you," she said. "I didn't want you to stay because I was afraid you'd be smarter than I am and do better in school and in sports. I couldn't stand the thought of competing with a twin and coming out second."

"You're taking a terrible chance by sending that poem and the affidavit to the regional contest," I said. "What if one of the judges recognizes the poem? You'll be publicly humiliated. Think what that would do to your parents. It would be a lot easier if you admitted what you did now instead of getting caught later."

"I'll withdraw the poem," she said. "I'll tell the judges I sent it by mistake. That way, Mom and Dad won't have to know. They'll just think I didn't win."

I looked at my sister. Even now that her plagiarism had been found out, she wasn't willing to take responsibility for what she had done. *Twinkie, Twinkie, little Starr. How I wonder who you are.* I didn't know the girl who sat in front of me. I no longer wanted to know her.

"Thanks for not telling on me," she said.

"Good-bye, Starr," I said.

20

Rita was waiting at the baggage claim, as we had agreed. I spotted her as I rode down the escalator.

She opened her arms and I rushed to hug her. Then she held me at arm's length and said, "What did you do to your hair?"

"As soon as I shampoo it twenty-two more times, it'll be back to my natural color."

The drive home took nearly two hours, and we never stopped talking. Rita told me she had notified the police about the bag of money I'd found.

"Did they know who it belongs to?" I asked. "Do I

have to give it back?" I hadn't thought about telling the police.

"Nobody had reported the loss and the amount didn't match any robbery, so it's yours to keep."

"Good, because I spent most of it getting to Starr's house."

"I'm in a peck of trouble with Hiss," Rita said.

"You told them I was gone?"

"Well, of course I did. I had to try to find you."

"Are they going to let me stay with you?"

"Yes. When they found out that you had voluntarily called and asked to come back, they agreed that we could try again. We're on probation for six months, though. If you leave again, they'll . . ."

"I'm not leaving again," I said. "Where would I go?"

"Who knows? Maybe you are one of triplets and there's a brother somewhere that I don't know about and one day you'll take off, looking for him."

"I don't blame you for being mad at me."

"I'm not mad at you, but I'm disappointed that you didn't feel you could tell me the truth. I would have helped you find your sister. I would have taken you to meet her."

"I know. I wish I'd done that, and I'm glad you're willing to give me another chance."

"I figured if I let you come home, I'd get Snickers, too," Rita said. "Ever since I arranged to work from home, I've wanted to have a dog."

"You're going to love him," I said.

"I'm sure I will."

"I thought my search for Starr would have a perfect, fairy-tale ending and we'd live happily ever after."

"You pursued your dream," Rita said. "It didn't turn out the way you had hoped, but now you can go on to other dreams."

"Is it too late for us to do the tennis lessons?"

"No. We can still do them."

"I'm going to write about my trip to find Starr," I told Rita, "and turn it in this fall for extra credit."

"That's a fabulous idea," Rita said.

"I thought about it on the plane," I said. "It might be too long for an essay. I might have to write a whole book."

Rita looked shocked.

"I already know the title and how it starts," I said. "I'm going to begin by saying my life was transformed by a craving for Twinkies."

"Twinkies?" Rita looked repulsed. "What do Twinkies have to do with searching for your sister?"

"You'll see when you read my book. I'm going to call it *Runaway Twin*."

"Good title," said Rita. "I can't wait to read it."

When we got to Rita's house, she said, "I have a welcome-home present for you." She handed me a bagel bracelet. "I used yellow yarn," she said. "For Sunny."

The bracelet was covered with buttons shaped like rainbows and little suns. I slipped the bracelet on my wrist. "Thanks, Rita," I said. "Thanks for everything."

"We'd better get to bed," Rita said. "I told your pal, Charley, that we'll be there tomorrow evening."

I walked into my room. My room. I looked around at the desk and the bed with its purple spread, and the Lava lamp. Then I noticed a new addition to my decor: a large dog bed with a cedar-filled pad sat next to my desk.

I'm home, I thought. *At last, I'm really home.*